Secrets of the Heart

Dana Wayne

Book Liftoff
1209 South Main Street
PMB 126
Lindale, Texas 75771

Interior Book design by Champagne Book Design
Cover design by Just Write.Creations

Library of Congress Control Number Data
Wayne, Dana
Secrets Of The Heart / Dana Wayne.
Contemporary—Romance—Fiction.2. Supense—Romance—Fiction.
BISAC: FICTION / Romance / General. | FICTION / Romance / Contemporary.
2018937811
2nd Edition
Second publication 2018

ISBN 9781947946385

www.danawayne.com
www.bookliftoff.com
Book Liftoff

Books by
Dana Wayne

Secrets Of The Heart

Mail Order Groom

Whispers On The Wind

To my wonderful, supportive husband who always believed
in me;
Especially when I doubted myself.
Thank you, sweetie for your love and support as
I chased my dream.

Chapter One

Houston, Texas present day

THEY DIED TWO YEARS AGO TODAY.

Tori didn't need the calendar to remember the date. Her heart ticked away the hours one anguished beat at a time then stuttered and skipped each September fourth at 7:01 p.m.; the day her husband and seven year old son were murdered.

She sucked in a lungful of air and forced back the tears threatening to crush her resolve.

No more tears. Time to move forward.

Tori stared at the half-packed suitcase on the bed, each item new and chosen for this journey, symbolic of her mission to start fresh. She was certain her best friend since forever would understand and support her decision. Obviously not the case.

"Oh my God, Tori! Have you lost your mind?" Sasha paced in front of the closet, fingers pressed to her temples. "I am so not believing this!"

Her reaction mirrored the one from Tori's family last night. Going to Montana was one thing, keeping it secret until the night before she left was a lot to accept. Apparently.

Hands on her hips, voice rife with tension,

Sassy—personifying her nickname—raved on. "I mean, really, what do you even know about this guy?" She crossed her arms, right foot tapping out a staccato. "How do you know he's not some wacko serial killer or if he even *has* a sick mother?"

She didn't give Tori time to take a breath much less respond.

"I can't believe you didn't tell your best friend in the whole world about this hare-brained idea weeks ago instead of the *day* before you leave."

"You know why." Tori held up her hand. "You're worried, Sassy, I get it. But I have to do this." She placed folded pants in the suitcase and walked back to the closet, staring at the unfamiliar items hanging there. "The past two years have been a never-ending nightmare." She wrapped her arms around herself and struggled to remain calm. "Joey died in my arms." Tori blew out a breath. "I didn't know a human could endure that much pain and live. I never thought their killers would go free, but they did and I survived that, too." Her voice dropped to a soft whisper. "I'm just existing, Sassy. I'm not living anymore."

"Rico is still out there. You know you're a loose end he wants tied up."

"I talked with Captain Lockhart last week and Rico hasn't been seen in months. Word is he took his drug plans elsewhere. Maybe even as far as Canada." She turned back to the closet and pulled a blouse from its hanger, folded it, shook it out then refolded it. "When Joey and Eddie died, a big part of me died, too." She took a breath and tried to speak without crying. "I know I can never get that back. But this job will give me a chance to…re-group, get grounded again."

"But *Montana*?" Sassy stood in front her. "It's colder 'n hell there and snows like a gazillion feet a year! What if you need to go to town or get sick or hurt?"

Tori threw the blouse on the bed and faced her friend. "I can't stay here any longer!" She trembled with the effort it took to control the pain that had defined her life the last two years. Eyes blurring with unshed tears, she blinked several times, sucking air through clenched teeth. "Everywhere I go, everyone I see is a constant reminder of all I've lost. And my family, Sassy…they're smothering me."

"They love you. We all do."

She gripped her friends' shoulders. "Then *please*. For my sake, try to understand. I lost a big piece of myself that day and lose a little more each day I stay here."

Several seconds passed before Sassy placed her hands over Tori's and squeezed. "All right. But promise you'll call if you need anything, *anything* at all."

"I *promise*. Now, are you going to help me pack or what?"

"Fine. I'll help, but I want the whole story, start to finish. How the hell did you get hooked up with some cowboy from Montana?"

Tori released a long held breath. "It's not a big deal." She picked up the discarded blouse and refolded it. "Ted Freeman, Chief of Staff at Memorial?"

"Oh yeah, the yummy one that looks like Richard Gere."

She nodded. "He has this friend in Butte who knew about a family, the McBride's' that wanted a live-in nurse for his elderly mother. She has terminal cancer. Pretty advanced."

"They don't have nurses in Montana?"

She ignored the sarcastic comment. "He mentioned it to Ted who mentioned it to me in passing. I asked for more information, made a few calls." Tori shrugged. "And off I go."

Though not that simple, the explanation seemed to satisfy Sasha for now. True, she insisted on a background check and made a few discreet inquiries herself but not until she'd accepted the position. Tori realized significant steps had to take place if she were to have any chance at *normal* again. This was a significant step. A little rash maybe, but significant, so, no second guessing it now.

It was an ideal solution for her current state of mind. She would live in the McBride home and care for Mr. McBride's sister and mother, receive an acceptable salary, a private room and meals. Most important of all, she'd be free from constant reminders of her loss and well-meaning friends and family—namely her mother—now determined to *fix her up* with someone.

But she lacked the motivation, and, though loath to admit it, the confidence, to pursue another relationship. Eddie was her first love, and her only lover. Hell, she'd never even kissed another man—not like *that*—and even the thought of doing so now made her palms sweat and her heart race.

I'm a thirty-three year old coward.

"Hello in there?" Sasha tapped the side of her head. "Anybody home?"

Tori blinked. "Huh?"

"Answer me."

"I'm sorry, my mind was wandering. What did you ask?"

She heaved an exasperated sniff. "I *said* tell me about this McBride fella. What does he look like, is he married? And I want the good stuff, too, not whatever sugar-coated version you gave your parents."

Tori hesitated.

Sasha poked her shoulder with her index finger. "Out with it. What are you hiding?"

"Nothing." She studied the closet's contents without seeing them. "There isn't much to tell. He runs the family ranch. His brother was the sheriff before he and his wife were killed three months ago." She took a sweater and studied it. "That's about it."

"And you never met 'im?"

"Uh-uh, just spoke with him on the phone. Got the majority of my information from his sister, Sheila. She had some sort of accident, too and needs PT."

"Okay then, what does he sound like? Old? Sexy? Gay?"

"You're incorrigible."

"Well?"

"I guess…hell, I don't know." She swapped the sweater for blouse. "It's hard to describe." *Liar. You know exactly how it sounds; a deep baritone with a huskiness to it that flows through you like fine wine, raises gooseflesh on your arms, leaving you off-balance, a strange tingling sensation racing through you.* She placed a hand at her throat and tried to breathe normally as guilt over such forbidden feelings overwhelmed her. *If just the sound of his voice on the phone has such an effect on me, what on earth will happen when I meet him?*

"Dammit! You're not listening again."

The declaration, complete with a heavy sigh, pulled Tori from those disturbing thoughts. "I'm sorry. What did you say?"

Sasha rolled her eyes and made no attempt to hide her frustration. "I said, give it to me."

"Give what?"

"I know good and well you at least got a picture of him

before sashaying across the country to meet him, so gimmee."

She looked away, said nothing.

Her best friend held out her hand and snapped her fingers. "Hand it over, girl. I wanna see the man who could persuade my reasonably intelligent—"

"*Reasonably* intelligent?"

Sasha cocked her head to the side, one delicately arched brow raised.

"Point made."

"As I was saying, persuade my reasonably intelligent best friend to hightail it to Montana in the dead of winter." She wiggled her fingers and grinned. "I can't wait to see him."

Tori glanced at the outstretched hand and reached for her purse. She didn't bother to glance at the photo as she passed it over; didn't need to. Her mind's eye provided a vivid picture. *Wind-blown ebony hair, streaks of grey at the temples. Strong, defined cheekbones anchored by heavy brows. Sky blue eyes framed by killer lashes. And his mouth. Oh God.* What was it about his mouth that intrigued her so?

Full lips parted in a sexy smile that lit up his face and made her breath catch. She gave herself a mental shake and tried to focus on the task at hand. "His sister sent it. He's the one on the left. The other one is his late brother, Isaac."

"Holy-moly girlfriend! No wonder you can't wait to go. Talk about your tall, dark and handsome. He's what…six feet at least; bedroom eyes if ever I saw 'em, come hither smile… daaa-yum! I bet he's got a killer ass, too."

"Sassy!" Tori reached for the picture but her friend moved away, still studying it.

"What did you say his name is?"

"Wade McBride."

"Well, Mr. Wade McBride, you are one delicious lookin' cowboy." She made a show of fanning herself with the picture. "And I'd be on 'at puppy like mornin' glory on a fencepost."

Her face grew warm and she shook her head. Sasha had a one track mind of late and did her best to get Tori on the same track.

"Damn. Damn. *Damn!*" She handed the picture back. "Sure you don't want me to come along? You're a bit out of practice you know, and he may be more than you can handle alone."

"It's nothing like that and you know it. It's a job."

"Yeah, well, it *should* be." She rummaged through the contents of a dresser drawer and tossed a filmy nightgown at Tori. "Better take this along. Winter or not you'll want it 'fore this is over."

"Good grief! Is sex all you think about?" She tossed the garment back to her and pulled out a pair of sweat pants.

"Hell yeah when I see a Timex man."

Tori ducked her head and sighed. "I know I will regret this, but…a Timex man?"

Sasha giggled. "Think a can of Redi-Whip topping, some chocolate syrup…a strategically placed cherry." She paused for effect. "And see if 'at cowboy can take a lickin' and keep on tickin.'"

Her face flamed as an image of McBride lathered in whipped topping and chocolate syrup formed. "Oh my God, Sasha! Where on earth do you come up with this stuff?" She extended her arm, palm up. "Never mind. I don't want to know."

"Trust me…one day you'll thank me."

"No. I won't. Besides, he has a lot on his plate with his

sister and mother both ill and the ranch. He needs a nurse, not a lover."

"Says who?"

"Sassy, please."

"I've said it before and I'll say it again; you were too good for Eddie." She waved her hand back and forth to silence Tori's rebuke. "I know, I know, it's wrong to speak ill of the dead. He was a good cop, a decent father, but a crummy, cheating husband."

Tori sat on the edge of the bed and said nothing as her friend continued. "You've got the kindest heart of anyone I've ever known." Sassy joined her on the bed, her smile reflective. "I guess that explains why you put up with me all these years. And you have a capacity for caring I truly envy. It's why you are such an awesome nurse. Well, that and the reasonably intelligent thing."

Tori snorted. Sassy would never change. Thank God.

"I know you loved Eddie. I never understood why, but I know you did. But he's gone, Tori. You need to let him go and love again."

"I…I don't know if I can. Every time I think about moving on, of getting involved with someone, I feel guilty. Like I'm…betraying him. I know it sounds silly to you, but it's how I feel."

Sasha slid an arm around her shoulders and squeezed. "I don't think it sounds silly at all. He was your husband and you loved him. But he's gone." She blew out a breath. "You're my best friend in the whole world. I want you to be happy. I want to see your eyes smile again."

"I know you do. And I appreciate that." She leaned her head on her friend's shoulder. "I'm not interested in a relationship right now." She sighed. "I don't think I even remember how to kiss anymore so a relationship is out of the question."

Sasha looked at the picture and grinned. "Wanna bet? Besides, kissing is like riding a bike, once you do it, you don't forget how." She giggled. "And if you did, I'm bettin' this cowboy is one hell of a teacher."

♡

Tori placed the last bag on the cart by the door and called for a taxi. She stood in the middle of her living room, staring at the expensive set of matching luggage she'd splurged on, mentally checking off her preparations. Her rent was paid up for six months and the mail forwarded to her parents who would take care of any bills. Her friend had a key to the apartment and would keep an eye on things while she was gone.

She suffered no misgivings about leaving. In fact, her excitement grew as departure time approached. The need to take control of her life was of major importance right now. When she heard about the McBride's needing a nurse, it was like a rainbow following a thunderstorm proclaiming the worst was over.

Maybe it was the prospect of change itself making her tingle with anticipation or something else altogether. Wade's enticing voice notwithstanding, exactly what pulled her to Montana remained a mystery. She only knew she had to go.

The doorman rang to say the taxi arrived. Tori grabbed her purse, the cumbersome luggage cart and headed out the door. As it shut, she heard the phone ring.

She let it go to voicemail.

Chapter Two

WADE McBride threw the worn Stetson toward the nearest chair and paced in front of the fireplace. Anger rolled off him in waves, pulsing with each beat of his heart.

He was way beyond royally pissed. *How could she do this to me?*

He stopped and stared at his sister, unable to speak.

"I'm sorry, Wade." Sheila didn't meet his gaze. "I was just trying to help." She looked up, raised her hands in a pleading manner and lowered them. "You know I can't stand Lucy Tate. When she started gushing about making a home for Cody, well, I said it before I thought."

"And now Mother thinks I'm bringing home the woman I plan to marry to care for you both." His voice resonated with tightly controlled anger, the words forced out one at a time through clenched teeth.

"Well how was I supposed to know she'd say something to Mother?"

"Dammit, Sheila! You should've known. You know how she is."

"Which is why I couldn't let her think she had a clear path to your bed."

"Sheila!"

"Well, I couldn't," she shouted. "She's had her eye on you ever since the day Isaac and Karen got married. And since your little lapse in judgment, she's been worse than ever."

"I. Did. Not. Sleep. With. Her." With each clipped word, his control slipped.

"Well, she claims you did."

"I was drunk and sick with grief. But not *that* drunk." His hands trembled with the effort needed to maintain control.

"According to her, you were sober as a judge, and, let's see; how did she put it? Oh yeah… put her stallion to shame."

"Enough." His roar would've sent any ranch hand scrambling for cover.

Sheila merely stared at him.

He wanted to shake her until her teeth rattled.

Or hit something. Hard.

"I'm not a child, Wade. I'm a grown woman and I aim to speak my mind." She stopped, then added. "And you're as much to blame for this mess as I am."

The statement was so ludicrous it took a moment for him to process it and yet another gulp of air to keep from strangling his younger sister. "You cannot seriously blame me for any of this."

She stared at him and didn't reply.

Wade flung his hands in the air and stomped to the fireplace, gripping the mantel till his knuckles turned white. "I can't believe you would think I slept with her."

"She's bat shit crazy, Wade. We all know that. And for whatever reason, she insists you did and that's why I had to do something to get her off your tail."

He pushed away from the mantel and faced her, hands

on his hips. "Well, you've certainly thrown a wrench in the works this time." No longer shouting, his words nonetheless vibrated with tension. "I can't let Mrs. Morgan come out here now."

"Why not? She's by far the best qualified of anyone who applied and is willing to stay here until…"

"And how do you propose I get her to agree to this?"

"Talk to her, explain what happened."

The death-grip on his temper faltered and he paced to where she sat in the wheelchair, innocent looking face turned up to him. "*Talk* to her? Of course. Why didn't I think of that?" He paced back and forth in front of her. "Right. I'll just march up to her and say, 'by the way, Mrs. Morgan, some things have changed since your last conversation with my interfering sister. For a while at least, I need you to pretend to be my fiancée because my mother smiled for the first time in months when she heard the news and to tell her otherwise would hurt her. Oh, and we forgot to mention something else; there'll be a six-year-old boy running around who's sure to remind you of your own dead son.' He stopped and looked down at her. "And let's not forget Lucy Tate, my dead brother's looney sister-in-law who will do anything to get me to marry her."

His face now inches from hers, he snarled. "Did I leave anything out?"

She avoided his lethal scowl and had the good sense to keep quiet.

"Dammit it all, Shelia! How the *hell* could you do this to me?" He straightened and ran his hands through his hair. *What a bloody mess.*

She ducked her head. "I'm sorry. I don't know what else

to say." She chanced a quick glance at him. "You're my big brother. There's nothing I wouldn't do for you. I want you—us—to be happy again." She reached in her pocket and took out the picture Tori sent. "Look at her, Wade. She learned to smile again in spite of what she went through."

Wade didn't need to see it, her image was already embedded in his mind; the proud tilt of her chin, the dimple in her left cheek, the rich fullness of lips spread in a delightful, teasing grin that was playful, even sexy, and hypnotic hazelnut eyes sparkling with…something that tugged at him the first time he gazed at the photograph.

How does anyone smile again after what she went through?

He looked toward the window overlooking the entrance to his beloved Haunted Mesa ranch. "Why do you think she's the answer?"

"I don't know. I know it's asking a lot." She rolled her wheelchair beside him. "I can't explain why, but I really want her to come."

Wade remembered his mother's radiant smile when she told him how happy she was to know he'd found someone.

He couldn't bear the thought of taking that smile away.

But what if Mrs. Morgan did agree to stay and play the part thrust upon her? He would be forced to play a very intimate role with a total stranger, to lie to his mother, all so she would die in peace.

In the next heartbeat, his life went from sugar to shit.

And there wasn't a damn thing he could do about it.

Chapter Three

WADE PACED THE SMALL WAITING AREA AT THE airport, slapping his hat against his thigh. Four hours wasted waiting for the damn plane. *Four hours.* He should be back at the ranch by now. Better yet, he shouldn't even be here.

How the hell did things get so screwed up?

The feeling of helplessness overwhelmed *and* pissed him off. If she stayed or if she left, he was screwed.

He paced and waited. The thought of addressing this in person made his teeth clench. *How the blue-blazing-hell am I going to do this?*

"Mr. McBride?"

Startled by the light touch on his arm, he turned to find Mrs. Morgan staring at him.

Damn. The photo didn't do her justice.

She stood a good five-eight or so, with curves in all the right places even the bulky purple sweater didn't hide. Rich, auburn hair fell below her ears, disheveled from travel, her face flushed to a rosy glow and rich, coffee-colored eyes immediately drew him in. She had to speak again before he came to his senses.

"I'm Tori—Victoria Morgan." She spoke cautiously, the

tension evident in her strained features as she gazed at him, one hand clutching a small carryon bag.

"I've been waiting here for hours." He winced at the gruffness of his tone, and it wasn't until she let her hand drop that he realized she'd held it out to him.

Way to go, dumb ass. Some first impression you're making.

"Well, yes, um, I guess you didn't hear about our problem in Denver?"

"They never said why you were delayed. Only that you were."

"Some sort of mechanical thing." She waved her free hand around as she rushed through an explanation of the delay.

He fixated on her voice; smoky, breathy and sexy as hell.

I'm in deep shit already.

"They kept us on the plane for the first hour; then we had to get off and wait, and wait some more before they put on another plane and it *finally* took off and, oh my goodness the flight was horrid! I don't think I'll ever be able to fly again."

He forced himself to focus on what she said and not how it sounded coming out her mouth. "Unfortunately, you may be flying again sooner than you think."

"We're flying to the ranch?"

Wade slapped his hat against his leg and looked everywhere but at her. His behavior bordered on rude but he didn't know how to approach the subject. "Look, some things have changed. We don't need you after all."

"Oh no…your mother…?"

He ignored her question and headed in the direction of the nearest ticket counter, slapping his hat on his head. "I'll get you booked on a return flight as soon as possible."

"Not so fast."

He turned at the sharp command and stared at the transformation in the woman striding toward him. Her coat, purse and carry on lay where she'd dropped them. Her faced was flushed with anger and her eyes flashed with a fascinating intensity and made his groin tighten.

She stopped in front of him, hands on her hips, swiped an errant curl behind her left ear, and, using her fingers, ticked off her list of issues with him.

She had several.

"I quit my job; I left my family. I put my whole life on hold to be here only to be treated like something you got on your boot in the yard. Now you're sending me back just like that." She snapped her fingers for emphasis.

Wade wisely kept silent and ignored his body's ill-timed reaction to the electricity bouncing off her as the rant continued.

"I've endured the travel day from hell. The last three hours I've been scared out of my wits, bouncing around the sky like a noisy metal ball. More than once I thought that damn puddle jumper would drop like a rock." She crossed and uncrossed her arms. "At the very least I deserve some semblance of an explanation." She swatted at the rowdy curl again. "And a little courtesy wouldn't hurt either."

The top of her head, tilted slightly to look him in the eye, would fit right under his chin if she stepped closer. Her chest rose and fell with each measured breath, hands clenched at her sides as she visibly struggled for control.

His groin tightened again. *Shit.* He couldn't remember the last time a woman, a stranger no less, had affected him this way.

From the corner of his eye, Wade noticed several people observing their display with delight apparently mistaking this for a lover's quarrel. "Look, the whole situation is fu—uh, complicated beyond reason. And under the circumstances, I think it will be best for you to go back to Houston and forget it ever happened." He spoke softly and tried to remain calm and rational so perhaps she would as well.

"I believe I'm entitled to answers, Mr. McBride, not BS." She folded her arms across her chest and looked him in the eye. "You can start anytime."

He changed tactics. "I know you've got to be exhausted." He reached for her arm and started in the direction of the dropped luggage. "Why don't we find a place to sit and talk?"

She didn't move. "Is an explanation included in that?"

Wade removed his hat and swatted it against leg. He was not helping the situation. If he asked her now she'd probably tell him to go to hell…with good reason.

Without preamble, a little gray-haired woman stepped forward from the onlookers. "Pardon my intrusion, young man, but it's always best to be honest. Otherwise, you'll never know if it might've worked out."

A sharp mind-your-own-business rolled around the tip of his tongue, but he swallowed it. No getting around the problem. "Look, it's late, you're beat and it's still a two hour drive to the ranch. I took the liberty of booking some rooms since I had no idea how late you might be. It's not far from here. Let's get your luggage. We can talk later."

He picked up her coat and purse and passed them to her.

She took them without a word and started toward baggage claim.

Grabbing the carry-on, he followed in silence. Once her

bags were retrieved, they headed for the door, the heavy silence increasing with each step. "Wait here," he said as they approached the door, "It's pretty brisk outside; I'll bring the truck around."

The early winter chill outside didn't compare to the inside of the pickup. Wade peeked at her a time or two and found her looking straight ahead, gnawing her lower lip, hands folded in her lap, and her face flushed.

Her expression changed with her thoughts and he couldn't help but wonder what track they took.

"This is it," he said as he pulled into the parking lot of the chain motel. "It's small but clean and has a decent restaurant."

The check in process went smooth, despite a leer from the clerk as he handed Wade the keys to adjoining rooms.

He handed Tori a key. "Go ahead. I'll bring the luggage."

He knocked on the door and was greeted with a tense silence and the smell of brewing coffee.

She stood aside for him to enter and walked to the picture window, gaze turned outward.

He pulled her luggage into the room and placed the bags against the wall by the bed and removed his hat. "Um, when you freshen up we can grab supper if you like."

"What I'd like," She turned to face him. "Is an explanation. And I don't think I'm asking too much."

He had to give her credit; she didn't waste time or mince words. He wished he had some of her gumption right now. He looked around for a place to sit. There were two chairs at a tiny table and one of them held her purse. He glanced at the bed and immediately regretted it for the image that crystalized sent a surge of heat through him.

He remained standing, rolling his hat brim around in his

hands. "It's a…complicated story."

She crossed her arms and stared at him.

He took a calming breath. "Everything was fine until yesterday."

"What happened yesterday?"

Wade ran his fingers through his hair and avoided looking at her as he relayed the recent developments.

"Let me get this straight," she said, coming to stand in front of him, arms crossed, eyes locked with his. "Your mother and sister are excited about my coming and you want to send me back because you think your nephew or crazy sister-in-law will upset me?"

"…Yes."

"That's hardly a deal breaker."

Her curt response put him on edge. *Well, just fine then. Time for the kill shot.* "Mother thinks you're my—my fiancée."

"What?"

"I said my mother -"

"I heard what you said." Her voice edged up a notch and he didn't miss the slight crack in her composure. "Where did she get such an idea?"

She didn't move as he explained how Sheila's plan to dissuade Lucy from pursuing him had backfired when she'd immediately gone to their mother for confirmation.

"I'm sorry things go so out of hand. I tried to phone before you left but missed you."

His heart hammered as he braced himself for the explosion sure to come next; almost like that time he walked through a mine field, wondering which step would be his last.

She stared at him for several heartbeats, eyes wide, lips parted. With a shake of her head, she blinked twice. "What will you tell your mother?"

Her simple question took him completely by surprise and it took a moment to process. "What?"

She closed her eyes again and inhaled, then blew it out through pursed lips once, twice.

He admired her control. The helpless feeling engulfing him since yesterday threatened to send him over the edge. His palms were sweaty, his heart pounded like a jackhammer and getting enough air in his lungs took monumental effort.

Yet she just took a couple of deep breaths and acted, well, *normal.*

"What will you tell your mother when I don't show up?" She opened her eyes and shoved her hands into her back pockets, her gaze sweeping him before focusing on something outside the window.

He had no practical answer so remained silent.

"She appears to be expecting me. And her health…"

He tried to shake the fog from his brain. "I'll think of something."

Of course I will. I'm a magician and have complete control over everyone and everything in my life.

"But you said she hasn't smiled much until she thought you…had a…"

"Fiancée, Mrs. Morgan. She thinks you're my fiancée." He ran his fingers through his hair again, unable to meet her dumbfounded gaze. "And…it was love at first sight."

He braced himself again, ready for her to lay into him this time. She had every right to do so.

Instead, she stared, mouth gaped open, and said nothing. Hell, he wondered if she was even breathing until her nostrils flared out.

God, she's beautiful. He clenched his jaw and willed away such a troubling thought. *Wrong time, wrong place, wrong woman.*

She moved to the little alcove where coffee beckoned.

He noticed the slight tremble in her hands when she poured some into one of the plastic cups before she offered it to him, all without looking at him.

"Sugar and creamer are in the little basket." She poured the remainder into the other cup and went back to her spot by the window.

"Mrs. Morgan, I'm—I'm so sorry… about all of this. And you have every right to be mad as hell. I'll pay you a month's salary for your trouble as well as airfare home."

Her back to him, she asked, "Is there anything else you haven't told me?"

His face grew warm and he ducked his head. "No," he lied, "nothing else."

She remained quiet.

After a moment of strained silence, he joined her by the window. "My mother is…is dying, Mrs. Morgan. If she makes it to Christmas it will be a miracle."

The coffee now tasted like sawdust as he struggled to swallow past the lump in his throat. "When I hired you, my main concern was her physical comfort. It never occurred to me she might need, I don't know, something more." The enormity of that realization swept over him again. "Until yesterday."

It took two attempts to draw a decent breath, powerless to stop the outpouring of words. "I was married once. When I first got out of the Army." He drew a wavy line in the moisture on the window then erased it. "She hated ranch life. I couldn't leave it." He omitted the part about the affair. Even now, the hurt ran deep.

Another line traced, erased. "Eventually, it came down to a choice."

She chose to run off with her lover, I chose to let her.

He paused and glanced sideways at her.

She still looked straight ahead, a bright spot of pink high on her cheekbone.

"Mother blames herself for not doing more to make Kathy feel at home. Though in truth, I doubt there was anything she could've done to change things."

A sip of tepid coffee provided a chance to gather his thoughts. "When my father died this spring, she grieved of course, but seemed to handle it. But then Isaac and Karen died and she got sick…"

He was a strong man, an Army Ranger for God's sake, who walked through mine fields and fought a war. And still he couldn't keep the pain of watching his mother give up and wait to die from making his voice quiver when he spoke. "She—she just gave up. I don't think she has smiled once since then. Even with Cody's antics. Not until she thought I… had someone."

"That's understandable."

Her soft, matter-of-fact statement stunned him. "It is?"

She nodded but didn't look his way. "She's gone through a lot. This…situation is a bright spot. Something she can look forward to and be happy about. Even now." Her nervous gaze met his briefly and her hand trembled as she raised the cup to her lips.

What was your bright spot? How does anyone survive that kind of pain?

For whatever reason, Wade wasn't put off by the ensuing silence. Maybe because her calm acceptance of the situation kept him from embracing the impotent anger lurking just beneath the surface.

Or maybe he just enjoyed standing next to her sipping lukewarm coffee watching the sun dip below the mountains and for just one tiny moment in time pretend his life wasn't a giant sinkhole of shit about to swallow him whole.

"Well," she said at last, "this has been an interesting day."

He smiled in spite of himself. "That's got to be the understatement of the year."

She squared her shoulders and faced him. "So, what are our options?"

"Options?"

"What do you want me to do?"

"Do?"

"Oh for heaven's sake." she snapped, "can't you speak in words of more than one syllable?"

Resentment simmering for hours jumped to a slow boil. "How many syllables would you like?" he hissed.

"What I would like, Mr. McBride," she said with exaggerated calm, "is some indication of what you propose we do about this—this— situation."

He fought to keep from shouting. "The way I see it, Mrs. Morgan, I have very little to say about what happens in my life these days. I thought I did, but Sheila interfered. Then Lucy added her two cents worth." He ignored the coffee that sloshed out of his cup and dribbled down the back of his hand as he ranted. "Now, here I am, up to my eyeballs in bullsh— problems—none of which I am responsible for creating, and not a single solution comes to mind." His frustration escalated and by the end of his speech, he spoke through clenched teeth, holding himself together by sheer force of will.

"I'll thank you to remember *I* had nothing to do with *creating* those problems." Her quiet statement instantly quashed his rising ire.

And made him feel like the king of jackasses.

"You're right, of course. I don't…I'm sorry." He moved the cup to his other hand and wiped the spilled coffee on his pants. *What a mess.*

An uneasy silence ensued.

What the hell do I do now? How do I fix this?

He had to ask her stay, but how? His behavior up to now did nothing to endear him to her. What could he possibly say to entice her to even consider such a charade? *Just do it, open your mouth and say, Mrs. Morgan, will you stay and pretend to be my love-at-first-site fiancée until my mother dies?*

He almost laughed at the absurdity of it. He knew in his heart it would make his mother happy if they succeeded in this ruse. If it got Lucy off his back in the process, well, just icing on the cake. Plus, with his mother and Sheila being cared for and Lucy out of the picture, he could devote more time finding Isaac's killer before winter set in.

He couldn't believe he would even consider such an absurd scheme.

The bottom line was, he had no choice.

His mother's happiness meant everything to him.

He plunged ahead. "Mrs. Morgan, I—" A low rumble coming from the direction of her stomach caused his whole train of thought, not to mention his new-found courage, to evaporate in the blink of an eye.

Shit.

"Oh my goodness!" She covered her midsection with her free hand. "I'm sorry. I left so early and the flight was so bad I didn't eat."

Better late than never, Wade's manners kicked in. "It's after eight already. Maybe you'd like to freshen up and meet me downstairs for dinner?"

"Thank you for the offer, but frankly, it's been a long day. I'd prefer a hot bath and to have something sent up."

A mental picture of her in a giant tub surrounded by lots of bubbles materialized out of nowhere causing more discomfort. Again. *What the hell is wrong with me? I've never had such a short fuse around a woman.*

"Of course." He started for the door. "We have adjoining rooms. I'll leave my door unlocked in case you need anything—I mean, if you have any questions or anything."

"Thank you, Mr. McBride. I'm an early riser so what time would you like to meet for breakfast?"

"Whatever works for you."

"How about eight?"

"Eight's fine."

"We'll talk then."

He stared at her for a heartbeat before it dawned on him. *She hadn't said no.*

He nodded and left, amazed he could walk so straight with the weight of the world on his shoulders.

Chapter Four

TORI LEANED AGAINST THE DOOR, AND STRUGGLED TO breathe. *Oh my God? Did he notice how my hands trembled when I handed him the coffee?* She closed her eyes and the sexy timbre of his voice resonated through her body making her quiver like a school girl meeting the handsome football hero for the first time. Warring emotions set off waves of guilt over her intense awareness of him.

The precarious situation in which she found herself came crashing down.

Oh my God! His fiancée. Love at first sight?

The coffee she drank earlier now roiled in her empty stomach and she placed both hands over it as if to keep things where they were. *Think, Tori, think. There must be a way out of this.*

She looked toward his now-vacant spot by the window and reflected on their conversation. His love and concern for his mother's well-being showed in the tender way he spoke about her. The natural healer within moved her to offer solace despite any personal ramifications.

Sassy's image flashed through her mind and she grimaced. No doubt she'd find this complication ironic if not downright entertaining.

She rummaged around her bag for her favorite sleeping attire—faded football jersey and sweat pants—unfolding the shirt, a silky black nightgown, no doubt hidden there by her friend, cascaded out. She ran her fingers over the delicate fabric, an impulse buy at her one and only trip to Victoria's Secret.

What on earth was I thinking? I'll never wear this. She wadded it up and stuffed it back in the bag before heading to the bathroom to draw a bath.

Once submerged in the soothing waters, Tori assessed the situation. She didn't want to go back. If she stayed, she might be biting off more than she could chew given the strange turn of events. Her patients posed no significant problems. His nephew's presence had the potential for snags, however she was confident she'd handle things in a professional manner. The healer—and mother—in her took over. The child had recently lost his parents and might need her.

Lucy, was a different matter altogether. She had no experience dealing with people who, for whatever reason, didn't want her around, so it would be a very different test.

Tori's main concern centered on Wade McBride himself. The onslaught of emotions experienced in this short period of time caught her unprepared. She slipped lower in the warm water, letting the memory have full rein.

He stood six-four at least; flannel shirt stretched tight across the broad expanse of his chest, tapering down to a slim waist. Strong and rugged looking, he possessed an earthy sensuality that made her pulse jump. And when he spoke… deep and masculine, the words flowed through her like warm, honey-laced whiskey, and even angry, held the power to make her tingle.

A dangerous sign a reasonably intelligent woman would heed.

Thoughts of Eddie, different from McBride in so many ways, erased the smile and guilt took center stage. She lay her head back against the tub and squeezed her eyes shut, willing the tears back once more. *Can I do it? Will I ever be able to move on with my life?*

Innocent flirting with a few male co-workers summed up her experiences with the opposite sex and she had yet to date since her husband's death. Over the last few months, a few brave souls had asked her out but she declined, which made her attraction to her new boss all the more troubling.

The man exuded masculinity and a potent sexuality that made clear thinking difficult. When he walked away from her at the airport, despite being irritated with him, she still noticed the way his faded jeans hugged his well-defined butt and muscular thighs.

Oh, yeah, Sassy, he definitely has a killer ass.

She dipped her head under the water forcing herself to focus on the main objective—he wanted his mother's last days to be happy. Although he hadn't come right out and asked, she intuitively understood he wanted her to stay and play the part. Perhaps because she knew first-hand the anguish of losing a loved one, what to expect and how to prepare. But nothing ever completely prepared a person for something so heart wrenching.

Plus, he hid something from her. After years of practice with Eddie, it was clear to her there was a piece missing to this puzzle. *What is he hiding? Does it really matter?*

She hated lying and being lied to. When the time came, could she be convincing? She recalled countless words of encouragement and hope whispered to patients who had neither and knew she would do what needed to be done. *It doesn't matter if you're healing the body or healing the heart, sometimes it's one-in-the-same.*

The coolness of water made her shiver so she stepped out, dried off and dressed. *I have to tell him now before I have time to think about it anymore.*

She wrapped a towel around her head turban style and started out, stopping when the door to the adjoining room caught her eye. After a brief hesitation, she twisted the lock and pulled it open just enough to see the other side.

His door stood ajar and the lights were on.

She knocked lightly. "Mr. McBride?"

No answer.

She rapped harder and pushed it open further. "Mr. McBride?"

Still no answer

Rats. He must have gone down to the restaurant to eat.

When she heard the shower going, the mental image materializing made her cheeks burn.

She nibbled her lower lip. *Should I leave the door open and hope he sees it or what?*

Curiosity got the upper hand. She stepped inside the room and looked around. Larger than hers, it had a small table and two chairs by the window along with a small couch. The rumpled bed with covers turned back, indicated he must've laid down before his shower. A pair of jeans and a shirt lay across the foot of the bed, boots and socks on the floor.

The shower image returned and make her breath catch.

A knock on the door startled her, and she brought a hand

to her mouth to stifle a squeal.

Another knock, louder this time.

I bet its room service and he can't hear it in the shower.

A split second decision sealed her fate. She unlocked the door.

The shower shut off as she pulled it open.

Shit. Not room service.

A curvaceous red-head wearing a skirt so short it couldn't possibly be legal, a blouse cut low enough to show the rounded globes of ample breasts stood there holding a bottle of champagne and two glasses.

Chapter Five

"WADE, DARLING." THE REDHEAD STEPPED INTO the room and turned to face Tori. "Oh, I'm so sorry. I thought this was Wade McBride's room."

Tori squeaked, "It is."

The situation took a downward turn when the man himself walked out of the bathroom wearing nothing but a towel around his waist, rubbing his hair with another.

Her eyes locked on his bare chest, the dark curls glistening with tiny droplets of water. Her mouth went dry. His chest was a work of art.

He stopped short when he saw the two women, eyes darting from one to the other before locking on the newcomer. "What the hell are you doing here, Lucy?"

"Who is she?" The redhead pointed an accusing finger at Tori.

Her new boss switched his scowl to Tori who wilted against the door frame. Eyes downcast, she couldn't meet his gaze. *Oh my God! What must he be thinking?*

"Well, who is she?"

He turned back to Lucy. "What you are doing here, and how did you get in my room?"

Tori's voice trembled with embarrassment. "I let her in. I thought she might be room service." Belatedly, Tori realized this must be Lucy Tate, the person who, in a rather round-about way, placed her in this awkward position. *Pop said when trouble comes, face it head on.*

Trouble, in this case, stood in front of her waving around a bottle of champagne.

She took a step forward and faced the angry woman. "I'm Tori Morgan. You must be Lucy Tate." She held out her hand. "Wade has told me so much about you."

Lucy ignored the offered hand. "I thought you weren't coming until tomorrow."

It took Tori a moment to process her statement. *Oh, right; the complicated situation we have to deal with.*

"Well." She let her hand drop. "We wanted some time alone before going to the ranch." Tori smiled, and inadvertently glanced at the bed.

Lucy's face flushed and her eyes narrowed. The hatred pulsing from her was almost palpable.

Tori shivered.

"For the last time, what the hell are you doing here, Lucy?" Wade's formerly seductive voice turned hard as stone.

"I—I thought we might have dinner—or something. I didn't know…"

"Ahem." All heads turned to the young man at the door. "Room Service, Sir."

Wade picked up his clothes and headed back to the bath-room. "As you can see, Lucy, we have ordered dinner. Tori, would you sign the ticket?" He didn't glance at Lucy when he walked by her. "Be gone when I get back."

As the bathroom door shut, Lucy turned to Tori, the

animosity in her eyes frightening. "You may have gotten him in bed, but he'll never belong to you." She stomped out the door.

Tori motioned for the young man to set the tray on the counter holding the coffee pot and signed for it with shaking hands. She leaned against the closed door for support. "Good grief. What have I gotten myself into?"

"Are you okay?"

She whirled around. "When you said she was crazy, I thought you meant— I didn't think…"

"I'm sorry. I never thought she would show up here."

"She's dangerous."

"I don't think she's dangerous, she's—"

She moved on the couch. "We need to talk."

Wade took the tray from the counter and placed it on the table and hesitated before sitting in the chair. "Okay."

She looked at her hands, the window, the door, every-where but at him. Even though he was now dressed, in her mind's eye, McBride still wore that damn towel. "I don't seem to know where to start."

"How about how you came to be in my room when Lucy knocked at the door?"

Her face burned. "Oh, yes, well." She stood and paced in the small area between the couch and table, navigating cau-tiously around his bare feet. "I wanted to—to tell you—I'm willing to help your mother." She stopped beside the table and looked at him. "In spite of the fact I feel certain there is more you're not telling me."

His expression never changed.

What is he hiding? Does it really matter? "And I don't think it has anything to do with Lucy Tate, although I do think you glossed over the fact that she's obsessed with you."

Wade removed the cover from the dinner tray. "Go on."

The enticing aroma coming from the plate caused her stomach to grumble again, reminding her she still hadn't eaten.

"Well, I didn't want anyone to see me in the hall like this, and I remembered what you said about adjoining rooms." The image of chicken fried steak, gravy and mashed potatoes followed as she resumed pacing. *Is that apple pie under the plastic wrap?* She looked away to keep from drooling, words pouring out in a rush as she hurried through an explanation.

She paused for a quick inhale which brought with it the intoxicating smell of soap and man mixed with mouth-watering food, and for a moment, lost her train of thought. *I don't know which is worse, seeing food I can't have or him there barefoot, shirt unbuttoned half way down.* Fingers curled into her palms as she thought about running them through the dark curls visible through the vee of his shirt. She drug her gaze back to his face…and lost her train of thought again when she found him watching her, a wry grin on his face.

"Have you eaten?"

"What? Oh, uh, no, I meant to call when I finished my bath. I'll go now. I'll see you at breakfast." Her pacing loosened the towel around her head. When she turned to step around the table, it came undone and slipped over her eyes. Blinded, she stubbed her toe on a chair leg. "Dammit!" She tried to uncover her eyes with one hand and brace for a fall with the other. Instead of the hard floor she expected, the soft firmness of his shoulder met her hand when he caught her about the waist and pulled her to him.

Heat seared her face when she realized she straddled his

lap in a very unladylike fashion. The towel hit the floor and she found herself face to face with him, hands planted on that very impressive chest for balance.

"Are you all right?" His warm breath on her face smelled faintly of mint toothpaste.

She struggled for air as heat from his chest raced up her arms, travelling with lightning speed to settle low in her belly. "Um, yes…you can let me go."

"Are you sure?"

When he spoke, the soft rumble in his chest added sharp tingles to the heat pulsing through her, like the time she touched the electric fence around her grandfather's hog pen.

"I'm sure." *Is that rusty squeak really me?*

He helped her stand and let his hands rest a little longer on her waist than was called for, before he reached down and grabbed the pesky towel. He held it out to her, the edge of his mouth kicked up in a sexy smirk.

Her stomach fluttered.

"I never understood how women made that whole head wrap thing work."

It took a couple of heartbeats for her to reach for the towel. She caught it in one hand and stepped back, running shaky fingers through her hair with the other. "Well, as you can see, it doesn't always."

He sat back in the chair and looked at her without speaking.

Her anxiety level shot through the roof. She had to keep going before she lost her nerve. "I know it's late," she said at last, "but, well, I have some questions if you don't mind."

"Ask away."

"Well," she stared at her hands and heat percolated up

her neck. "I know what I am expected to do with regard to caring for Mrs. McBride."

"Willimena. But everyone calls her Miss Willie."

"Oh, okay." She paused. "I know what to do with Sheila and her physical therapy; what I want to know is—what does Miss Willie—think about me…us?"

When he didn't answer right away, she looked at him.

He looked toward the window, left hand resting on the edge of the table. At last, he came back to her. "Until yesterday, all Mother knew was she had a new caregiver coming. Hadn't seen the picture you sent. Didn't want to. She'd had nurses before. You were just one more."

He stood, hands pushed in his pockets and looked away from her. "Then Sheila opened her big mouth. Lucy went straight to Mother to ask if it was true." He removed his hands from his pockets, crossed his arms over his chest, and then shoved them back in his pockets. "I had no idea what was going on when she asked me about it and had to tread carefully until I got the whole story." He shook his head and blew out a heavy breath. "I had every intention of telling her it was all a lie to get Lucy off my back…"

"Why didn't you?"

He ran his fingers through his hair, like he seemed prone to do when under stress or deep in thought. "Because of the look in her eyes when she asked. For the first time in months I saw real emotion there. I saw hope—and hurt. She didn't say anything, but it I saw it. If I denied it, she might think I wanted to keep it from her. So, I told her it was more or less true and didn't want to say anything until we were sure because everything happened so fast." He expelled air in a slow, steady hiss. "I still can't believe I didn't set her straight right away."

He continued to look out the window as he spoke. "She just… lit up when I didn't deny it…"

He came back and sat on the couch in front of her, elbows resting on his knees, hands clasped in front. "I know it's asking a lot—if it's more money I'll -"

"It's not the money. The arrangements we made are fine. It's, well…" She paused and moved to the chair he'd vacated. "I guess I'm more than a little nervous about the… personal aspect of this." She rolled the towel she held in her hands. "I married the only man I ever dated. I haven't dated anyone since his death." She faced him. "I'm not sure I'll know how to— behave— with someone else." She waited for his reaction— a short lived look of surprise—before continuing. "So, if you want to call this off, *now's* the time."

"What do *you* want to do?"

"Well, to be honest, run like a scared rabbit."

"Will you?"

She thought about Houston, her life there and the emptiness of it all. She understood what they'd be going through over the next few months and she'd be able to help them through it. But what about her? Could she deal with what might lie ahead?

Why am I even considering this? Can I really play the part of his fiancée for the sake of his dying mother? A total stranger…who touched in ways she didn't understand. As she studied his rugged features, she knew she played with fire.

But what was more satisfying on a cold winter's night than a roaring fire?

"No," she said at last, "every new job has its challenges. This this one is off the charts different, but it's still just another challenge."

"What made up your mind?"

"I don't know exactly." She heaved a sigh. "I detest dishonesty. But, your concern for your mother's welfare... I believe what you said. I...I understand what it's like to see someone you love suffer, and know there's nothing you can do to help them." She folded and unfolded the towel in her lap, the image of Joey and Eddie so vivid in her mind. "I have come to believe everything happens for a reason, and you are not always powerless." She paused and nibbled her lower lip. "Honesty with those you care about is crucial. But sometimes..." She raised her head and met his steady gaze. "Sometimes... healing the heart is just as important as healing the body." Heat crawled up face and stood to leave. "I'm sorry, I didn't mean to -"

"Mrs. Morgan."

She stopped without looking at him.

"It's nine. The dining room is closed. Sit down and let's eat."

"What?"

"The dining room closes by nine on week nights, sometimes earlier if they aren't busy." He stood beside the table and held out the chair she vacated. "It's too late to get something to eat and I have more than enough to share. Sit. Please."

"I couldn't eat your dinner, Mr. McBride."

"You can and you will." He took her arm, guided her to the chair, and she sat down. "You said yourself you haven't eaten all day. After all you have been through, the least I can do is share a meal."

He moved the other chair beside her and sat down pulling the platter in front of him. He slid half the potatoes to one side along with half the chicken fried steak, then cut the apple pie in two and his steak into bite-sized pieces before plac-ing the knife and fork on her side, the spoon on his. "I made some coffee earlier. Or would you rather have water?"

She smiled for the first time since Lucy's appearance. "Coffee's fine, Mr. McBride. Hazard of being a nurse on the night shift. I drink too much of it and can't seem to get by on less than a gallon a day."

"Me, too. And call me Wade. If we stand any chance of pulling this off, you better stop calling me Mr. McBride."

"Alright— Wade. I prefer Tori over Victoria." She was so hungry she could've devoured the whole meal by the time he brought coffee to the table. However, she made herself wait.

He placed the cups on the table along with the basket of sugar and creamer. "I don't know how you like your coffee. You drank it black earlier."

"Sometimes with cream in the morning, but black the rest of the time. Never with sugar."

Wade smiled. "Black and strong, though hotel coffee doesn't quite hit either mark."

"I guess those are things we should, well, know." She cursed the flood of heat warming her face—again. *Good grief! I blush like a school girl on her first date!*

He joined her at the table and sat down. "Yeah, guess so."

She tried not to notice his hip touching hers or the man-fresh-from-a-shower-smell competing with the food for her attention as they adjusted to eating off the same plate. He switched to eating with his left hand which made things less awkward until they both reached for a roll at the same time.

"Sorry, go ahead," he said.

"You first. It's your dinner."

"And two rolls." He took the saucer and held it to her.

She took one but declined the butter which he added to his.

More than once, she found herself glancing sideways at his mouth as he chewed or licked gravy from his lips, something about the action so suggestive she squirmed in her seat.

They finished the meal in relative silence then sipped the remainder of their coffee. The natural activity of life-long friends instead of strangers who just met.

Strangers who would soon pretend to be lovers. Her nipples puckered as images of that formed vividly in her mind.

She stood suddenly, arms crossed over her chest, towel clutched in one hand. "It's late. I should turn in. We can discuss the particulars of our whirlwind courtship tomorrow. Thanks for dinner."

He stood and shoved his hands into front pockets. "You're welcome. The weather shouldn't be bad, no snow, but cold, so dress comfortably."

"I will." She turned to leave and was stopped by the burning question in her mind. "What would you have told your mother if I didn't do this?"

He rolled his head slowly from side to side, one brow slightly raised, his expression glum. "I don't know," he murmured.

Compassion closed her throat. What was it about him that affected her so? His love for his mother? Her natural tendency to console? Or the blatant sensuality she sensed in him from the beginning that even now tugged at her. *I'm not ready for this; I have to get out of here.* She nodded to acknowledge his reply. "Goodnight."

"Mrs. uh, Tori?"

She turned and unexpected longing whispered through her.

"Thank you."

Not trusting herself to speak, she nodded again and closed the door behind her.

Holy crap. What am I doing?

Chapter Six

THE MORNING DAWNED GRAY AND OVERCAST. WADE hoped it wasn't a bad omen. Tori's mood at breakfast seemed apprehensive at best and though she tried to hide it, he got the impression she might be second-guessing the deal. When he told her it wasn't too late to change her mind, she sighed and said unless *he* wanted to call it off, she'd see it through.

After they ate, he stopped by Dr. Calhoun's office. He'd been expecting them and had prepared a list of his mother's medications along with detailed instructions of her care, as well as Sheila's physical therapy.

Tori impressed him with her level of understanding of what he considered *doctor talk* and Doc seemed impressed as well.

At Wade's request, Doc and Tori had spoken on the phone a month ago and he'd deemed her qualified to care for his favorite patient. Upon his recommendation, Wade hired her.

A quick stop at the post office and another at the local drug store and they were on their way.

The drive held periods of silence and idle chatter, but they managed to put together a plausible story.

He had traveled to Houston the previous summer to attend a cattle buyer's convention, which put him in the right place. Tori had attended an oncology workshop in the same hotel and they'd met in the elevator, hitting if off right away.

Neither wanted to discuss the particulars of how it all transpired, simply agreeing it had. When Wade returned home, the long distance romance continued which was substantial enough for now.

The conversation turned to trivial things and he noted points of interest along the way.

"I can't wait to see the ranch. I bet it's beautiful."

Her enthusiasm pleased him. He loved his home but it wasn't for everyone. "Just to be clear, I wasn't exaggerating when I told you we're pretty isolated. Our closest neighbors are over five miles away and the nearest town a good forty-five minutes."

"I'm fine with that." She inched forward, straining against her seat belt to look beyond him. "I have never seen mountains in my life! They are magnificent!"

"It's part of the Flathead Range. You'll have a great view of them from your bedroom window."

The bedroom next to mine. That doesn't have a lock on it.

He focused on small talk. "The clouds are hiding the best views. In a day or so when the weather clears, you'll see some *mountains.*"

She laughed and the sound was musical to him.

"When I was growing up, I spent a lot of my summers on my grandparents' farm. There was this big hill on the back of it that they called Barton's Mountain. I used to ride all over it." She chuckled again. "That thing wasn't even a hill compared to this."

"Do you like to ride horses?"

She laughed. "I'm from Texas! I love to ride. Haven't gotten to do much of that since—well in a long time. But I do enjoy it."

"There are quiet few trails around we can ride. Snows won't begin for a few weeks yet. It will be cold of course, but should be able to get some rides in."

"Cool."

As they drew closer to his home, she grew quiet and kept fidgeting, pulling at a string on the old seat cover where the stitching was loose.

He noted his own apprehension level rose with each passing mile. He had to admit, at least to himself, the idea of pretending to be in love with a woman like Tori Morgan had its advantages.

She was unlike anyone he had ever known. No shrinking violet, he sensed an inner strength and independence of mind, and that piqued his interest. At the same time, she possessed a vulnerability which made him want to shield her, protect her. From what exactly, he had no idea. The image that haunted his dreams last night jumped front and center; Tori wearing only that jersey, straddling his lap, lips pressed to his…he caught himself before he groaned out loud, and shifted in the seat to ease his discomfort. *Wrong time, wrong place, wrong woman.* He repeated what he now considered his mantra; *wrong time, wrong place, wrong woman.*

Why did he find the image of her in his hotel room wearing an old football jersey and sweatpants, hair wrapped in a towel, more appealing than any sexy nightgown? Perhaps it spoke of a charming naiveté or trust…or both.

The fact she instinctively knew he hid something from

her nibbled at his conscience. He justified the deceit with the old *it's for her own good* adage. His suspicions regarding Isaac's death and Sheila's accident were just that, suspicions. Saying anything at this point would serve no useful purpose and might hinder efforts to uncover the truth. As soon as Doug returned, the search would continue.

"Wade? Is something wrong?"

Lost in thought, he jumped at her quiet question. "What?"

"You seem so…distressed. Are you having second thoughts about this?"

"I'm all right. A little nervous. Not unlike you."

"Yes, I guess I am." She looked away. "Do you really think we can pull this off?"

He hesitated. "To tell you the truth, I have no idea. I've thought about what you said about a bright spot. Maybe you're right. Maybe she does need to know…" He didn't finish the statement. He'd resigned himself to his mother dying, but discussing it openly was hard to do.

"Then I know it will help," said Tori with firm conviction, "and I'll do whatever I can to make sure she thinks we're—I'm—"

Her confidence faltered and he noted she blushed again.

"I've never known anyone who blushes like you do." Immediately, he regretted the statement. It sounded critical, even to him.

She turned her face away. "I can't help it. It just happens."

"I'm sorry. I didn't mean that the way it sounded. It's, well, older women don't usually—"

She glared, brown eyes flashing. "*Older women?*"

"What I mean is, women today -" He stopped before he

made things worse. "Look, I can't remember the last time I saw a woman, any woman, any age blush. It's kinda nice. And a blush looks good on you."

It took a moment but she gave him a half-smile and a muttered "Thank you, I think," before training her eyes on the road ahead.

The silence was almost to the uncomfortable point when she spoke up. "A doctor friend told me once that blushing results from an overactive sympathetic nervous system. Said it explained why I was such a good nurse." She snorted. "Personally, I think it was BS but at the time, I believed him." She favored him with a timid smile. "I do seem to do it more than I used to, but it is what it is."

He accepted the olive branch she offered. "As I said, it looks good on you."

She promptly turned pink and darted her eyes toward him. "Had to do it, didn't you?"

He laughed. For the first time in months. He laughed. It felt good. *I could get used to having her around.*

"That's the entrance up ahead." His heart rate escalated and perspiration coated his brow despite the chill in the air. He turned down the lane and glanced at Tori to get her reaction when the house came into view.

She leaned forward in the seat and he slowed to give her a better opportunity to observe her new home.

"Oh, Wade, it's beautiful!"

He was proud of his home, his heritage, and couldn't hide it. "My great-great-grandfather built the little cabin out back around 1860." He didn't mention the original contents were still nestled inside which served as a unique memorial to the McBride legacy; bits and pieces of a heritage spanning over 150 years. It was his quiet space where he went to clear his head and make important decisions or to escape and enjoy the solitude.

"They started the main house around 1870. The original bunkhouse burned thirty years ago, and we built the replacement like a modern version of the original. Same with the house. Each generation has added their own piece to it, and it now covers almost three thousand square feet."

Corrals to the right held riding stock, and the barn behind them held all the tools of the trade, some of them heirlooms, some modern contrivances designed to make ranch work easier, but with none of the romantic allure of their predecessors. A cedar rail fence lined pastures on both sides of the road where horses and cows roamed, grazing on the thinning grass.

Trees planted by his ancestors shaded the house, and chickens still grazed in the side yard as they had for generations. Majestic mountains in the distance were concealed by overcast skies but he knew they were there; knew every line and curve.

He loved this land with a passion no one understood. More than his heritage, it exemplified all he wanted to be.

Tori turned to him as he pulled to a stop in front of the house, her eyes bright with excitement, a smile lighting up her face. "This is magnificent! So beautiful! And it looks so… old."

For a moment he was speechless, hypnotized by the unadulterated joy reflected in her face, that reached out to him, made a hole in the wall around his heart and perched there. He had to clear the knot from his throat before he could speak. "We tried to build every addition as it would've been built during the period. It's like a family tradition, I guess. We did have to make allowances for modern conveniences, but we tried to hide them."

"Does this porch wrap all the way around?"

Her uninhibited delight caused the dread weighing him down to dissipate a bit. "It does."

"It reminds me of my grandparents' farm back home. Although theirs isn't near this grand. And those rockers! Oh my. I love them."

"We finished the porch last year." He stopped before emotions got the best of him. This section of the porch was his favorite part of the house because it was the last thing he, Isaac and his father worked on together. "We better get this show on the road. I'm sure they know we're here by now."

"Yes, of course. How long before dark? Do you think there will be time for a look around?"

Her eagerness warmed his heart. The other nurses, Montana natives no less, had considered the premises isolated, and Wade struggled to keep them satisfied so they would stay. Tori's predecessor, obviously anxious to be on her way, had called when they almost there and spoke with Tori to bring her up to speed before she left for town.

"It won't get dark for several hours, so there should be time once you're settled in." He paused, "I guess we should go see Mother."

Tori's face lost some of the previous gusto. "Of course. We should talk to her first."

Wade parked and moved around to help her as she gathered her things. He took her hand not surprised to find a slight tremor there, and guided her to the porch. "I want you to know how much I appreciate what you're doing. All of it."

She squared her shoulders cast him a quick glance. "I'm doing this as much for me as I am for anyone else."

"What do you mean?"

The huge front door swung open before she got the chance to answer. "At last. I didn't think you'd ever get here!" A younger, female version of Wade rolled a wheelchair out the door.

"Hello, Sheila," Wade said, then stood aside for Tori to enter. "This is Tori Morgan. Tori, my meddling sister, Sheila."

It was Sheila's turn to get red-faced as she held out her hand. "I'm so glad you came. I -"

"Uncle Wade!"

His nephew bounded up the walk from the barn. Wade dropped the bag he held and scooped him up in his arms; tossed him in the air, caught him, and tossed him again, his squeal of laughter music to his ears. "How ya' doin', sport?"

"I missed you, Uncle Wade." Cody said, hugging his neck. "Did you bring me a present?"

"A present?" he asked as he tossed him up again. "Is that all you think about?" He settled the laughing child on his hip. Wade gestured toward Tori. "Cody, this is Miss Morgan. She's going to be staying with us for a while. Tori, this is my nephew, Cody."

He didn't know what sort of reaction he'd get from her and tried to prepare himself for anything. Cody had to be dredging up painful memories for her. *Dammit. I can't believe we didn't think to tell her about him before she got here.*

"Hello, Cody." Tori held out her hand. "I'm very glad to meet you at last. I've heard so much about you."

He ignored the outstretched hand and spoke to Wade. "I don't like her. She's gonna take you away."

"Whatever gave you that idea?"

"Aunt Lucy said she digs for gold and she wants to take you with her."

He gritted his teeth at those innocent words. Lucy wasted no time stirring up trouble. "Aunt Lucy is mistaken."

Cody grabbed him around the neck and squeezed. "I don't want her to take you away!"

Tori stepped forward and touched Cody's thin shoulder. "Cody, please look at me."

It took a moment for him to respond and it was only a sideways glance.

"I've no intention of taking your Uncle Wade anywhere. This is his home and you are his family. He'd never leave you for anything, or anyone."

"What about when you go digging for gold?"

Wade noticed her knuckles tighten as she gripped her purse but she remained calm and steady. His admiration hitched up a notch.

"I gave up digging for gold a long time ago."

His nephew caught his gaze. "Is it true?"

"I promise you, sport," his voice vibrated with suppressed emotion. "I'll never leave you. We're partners, and partners stick together. Right?"

"Right!"

Cody squinted slightly, his mouth moving side to side. Wade could almost hear the thoughts racing through his mind. After a moment, he looked at Tori. "Are you gonna marry Uncle Wade?"

His heart skipped a beat as his mind raced to come up with an answer. Tori again saved him the trouble.

"Your Uncle Wade and I are very special friends. And

when friends ask for your help, you do whatever you can for them, right?"

"Uh-huh."

"Well, right now, he asked for my help with your grandmother, and Aunt Sheila and I said yes. And to be honest, I'm not so sure I won't need some help myself."

"Why?"

"Well, Uncle Wade will be busy with the ranch, and Aunt Sheila, well she won't be much help for a while, so I'll want someone to help me out. You know, show me where things are, and carry things in to Miss Willie, lots of different stuff."

He straightened and sparkling blue eyes lit up his face. "I can show you. I know where everything is."

"Really? I'd appreciate that so much. I'm sure you have chores to do around here, and I'll try not to bother you too much, but I'm afraid I may have to depend on you a lot, at least until I can find my way around. This place is so big, I'll be lost all the time."

"No you won't." He wiggled and slid from Wade's grip, not quite meeting her gaze. "It's easy. Want me to show you your room?"

"If you don't mind, I would certainly appreciate it."

Cody eyed the bags on the floor and opted for the smaller carry-on. "I can take this one."

Wade hid his smile as his ward struggled to half-drag half-carry the bag down the hall to Tori's room. He glimpsed the faint sheen of unshed tears before she followed Cody down the hall. He inhaled to calm his racing heart, and erase the image of unbridled pain he'd briefly glimpsed. *What a selfish ass I am. This has got to be unbearable for her.*

"I'll go let Mother know you're here," said Sheila, "Lucy's been in and out all morning." She let the statement hang in the air and rolled her wheelchair toward their mother's room.

"What have I done?" he whispered to himself as he picked up her luggage and followed them. "What have I done?"

Chapter Seven

TORI FOLLOWED THE YOUNGSTER DOWN THE HALL and made a concerted effort to maintain control. Lucy's interference she could handle. Cody, however, was another matter altogether.

This is going to be so much harder than I thought.

He was younger than Joey, maybe six, with bright blue eyes like Wade and inky black hair badly in need of trimming. His tee shirt, smudged with dirt, bore the name of a local feed store and his pants needed a rip repaired on the knee.

She managed to quell the impending tears as she gazed at the child in front of her, but the pain in her chest made it difficult to breathe. She slowed her step, inhaled and exhaled, once, twice.

His bright laughter, carefree smile and unrestrained curiosity were heartbreaking reminders of her loss. So much like Joey at that age, who was all boy, wouldn't stay clean for more than a few minutes at a time and always needed some rip or tear mended.

She pushed the painful memories to the shuttered corner reserved for them. *I have to think about the problems at hand, and save those tears for another day.* A simple action she used to survive the last two years and would use it now to make it through this.

"Here it is." Cody drug the heavy bag into the room. "It was my dad's when he was little."

She entered the room while he continued his guided tour.

"That's the bathroom. You have to share it with Uncle Wade cause his room is on the other side."

That statement seemed more like an order and she almost smiled.

"That's the porch. You have to share it, too." He walked to the foot of the bed. "Aunt Sheila's room is across the hall from Miss Willie's."

"You call your grandmother Miss Willie?"

"Uh-huh, ever 'body does."

Tori took in the room's rustic appointments, and loved it right away. A four-poster bed rested between an antique armoire and dresser on the north wall while the west one featured French doors which she assumed opened to the porch. A small settee to the left of the doors held a colorful quilt with coordinating throw pillows. Braided rugs on gleaming hardwood floors completed the furnishings.

She ran her fingers over the intricate stitches of the handmade quilt draped over the foot of the bed. "This is beautiful."

"Miss Willie's mama made it before my dad was born."

"It's exquisite."

Wade appeared with the rest of her luggage. "It's old, but warm." He placed the bags on the settee. "I'm sure this room isn't what you expected. If you want to change something -"

"Oh no, I love it."

"Well, if you need anything, let me know." He hesitated, and motioned toward the adjoining door. "It's a Hollywood bathroom. There's a vanity and mirror in the hall and the bathroom is through the door behind it. There's only a shower, no tub. But, uh, there aren't any locks." He looked away.

She had the distinct impression he blushed and bit back a grin. *I never pegged him for a blusher.* Then the reality of what he said sunk in and she suffered a moment of panic.

"I, uh—this arrangement is Mother's idea. The other nurses stayed in a room next to her."

She swallowed hard. *It's just for appearances. It means nothing.*

"My room is across the hall." Cody's comment eased the awkward moment between them. "I have to use another bathroom cause Uncle Wade says I'm messy."

"You *are* messy."

"Na-uh."

Tori smiled at the exchange and moved to the French doors. She pulled back the lace curtains and peered outside. "Are those mountains I see through the clouds?"

Wade nodded. "More of the Flathead Range we saw earlier. When the clouds clear up, it's a pretty awesome sight."

"My daddy took me riding there, but he died." Cody reached for Wade's hand, head down.

Tori turned to the boy and her heart ached at the sadness reflected in his once happy eyes.

"Will you make Miss Willie well again?" he blurted, changing the subject before she could process a response about his deceased father.

She looked at Wade for an indication of what she should tell him.

"We've talked about this, sport -"

"I don't want her to die!" Cody stood in front of Tori, his

eyes filled with tears. "You have to make her better! You have to!"

Tori knelt and placed her hands on his shoulders. "I'm so very sorry, Cody. I wish I could make her better, but I –"

"I don't want her to die!" he whimpered.

His sorrow tore at her heart.

"I love her. Uncle Wade said you would help her."

"Cody," Wade took a knee beside her. "I know it's hard for you to understand -"

"No!" He pulled free and dashed out of the room.

"Well…getting off to a rocky start are we?" Lucy stood in the doorway, malicious smile in place.

"What do you want, Lucy?" Wade's deep growl thundered in the small room as he stood and assisted Tori up.

"Why, Wade, darling," she cooed as she stepped toward Tori, "what kind of relative would I be if I didn't offer your fiancée a proper welcome?"

Tori faced her antagonist. "Hello, Lucy." She revealed none of her inner turmoil.

"I noticed how you were with dear Cody. It's obvious you've been around children before." Her words were calculated and cold, designed to inflict pain. "But then, you had a son didn't you?"

"What are you doing here?" Wade barked.

"I only wanted to express my concern for your intended's well-being, darling. My sweet nephew must be such a horrid reminder -"

"Enough." Wade's order sizzled with anger.

"I have to offer my condolences and let her know -"

"How long will you be here, Lucy?" Tori's hands trembled as she placed her arm through Wade's. She needed his strength more than she wanted to admit.

He responded by placing his free hand on top of hers as they stood there. "She's leaving tomorrow," he commanded, "and there won't be any need for her to return."

Before Lucy could respond to his ultimatum, Sheila wheeled to the door.

"Uh, Wade, Mother is waiting for you."

"We're coming."

As they headed out the door, he turned back to Lucy. "Tori can handle things here."

Tori didn't look back as Wade led her down the hall.

But one thing was crystal clear; Lucy Tate was hell on high red wheels and they had not seen the last of her.

Chapter Eight

THEY WERE ALMOST TO THE DOOR OF MISS WILLIE'S room when someone called Wade.

"There you are, boy. Been looking ever 'where for you."

Tori spotted a grizzled old cowboy wearing faded jeans and a well-worn hat walking toward them.

"I'm sorry to bother you and your, uh, friend, but we got problems."

"Tori, this is Hank Calloway, our foreman. Hank, this is Tori Morgan."

"How do, Miz Morgan," said Hank, removing his hat. "I'm right sorry to barge in on you folks like 'is, but I need Wade's help." He looked at Wade. "It's Shadow. I think she's tryin' to foal."

Wade tensed. "It's too early."

"Yeah, I know, but she's showin' some signs. I reckon you better take a look."

He turned to her, his dilemma obvious. "Tori?"

She gave him a timid smile. "Go. I'll be fine. It's better this way, anyway."

"Are you sure?"

"I'm sure. Let me know if I can help. I am a nurse, you

know. Human babies, horses, they get here the same way." She tried to keep it light, but inside her stomach knotted as anxiety snaked through her. *I can't face her alone! What if I blow it?*

"I'll be back as soon as I can." Wade opened his mouth, then shut it, and followed the foreman down the hall.

"Here's her room. I'll go in with you," said Sheila.

"I think it's better for me to go alone, but thanks anyway."

"I don't know what to say," Sheila whispered, "what you're doing…"

Tori's resolve of a moment ago waned. "Not now. We'll talk later."

Sheila nodded but didn't respond.

Tori hesitated then made herself knock. After hearing a quick "Come in," she hurried forward before she had time to change her mind.

The room resembled her own except a hospital bed replaced the rustic four-poster, and the wall in front of the bed displayed many photographs.

Mrs. McBride lay in the bed, her face turned toward the picture window to her left, her gray hair pulled back in a tight bun at the nap of her neck. The dark blue bed jacket made her pale complexion more ashen, but when she looked at Tori, her hazel eyes were clear and bright.

"Good afternoon, Mrs. McBride." Tori smiled and headed toward the bed. "I'm Tori Morgan."

Her patient pointed a gnarled finger at the chair next to her bed. "Sit down, please." As soon as she obeyed, Mrs. McBride fixed her with sharp, appraising eyes. "I understand you arrived yesterday."

Heat flooded Tori's face, and she couldn't meet the steady

gaze. "Yes, well, uh…"

"No need to explain, dear, I was young once myself." Wade's mother paused for a beat and continued. "Tori is an unusual name."

"It's actually Victoria. My older brothers said I was like a little tornado from day one so they called me Tori and it stuck." She smiled at the memory of Brad and Derek's constant teasing. "Of course, I don't agree with their description."

"How many brothers do you have?"

Her heart skipped a beat. "Just Brad now. Derek died in Afghanistan three years ago."

"I'm so sorry, I -"

"Don't be. It's a natural question while we get acquainted."

"Did you know Wade was in the Army?"

She nodded. "Yes, but, to be honest, we haven't discussed much about the past."

"No future in the past, huh?"

Tori shrugged. "The past makes up the present. Sometimes to deal with the present you have to rely on the past."

"Pretty insightful." She paused and continued. "I assume Hank found him?"

"He did."

"Good. 'Bout time he earned his pay."

"Excuse me?"

"Shadow's not foaling. I told him to delay Wade so we could get acquainted without his interference." She fixed those all-seeing eyes on her. "Do you find that distasteful?"

Tori had to smile at the woman's ingenuity. "No, in fact, I told him it was better this way."

"Why?"

"Maybe for the same reason you felt it necessary to lure him away."

"Lucy thinks you're a gold digger."

"So I heard. What do you think?"

The older woman inhaled and closed her eyes. "I want my son to be happy."

"So do I, ma'am," she said softly, "So do I."

Miss Willie opened her eyes and stared a moment. "Yes…I believe you do." Any further comments ended when she grimaced, and clutched the blanket covering her.

Tori morphed into nurse mode. "How bad is your pain? Do you need a shot?"

"No," she whispered, "will be over soon. Medicine makes me sleepy. Don't want it."

"You can have a smaller dose; it will help without putting you to sleep."

"No, not yet." She slowly relaxed when the pain began to subside, but her breathing appeared to be labored. She sank back into her pillow and looked at the pictures on the wall in front of her. "My whole life is there. My husband, my children…such happy times together." She glanced at Tori. "What's your favorite memory? The one that makes you smile when nothing else will."

Tori replied without thinking. "They day my son was born."

Miss Willie brightened. "You have a child?"

Tori's heart lurched. She never meant to say that. "I… He…he died two years ago."

"I'm so sorry, my dear. Wade didn't tell me." Her voice broke and her lips trembled.

"Please, don't worry about it. I'm sure Wade didn't tell

you because he didn't want to upset you."

Miss Willie blinked a couple of times, then drew a shaky breath. "I…I lost a son, too."

"I know."

"Wade told me you're a widow."

"Yes. My husband and son were killed in the same incident."

She stared at Tori. "We seem to have a lot in common. We both lost a husband and son and we both—"

Wade entered the room. His expression gave no indication if he were angry or amused by his mother's ruse. "Hello, Mother." He placed a kiss on her forehead. "How are you today?"

"Better, now that you're home." She looked at Tori, her expression unreadable. "Tori and I are getting acquainted." Her sudden gasp and wince put Tori back in nurse mode.

"Mrs. McBride, you need to take your medication now."

"Not yet…will pass."

Tori continued to watch her for other signs of distress. "Have you eaten today?"

"No appetite," She offered a small smile. "Mrs. O'Conner is a dear but her cooking…"

Tori looked at Wade for more information.

"Mrs. O'Conner has been here most of my life. She basically retired a couple of years ago and lives in a small house out back. She occasionally cooks for Mother and does what she can to help her."

"She is wonderful to me, but her meals lacks something…flavor I think."

"Well, Mrs. McBride, I'm pretty handy in the kitchen, what would you like? I'll see if I can whip it up."

"Everyone calls me Miss Willie."

"Okay. Miss Willie it is. What can I fix for you?"

The older woman trapped her with those perceptive eyes. "Why did you come here?"

Tori glanced at Wade, reading the apprehension in his eyes. *This was it.*

"Wade asked me to." She weighed her next words carefully. "And it seemed a like a good way for us to get to know one another." Not quite a lie, but not the whole truth, either.

"If you're going to marry someone you should know them pretty well already," Miss Willie said matter-of-factly.

Her mind raced to find the right words. "I couldn't agree more. Which is why I'm here." Tori folded her hands in her lap and considered her response. "You know, it's pretty strange when you think about it. I mean, here we are, two grown, reasonably intelligent adults who, well, frankly, just met and here we are considering a lifetime commitment." She chanced a quick glance at Wade then back to his mother. "I admit our relationship is… rather unusual." She loosened her clasped hands so the knuckles would not turn white. "We were smart enough to know we needed more time together to figure out exactly where our relationship was headed. When the other nurse said she had to leave, it seemed like a good time to find out." Again, not quite the truth, but still not a complete lie either. *Maybe this wouldn't be so hard after all.*

"Do you love my son?"

And then again, maybe it would.

She looked at Miss Willie and read in her eyes the need to believe what she said next. She gathered her courage and looked at Wade. "The first time I met him he was mad as a hornet." *Another truth. If truths out-number lies, will I still go to hell?* She took a quick breath. *Please don't let me blow this.* "And I thought, 'now here's a man who needs a swift kick in the pants.'" Tori noted the uncomfortable expression on his face and smirked. "And I thought, 'I'm just the woman for that job.'"

Wade huffed, but a quick look from his mother silenced any retort he might've considered.

She took a moment to gather her thoughts. "He's the simplest and most complicated man I have ever met. He is kind and considerate with strong family values" As she spoke, she *knew* it to be the truth, just like she suspected there was more going on here than he'd told her. She continued with new fortitude. "He has a temper like a wounded bear. And I trust him completely." She unclasped her hands and smoothed the covers of the bed with her left hand. She had to make herself look at Wade and smile. "Could I love a man who makes my heart do flip flops and my knees turn to Jell-O? Yes ma'am, I can."

To her surprise, the words came with ease; perhaps because she avoided saying the words, '*Yes, I love him*' or maybe because she spoke the truth.

She *could* love a man who made her feel those things. When she looked at him, she *did* feel those things. Panic rolled over her. *No, I don't. I can't. I don't know him.* Her heart rate accelerated, her palms grew moist and her mouth went dry.

When Wade reached across the bed, took her hand and smiled, it took all her willpower not to jerk away. Outwardly, she acted as though it were the most natural act in the world; inside, her nerves went haywire. Her hand must be over hot coals because heat raced up her arm and throughout her body with lightning speed at his touch.

The challenges of this charade had just escalated into the stratosphere.

Miss Willie watched the exchange with interest, then placed her hand on top of theirs. "I'm happy for you both."

Tori's chest constricted at the look in her eyes. *She believes us.* The farce had begun and must be continued to the end.

Another spasm of pain made her patient gasp so she prepared the injection to ease her distress. "No more arguments, Miss Willie. You need to rest. I want you to take it easy for a while and I'll fix your supper. Is there anything in particular you'd like or don't like?"

"Can you fix biscuits? O'Conner said they're bad for me—like it matters now."

Tori smiled as she placed the used syringe in the red container used for that purpose. "At the risk of bragging, I have to say you won't find a better biscuit maker this side of the Rio Grande."

Miss Willie looked at Wade. "You got a winner here, son. A real winner." She took a deep breath and closed her eyes, a faint smile gracing her lips as she drifted off in a drug-induced sleep.

Tori finished her assessment and logged the information on the chart started by the previous nurse along with the information about the dosage just given.

She glanced at Wade who stared at his mother such love it made her heart ache.

She reviewed Dr. Calhoun's instructions and arranged the medications in the cabinet by the bed. She noted the key in the lock and secured it before slipping the key in her pocket. "She's resting for now. I'd like to see about those biscuits.

Where is the kitchen?"

Wade bent and kissed his mother. "Come on. I'll show you."

The huge kitchen/dining area was a cook's dream. It boasted an L-shaped countertop with two built in ovens, a range top, griddle, microwave, dishwasher, and double sink. A large walk in pantry and utility room covered one end while French doors opened out onto another porch. A large center island work area doubled as a breakfast bar and an eight-foot table with wooden benches on each side sat in front of the doors. The red gingham cloth added a bright spark of color.

"The pantry is there and the freezer over there. I haven't had time to check and see what we have, but if you need something in particular, let me or Hank know and we'll get it."

Curious, Tori lifted the table cloth. The table appeared to be handmade, and very old.

"My great-great-grandfather made it when the ranch first started. Back then, all the hands were fed at the main house instead of the bunkhouse."

"How many hands do you have now? Who cooks for them?"

"We have four full timers plus Hank and maybe three or four that help with the branding and round ups. Mrs. O'Conner used to do all the cooking, but now they pretty much have to fend for themselves."

"Does the bunkhouse have a kitchen or do they use this?"

"It has a small kitchen and the boys have become pretty inventive with their meals."

"Who cooks for everyone here?"

"Unfortunately for them, I do since Sheila's been hurt."

"I see." Tori explored the kitchen as they chatted, checked the cabinets, pantry and refrigerator. "What time would you like supper tonight? Or do y'all call it dinner?"

"What do you mean?"

"I mean, what time would you like eat?"

"I didn't bring you here to cook for us."

"I know. I love to cook. I haven't had anyone to cook for since—well, in a long time. I've already told your mother I'd fix her some biscuits and it wouldn't be any big deal to fix supper for the rest of you as well. Unless, of course, you'd rather I didn't."

"I don't want you to think you have to."

"I know I don't. So," she put on an apron she'd found on the wall by the pantry. "What would you like and when would you like it ready?"

"Whatever you want to fix will be fine. But you really don't have to do this."

"I know. My patients will always come first so if it gets to be a problem, I'll let you know. In the meantime," she glanced at her watch "It's ten to four. Your mom should sleep for a couple of hours. How about supper about seven? Is it too late, too early? I don't know how things work on a ranch."

"Seven's fine. I still have stuff I need to take care of before dark."

Tori smiled. "Like Shadow?"

"How did you know?"

"She told me."

"I'm sorry."

"Don't be. I think it…it went well." Heat leached up her neck so Tori busied herself looking around the kitchen. "I think I'd like some coffee. You?"

"Maybe later. I need to get back to work. Just make your-self at home."

"There you are." Sheila wheeled herself into the kitchen and stopped at the bar. She pinned Tori with eyes as sharp as her mothers. "How did it go?"

"Okay, I think."

"I'm so sorry for this mess, Tori."

It's done. Move on. "I thought I'd cook tonight, and Wade doesn't have a preference. Do you?"

"You're cooking?"

"You needn't look so surprised. I told you before I'm a pretty good cook."

"I know, I -"

"Well, well, if this isn't a cozy little scene," Lucy snarled

"I need to get back to work." Wade gave Tori a quick brush of his lips on her cheek. "I'll see you later."

She knew the performance was for Lucy's benefit, but was surprised to discover how much she enjoyed such a sim-ple thing as a peck on the cheek. The warmth of his lips lin-gered, and desired flickered through her.

"Who all will be here for supper?" Tori asked.

"Just us. Well, maybe Hank, if you don't mind."

"I don't mind." She gave him a big smile and playfully pushed on his chest, intending to steer him toward the door. The minute her hands touched him, her minds' eye flashed to the image of that naked chest as he exited the hotel bathroom. Her breath caught and she struggled to get the next sentence out with any degree of normalcy. "If you don't get out of here, I'll never get supper done."

"Yes, ma'am." He grinned and placed the worn Stetson on his head. "I never argue with the cook."

Add that smile to the mental image dancing in her head and Tori couldn't think.

"I thought you were leaving." Sheila's sharp question brought Tori back around.

"I wouldn't dream of leaving her here alone to take care of everyone." The words were kind, but the coldness in Lucy's voice said she meant them otherwise.

"I appreciate the offer, Lucy, but I can handle what needs to be done here." She pulled out makings for coffee and spoke to Sheila over her shoulder. "You look a little pale, Sheila, are you in pain?"

"I'm a little tired, is all. This chair is the pits."

"I'm sure it is, Sheila dear," cooed Lucy, "why don't I help you to your room? You can rest while Tori and I get acquainted. After all, she'll soon be part of my *family*."

"I don't want your help, Lucy." She turned to Tori, the plea in her eyes clear. "Is there something—anything—I can do to help? I'm so tired of feeling useless."

"Well, I haven't decided what to fix yet. Do you have any suggestions?"

"Wade loves fried chicken."

"Sounds good. Fried chicken with all the trimmings is my specialty," said Tori.

"Sounds delicious. But, Mrs. O'Conner will have a fit."

"We'll see." Tori looked at Lucy and smiled again, making it saccharine sweet. "I think Sheila and I can handle this. I'm sure you need to get packed so you can be on your way in the morning."

Lucy stormed out of the kitchen without another word, eyes shooting daggers at her.

Tori sighed. *If looks could kill I'd be pushing daisies now.*

"Don't make her mad, Tori. She's crazy."

"I noticed that."

"Just be careful. I think she's dangerous."

"Wade doesn't think so."

"Wade still believes in Santa Clause and the Tooth Fairy!"

Tori laughed. "Who doesn't?"

Sheila took her hand. "I don't know how to thank you."

Tori lowered her voice. "Don't thank me, yet. This is just the beginning."

"I know, but you…here like this, well, it means so much to her. You should've seen her this morning. She had Mrs. O'Conner fix her hair and dig out an old bed jacket. She hasn't worn it since before Isaac—" Tears filled her eyes. "I'm really sorry I got you in this mess."

"What's done is done." Tori swallowed hard. Everyone had burdens to carry. Even her. "Right now, we've got supper to think about."

Before she could say anything else, a huge dog wandered into the kitchen and stopped in front of Tori, hackles raised, on full alert.

"Good gracious! Is that a wolf?"

"Only half. Meet Major. Wade's pride and joy. Raised him from a pup. Ignores everyone except Wade. Once in a while, he might let me pet him, but not very often."

"Well, hello there, Major." Tori, cautiously extended the back of her closed fist toward him. "What are you doing in here?"

"I'm sure he's hungry again. Mrs. O'Conner leaves him a bowl of scraps in the utility room. He pretty much has the run of the house."

Major inched toward Tori and sniffed her fist.

"Careful. He's never bitten anyone, but there's always a first time."

"Well, Major? You gonna bite me?"

He wagged his tail and inched closer, and she scratched him on the head.

"Well, now, big fella, I see you like to be scratched, huh?" The wolf-hound rubbed against her legs and tried to lick her hand. Tori squatted and rubbed his ears.

Major responded by wagging his tail so fast his butt wobbled and licked her face.

"Well, I've seen it all now," said Sheila, "he won't have anything to do with anyone except Wade."

"I love animals. Always had a pet; usually a dog of some kind. Anyway, you just have to let them know whose boss."

"Yeah, right."

Tori gave Major one last pat and said, "Go. I've got work to do."

When he walked into the utility room, Sheila smiled. "You've got a friend for life, there."

She washed her hands at the sink.

Hope so. I may need one before this is over.

Chapter Nine

WADE WALKED UP THE BACK STEPS TO CLEAN UP in the sink built for that purpose and reflected on the days' events. He'd had no idea his mother would react the way she did. He thought she'd be happy about his so-called *engagement* but never thought it would bring about such a change. For the first time in months, her eyes sparkled with life and her voice no longer held the hopeless tone that wrenched his heart.

Nor did he anticipate the depth of Tori's acceptance of her role. When Miss Willie asked her why she had come, Tori's reply was quick and convincing.

He replayed her answer to the question *'Do you love my son?'* over and over. He knew if asked the same question, he would stumble for words. Tori, however, replied right away. What she said and the way she said it was spoken with such quiet conviction, he almost believed her himself. As he considered the conversation with his mother, he realized she hadn't *exactly* lied. He even smiled at her ingenuity when she spoke of their first meeting. To listen to her, no one would guess they spoke at brief intervals on the phone for six weeks and never met face to face until yesterday.

The woman had grit, and he admired grit. But one matter

unsettled him to no end. His reaction to her statement, '*Could I love a man who makes my heart do flip-flops and my knees turn to Jell-O?*' The accompanying smile lit up her face and her eyes sparkled. For a heartbeat, he imagined the words *were* meant for him and his heart thumped hard and fast. Before he knew it, he reached across the bed and placed his hand over hers and every fiber of his body instantly reacted. *What the hell?* He had no interest in her as a woman; she was a means to an end. Nothing more. He repeated this over and over but his body remembered the feeling too well and held on to it.

He did feel bad for her, though, for she had the most difficult role. He recalled the brief glimpse of pain in her eyes as she turned and followed Cody. He accepted her statement that she could handle the situation because it suited his needs. Now, he realized what a selfish mistake he made and it was too late to remedy. He promised himself he would make it up to her later, but knew he it would not be possible to make up for what she would have to endure. As guilt threatened to undermine his plans, he remembered the look of pure joy in his mother's eyes and knew he would do whatever it took to keep it there.

He ducked his head under the cold water in an effort to clear out the doubts assailing him. The charade was on and he must play his part.

As he toweled off, Hank came around the corner and Wade smiled at his friend. "What did you do, you ole goat? Take a bath?"

"Well," drawled Hank, "I didn't want the Missus thinking we wuz both uncivilized, so I just freshened up a bit."

Wade's stomach tightened. He hated to lie to the man

he loved like a father, but at this point, the fewer people who knew the better.

"You not only took a bath, you shaved and changed clothes."

Even in the fading light of day Wade saw the flush making Hank's cheeks glow and smiled. "I hope this meal is worth it."

"Well, I happen to know she took an apple pie out the oven not fifteen minutes ago. I smelled it all the way to bunkhouse."

"Well, let's check it out."

As Wade and Hank walked in the back door, Tori returned from his mother's room with two empty trays. Sheila and Cody sat at the table but he didn't see Lucy. Maybe it would be a peaceful meal after all.

"Uncle Wade," said Cody, "look what Miss Tori did."

"This is quite a spread, Miz Morgan," said Hank with obvious anticipation as he followed Wade to the table.

"Thank you, Hank. And, please, call me Tori."

Hank smiled and ducked his head. "Yes 'em, Miz Tori."

Wade caught her eye and nodded to the table laden with fried chicken, mashed potatoes and green beans. "I didn't expect all this."

"Well, I always heard a working man needed a good meal to keep him going," said Tori as she placed the trays on the counter and removed a pan of biscuits from the warm oven.

"This should do it."

"She even made your favorite, Uncle Wade! Apple pie!"

"I can't take all the credit," said Tori, seating herself across from Wade, "Sheila helped."

"I peeled the potatoes and sliced the apples," said Sheila,

"Tori did the rest."

Once they were all seated, Lucy walked in. "My goodness, Tori, darling, you really outdid yourself." She sat on the bench with Tori because Cody, Wade and Hank were on the other side and Sheila's wheelchair occupied one end. "But all this fried food. I'd never keep my schoolgirl figure if I ate like this every day."

Wade heard a snicker from Sheila, but ignored it.

They ate in sporadic silence broken by occasional words of praise about the meal and chit chat about the ranch's operations. Tori asked a lot of questions and Hank looked happy to answer.

Lucy baited her at every opportunity but Tori kept her cool, though he wondered how long she could keep up the pretense.

The thought surfaced that maybe lying came easy to her. In a flash, it scattered like dry leaves in a winter breeze because he intuitively knew it wasn't true.

Lucy's presence made the meal awkward at times and he heaved a sigh of relief when Tori asked who wanted dessert.

"I do!" said Cody and Hank in unison.

"Me, too," said Wade, as he stood to help remove the dinner plates.

Tori brought the still warm dessert to the table while Wade brought saucers. The mouthwatering aroma filled the room as she placed the thick slices on each plate.

"Miz Tori," said Hank, swallowing another bite of pie, "This is, without a doubt, the best meal I've had in I don't know when."

"Thank you, Hank."

"Yes sirree, Wade done found him a real rancher's wife.

'Bout time, too."

Before Wade could summon a reply, Tori saved him by changing the subject.

"How long have you been on the ranch, Hank?"

"Well, ma'am, I came on 'bout the time ole Wade here made his first appearance in this world.'Cept for a hitch in the Army, I been here ever since."

"Our Hank is quite indispensable around here," cooed Lucy, "Why we would be lost without him, wouldn't we Wade?"

Her constant reference to *we* all through dinner grated on his nerves. Apparently not as much as it bothered Sheila, though.

"There is no *we* here, Lucy, and you best get that through your thick head!"

"Why Sheila, dear, I meant no harm. I'm sure Wade told Tori how *close* we are. Why, it's only natural for me to associate myself with him. And everyone else, of course. After all, I have been here for him *so* many times."

This time, he didn't underestimate the implication of her seemingly innocent statement and it sent him past the boiling point. He dropped his fork, about to tell her to go to hell when Tori reached across the table and placed her hand over his and squeezed.

"As a matter of fact he did, Lucy." She placed her other hand over Lucy's. "I can't tell you how much I appreciate it. Why, if you hadn't been here taking care of things, Wade and I would never have met and I wouldn't be here now." She smiled and looked at him. "We owe her a lot, don't we... darling?"

It took him a moment to pick up the cue. "That's right.

We wouldn't be here now if it weren't for Lucy." He smiled at their inside joke. "So thanks."

Lucy jerked her hand out from under Tori's and left the table.

"What's wrong with Aunt Lucy?" asked Cody. "Ain't she glad you're gettin' married?"

Wade patted the child on the top of his head. "Of course she is, sport, she's tickled pink." He caught Hank's look of caution before he turned his attention to his dessert.

When everyone finished, Tori stood and started to remove the dishes.

"Oh, goodness." She covered her mouth when she yawned. "I'm sorry. Guess I'm more tired than I thought."

Wade stood up. "You've done enough for one day. Why don't you turn in and I'll do the dishes."

"You didn't tell me you do dishes."

"You didn't ask. Now go. Cody can help me, can't you, sport?"

"Yes, sir. I can put 'em in the dishwasher and ever 'thing."

"Yes," said Sheila, "We can do all this. You should go to bed."

"Well, I am pretty bushed. I'm going to check on Miss Willie before I turn in." She turned to Wade and continued, "There's a fresh pot of coffee on the stove. Be sure you turn it off when you're done."

"Yes, ma'am."

"Sheila, we'll start your physical therapy tomorrow, say around 10?"

"Ten's fine."

She looked at Wade. "I'll spend most of the day with Miss Willie and Sheila so lunch will have to be on your own. But

I should have plenty of time to cook supper again, as long as you'll do the dishes."

"Well, if he don't," said Hank with a smile, "I will. I ain't had a meal like this in a coon's age."

"Good."

Major came in as she turned to leave but instead of going to Wade or to the utility room where his food dish waited, he trotted over to Tori and licked her hands, while his tail wagged so fast his back end waved with each swish. *What the hell?* Wade fought a sudden attack of jealously. Major was *his*. He never let anyone else near him. Until now. Score another point for Tori.

She reached across the table, and took a piece of chicken off the plate, then squatted on the floor and hand-fed him pieces of the tender meat. "Hi ya, big fella," She rubbed his ears while he scarfed up her offering. "I see you like fried chicken, too, huh?"

"Well, I'll be damned." Hank shook his head. "That old buzzard ignores everybody but Wade."

"Oh, Major's just welcoming me here." said Tori. She stood and pointed toward the utility room. "Go now and eat your supper. Go on."

Another lick, another wag and he obeyed her command.

"Now, if you'll excuse me, I'll go check on Miss Willie."

He watched the sway of her hips as she left the room. *Damn. Jeans never looked so good.* He looked away in time to catch the perceptive smile on Hank's face.

What have I gotten myself into?

Chapter Ten

Tori paced around her room, consumed by a restless energy she hadn't experienced in a long time. She glanced at her watch. *Nine o'clock. I'm tired but it's too early for bed. Maybe a hot shower will do the trick.* She turned toward the bathroom and her eye caught the moon rising over the mountains in the distance.

Captivated, she walked out onto the porch, past Wade's room, and down the steps. She chanced a sideways glance and noted his lights were off and wondered if he was in bed yet, then shivered at the mental image that generated.

She crossed the yard toward the corral and soon found Major at her side. She gave him a quick pat and resumed her relaxed stroll. By the time she reached the corral, she wished she'd brought along a jacket. She rubbed her arms to generate warmth and looked up to the most beautiful night sky she ever remembered seeing. The clouds of the day were gone and stars glistened like so many diamonds resting on a rich velvet cloth. The full moon rested above the highest peak, its misty glow embracing the valley below.

She closed her eyes and inhaled a deep breath, pulling the cool mountain air deep into every tiny crevice. She savored the crispness and unfamiliar, yet pleasant, aromas accompanying it and found it both soothed and comforted. Exhaling, she opened her eyes and looked around, again rubbing her arms for warmth. "I have never, ever seen such a beautiful night sky."

"I'm glad to hear that."

Startled, she jumped and lost her balance.

"Sorry." Wade offered a hand to steady her. "I didn't mean to startle you."

"Well, you did." She turned to Major and wagged her finger, "And *you* should have told me someone was coming."

He had the nerve to yawn and lie down.

Wade chuckled. "Some watch-dog, huh?"

"Yeah."

"I thought you were going to turn in."

"Couldn't unwind." Tori shrugged. "Thought a walk might help."

"Yeah, me, too."

"I love the stars…Almost like you could reach up and pluck one." She ducked her head. *Pluck a star? He must think I'm imbecile.* "Sorry. I get carried away sometimes and don't know when to shut up." She shivered again and looked toward the mountains.

"The nights get cold pretty quick after dark." He shrugged out of his coat and placed it around her shoulders. "Need to keep one of these handy."

"Thanks. I didn't realize it would get this cold." She pulled the oversized jacket around her. Immediately swamped with unfamiliar musky, man-smells—leather, sweat, and something she couldn't identify—that seeped into the withered corner of her core, and something stirred. The feeling, so primal, yet foreign, caught her off guard, and made her tremble.

"Won't you get cold?"

He shook his head and motioned for her to follow. They walked around the corral side by side, Major close behind.

"I know today was hard on you," he said as they walked. "I wish I could say it will get better."

"It wasn't that bad, not really."

"I'm sorry we didn't think to tell you about Cody."

She wasn't ready for that conversation. "Hank doesn't know."

"No," he said after a bit, "I almost told him, though."

"This lying stuff is not as easy as some folks think."

Her remark produced the slightest of smiles and she shuddered. *Oh my God…that smile with that voice is a deadly combination.*

"When we got here today, you said something to the effect you were doing this as much for yourself as anyone. Mind if I ask what you meant?"

They passed the barn near the wood-pile and she caught the tangy smell of fresh cut pine along with a whiff of manure. She skirted a stack of logs and leaned against a metal rack, eyes focused on the moonlit valley. "The last two years have been…difficult. I finally realized it was time to make some decisions about my life. Couldn't make them in Houston. Too many…distractions I guess. Then I saw your ad." She glanced at him and smiled. "I still can't believe I answered it."

"Why?" His brows drew together and he watched her much too closely.

"Well, for one thing, I'm not the sort of person who makes rash decisions, and, well, this was a rash decision."

His face revealed nothing of his thoughts as he waited for her to continue.

Something about him relaxed her and made her uneasy at the same time, the conflicting emotions kept her off balance.

"After we spoke on the phone and I agreed to take the position, I had second thoughts. I mean, it suddenly dawned on me I knew nothing about you except what you told me, which wasn't much, so—I, um, had you checked out."

"Checked out?"

She faced him. "I'm from a family of cops. I had you checked out."

He nodded. "Pretty and smart, too. I like it."

His off-hand compliment caused a new surge of heat that had nothing to do with being embarrassed.

"So, I guess you found out I'm harmless."

Another hint of a smile and her stomach clinched, eyes drawn to his mouth.

Harmless? I don't think so!

A quick mental shake and she was back on track. "As I said, I needed space and time and distraction. Your ad offered it all." *Heavy on the distraction part.*

"Are you sorry you came?"

"Well, obviously, I didn't think things would get so... complicated, and it bothers me to lie to anyone, but, no, I'm not sorry I came." She snorted. "Not yet, anyway."

"I promise to do my best to ensure you're not sorry."

His remark, coupled with an easy smile, had her errant mind conjuring up ways he might ensure she wasn't sorry. "I'll hold you to that." *Surely that breathy sound is not my voice?*

He winked. "Good."

Eyes locked, neither moved for several moments. The

attraction was intense. And mutual. A strong, chiseled profile darkened by five o'clock shadow, slight bump on the bridge of his nose indicating it might have been broken at one time, and a full, sensuous mouth all worked together to wreak havoc on her nerves. She blinked several times, tried to get control of raging hormones. *Get a grip, girl! Get a grip!*

She needed a distraction and for once Lucy was helpful. "I do think Lucy is going be a problem, though."

"She's definitely odd but I don't think she will be a problem."

"You really can't see she's totally obsessed with you?"

He chuckled, a deep melodic sound like those fancy metal wind chimes that were four feet long.

"I'll admit she's about as peculiar as they come, but I wouldn't call her *obsessed.*"

Only a man would be so naïve. "My gut says she's dangerous."

"What does your gut say about me?"

Was he teasing her? It didn't matter, Tori was in honesty mode. She was forced to lie to others but she wouldn't lie to him. "I believe you'd give your life for those you love; I can trust you with mine; you're hiding something from me, possibly because you don't feel you can trust me yet, which isn't surprising under the circumstances, and you're having a great deal of difficulty with this…situation, too." She paused to give him a moment to digest that. "Anything else you want to know?"

The corners of his eyes crinkled when he grinned. "Are you always so blunt?"

"Yeah, 'fraid so." She looked around the moon-kissed valley, convinced there could not be a more beautiful spot in all the world.

"May I be blunt as well?"

Something in his tone made her pulse jump. "Of course."

He faced her, hands stuffed in his front pockets. "I think we need a test kiss."

"A wh-what?"

He took a step closer, hands sliding out of his pockets. "A test kiss. You know, so when we have to do it front of anyone, and we will, it won't look fake."

She didn't move. Couldn't if her life depended on it. "I-I guess…" He was close enough she could see the dilation in his pupils, smell the coffee on his breath. "If y-you think—"

"I do."

His low, raspy murmur sent heat pooling in her middle.

He cupped her neck with both hands, thumbs lightly caressing her jawline as his lips descended upon hers, light, tentative, tracing the outline of her upper lip with his tongue.

Tori forgot to breathe.

He claimed her lips again with a lingering, sensual kiss no doubt invented to entice and enflame.

And it did.

Her hands fisted in his shirt as the kiss set off rockets of sensation firing through her. Coherent thought fled. Nothing mattered beyond the tangy taste of him and she took her fill.

Too soon, he pulled back, hands shaky as he sucked in air. "Yeah, um, yeah. I think we got it."

She stood there, staring at him, waiting for her brain to kick in and say something clever and insightful. "That was nice." *Nice? That* is what her brain considered clever and insightful? Her face burned and she was thankful for the darkness to hide its embarrassing color.

He smiled. A slow, sexy, self-satisfied smile. "Yes it was."

She took a step back and noticed her hands still clutched his shirt. She released it, automatically smoothing at the wrinkles. His heart thudded against her palm, and she had to resist pressing it firmly against him as the rockets threatened to fire again. She jerked her hand away and took another step back.

I'm not ready for this.

"Yes, well, we should go to bed…to sleep, I mean. I think I can sleep now." *Yeah. Right. I'm not wound up at all.*

She handed him his jacket with a terse "Thank you", and strode toward the house. She stopped when her rebellious brain finally had an appropriate thought. She took a breath and faced him. "When this is over, I want us to come up with a story—together—about why we aren't, we didn't…you know." She folded her arms across her chest. "I don't want everyone to know I, we, lied to them."

"Fair enough."

She hurried back to her room.

Yep. Just like riding a bike. Or a grenade launcher.

Chapter Eleven

WADE STARED AT THE LEDGER IN FRONT HIM without seeing it, so tired his vision blurred. The last two weeks had zoomed by. His days were filled with countless activities around the ranch or looking for any sign that his brother's killer was back. The sheriff wanted him to believe it was an accident but Wade didn't buy it. Isaac drove that mountain road a thousand times, knew every twist and turn. There was no way he went over the edge on his own. He'd found the boot prints and tire tracks but nothing else, and Sheriff Wallace said that was not enough to do anything with.

His nights were filled with Tori.

Or rather, dreams of her and that damn kiss. It was an impromptu urge, spawned by the play of moonlight on her expressive face, the way she smiled gazing out at the valley. Hell, maybe it was the way she breathed. One minute he was a sane adult having a normal adult conversation, the next a randy teen trying to steal a kiss.

And what a kiss it was.

Now, they danced around it and each other till he was ready to explode. Every time he was near her, desire flickered to life. It was like his brain was hot-wired to that moment in time. As a result, he was in a constant state of semi-arousal with no way to remedy it. A wounded bear had a better disposition than him.

Thankfully, they did not have to *perform* often for his mother's sake and when they did, it was light banter or maybe a quick kiss on the cheek.

Even that was too much for him. And not enough.

They spent an hour or so with his mother after supper each evening. He would sit quietly while she told some story of him growing up that, more often than not, had him ducking his head. Tori would laugh or tease him and his mother would smile. And that one smile was worth whatever discomfort he endured.

Tonight, though, she was not herself and that worried him. She was weaker than yesterday and Tori had to work to get her to eat anything at all. She asked for the pain meds, too. She never did that. His breath hitched at the thought of losing her.

Later, at supper, Tori was especially quiet and avoided looking at him. He didn't know if it was his mother or that damn kiss but made up his mind they would discuss the elephant in the room like adults. They kissed. They enjoyed it. Move on. *I wanna do it again.*

He sighed and turned back to the ledger.

♡

Tori finished the dishes and stared out the window. Miss Willie was fading fast and it broke her heart. She had such a wonderful outlook on life…and death. Tori loved her spirit, and her determination to make every moment count.

That thought brought her to the crux of her dilemma tonight.

The kiss.

It was never far from her memory. Swamped by emotions she hadn't experienced in years, she struggled to maintain balance. Out of her element, she wasn't sure what she needed to do. *Kiss him again.* Unconvinced she was ready for that, she did think they needed to discuss it and get past it.

She made a decision. Wade was in his office doing paperwork. She'd take him some coffee and play it by ear.

A few minutes later, she stood at the door and watched him before he saw her. His head rested on his left hand, staring at the ledger in front of him, tapping the pencil he held in his other hand on the edge.

"Ready for a break?" she asked as she entered.

He looked up and gave her a timid smile. "Absolutely."

She placed the cup within his reach. "I'm sorry if I'm interrupting. You seemed to be deep in thought."

"You're not interrupting. I needed this." He picked up the cup and sitting back in his chair, took a careful sip and watched her.

She noted the dark circles under his eyes, and fatigue was more evident in the lines on his face. The natural caregiver in her surfaced; he was under a lot of pressure with his mother's illness and caring for the ranch, and he always set his own needs aside. "You look tired. Are you sleeping all right?"

He flexed his shoulders and neck. "Some nights better than others." Then he grinned and winked. "Worried about me, Nurse Morgan?"

It took effort on her part not to show how that sexy little repartee affected her. "You work too hard." She stood behind his chair. "Put your cup down a minute."

He did as she asked. "Okay. What's up?"

"This." She placed her hands on his shoulders, noting the tense muscles. "Relax." She placed her right thumb on one side of his neck and fingers on the other, pressing downward, across his shoulder. She found the knots that needed to be worked out. Using her thumb, she massaged each one until it disappeared.

"Damn that feels good."

"Good old fashioned neck rubs work wonders."

"Uh-huh."

She shifted to the shoulder blade, using circular, kneading motions to release the tension.

Wade relaxed more with each pass and soon reclined back, eyes closed, arms resting in his lap. His head lolled back and rested against her chest, sending a frizzle of awareness to every nerve in her body.

His eyes popped open and captured hers; desire sparked like electricity between them.

She looked at his sensual mouth, lips parted, tongue tracing his lower lip, then back to his eyes which darkened to a deep azure blue. Her breath caught and her gaze returned to his lips, unable to quash the sudden need engulfing her.

Thoughts of Eddie warred with her resolve to move forward.

The desire to taste him again won the battle.

She bent lower, about to cross a line she could not uncross, but unable to stop.

So much for discussing this first.

He didn't move a muscle as her lips softly brushed his, testing his reaction.

Just like riding a bike. She kissed him again, letting her need guide her actions as her tongue lightly touched his.

Evidently that was the right move.

His hand came up and cupped her neck, pulling her toward him, his hot, open-mouth kiss reminiscent of the other night as shock waves of desire rolled through her.

She ended the kiss and slowly opened her eyes.

Holy mother of pearl. What have I done?

Wade's expression softened. "So much for the elephant in the room."

Once again, her noncompliant brain refused to function. "I'm s-sorry…I-I meant to talk…"

He smirked. "I like how you *talk*."

She took a step away, her backside against the desk. Her heart pounded, thoughts scattered to the four winds. *What am I doing?*

Wade pushed his chair away and stood. "Wanna talk some more?" He didn't do anything, just stood there… waiting.

She took a deep breath, forced herself to look at him, silently cursing the heat that radiated from her cheeks. "I didn't…I only meant to …discuss it."

"The elephant in the room?"

She nodded. "I'm not…I don't think I'm ready."

One brow raised slightly and his lips curled up in suggestive smile. "If that's your idea of not ready, I can't wait till you are."

She ducked her head as guilt and embarrassment washed over her. "I can't think around you…"

Fingers under her chin, he raised her head. "Look at me, Tori."

It took some effort but she did.

"There's a …connection between us. We both sense it and we reacted to it. There's no shame in that." He paused. "But I do understand where you're coming from. I won't push you into something you're not ready for." The smile returned. "But anytime you wanna *talk*, just let me know."

She managed a pitifully weak smile and slowly shook her head. "I can't think straight around you."

His left brow kicked up again and his grin widened.

"Aunt Tori," Cody's voice from the doorway broke the spell and she jumped. "You said you would read more *Treasure Island* tonight."

She took a breath, gave herself a mental shake and left the room, Cody in tow.

Oh my God! I told him I couldn't think around him!

She completed her nightly ritual with the child and Miss Willie before retiring to her room. Sleep was a long time coming.

Long dormant feelings surfaced and her body begged for his touch.

When sleep finally came, her dreams were peppered with images that had nothing to do with the job and everything to do with the man.

Maybe Sassy is right; maybe I just need to let go and do it.

<h1 style="text-align:center">Chapter Twelve</h1>

Tori closed the book she read to Miss Willie when Wade entered the room. "I thought you were checking fences today?"

He gave Tori a quick peck on the cheek. "Decided to spend some time with my favorite girls."

Since their *talk* in his office two days ago, they were a little more relaxed around each other and their banter showed it.

He sat on the edge of the bed and looked at his mother. "Have you had lunch yet?"

"Yes, Tori fed me already." She smiled at her nurse. "I'm so glad you came to us, my dear. You take such good care of me." She winced and closed her eyes briefly.

"Miss Willie? Do you need the paid meds?"

She took a halting breath and spoke softly. "No, dear, that one wasn't so bad. Passed quickly."

Tori glanced at Wade and saw the worry lining his face. She reached over and placed her hand on his and he gripped it tightly. "I was just reading to her from *Last of the Mohicans*. Shall I continue, Miss Willie?"

"Maybe after supper, dear." She saw the clasped hands and smiled. "Did you know Tori likes to ride horses?"

"I did. In fact, that was one of the reasons I came in." He turned to Tori. "I thought we might take a ride later this afternoon."

"A wonderful idea, son." Miss Willie looked at Tori. "Why don't you go ahead and go now? Sheila will be here and you know I will sleep most of the afternoon anyway."

"Are you sure? We were just getting started on the book." Undecided about what to do, Tori hesitated.

"I'm sure. You two go for your ride."

"We won't be gone long, couple of hours at the most," offered Wade.

She worried about being alone with him but wanted to ride…and be alone with him. "Um, Okay. When?"

"Whenever you say."

She glanced at her patient. "Are you certain you don't want me to read some more?"

"I'm sure. Enjoy your ride. You have been cooped up in here with me for too long."

"A ride it is, then."

"Great." Wade spent a few more minutes visiting and joking with his mother then rose to leave. "I'll meet you in the barn in half an hour." He turned to his mother. "I'll see you at supper."

"I love you, son." Her voice was weak but her eyes sharp.

He kissed her brow. "I love you more."

After he left, Tori busied herself making sure everything was put away and her patient comfortable.

"Thank you for being here with me, my dear."

The heartfelt words sliced into Tori's soul, stealing her breath. "I love being here." She covered a gnarled hand with her own and smiled. "You are a very special lady and I treasure the time we have together."

"I feel the same way about you." Miss Willie smiled. "Now go for that ride."

Tori brushed her cheek with a kiss. "I'll check on you later."

True to his word, Wade had her horse ready and waiting when she arrived. A beautiful black and white mare sniffed her hand when she approached. "Oh, Wade, she's beautiful! Is she a paint?"

"Pinto-Paint mix. Very easy to ride. Her name is Bonnie."

"I love the markings. That jumble of black and white is so striking." She pulled a sugar lump from her coat pocket. "Can I give her this?"

"Sure. She loves it. When you get mounted I'll see if I need to adjust the stirrups."

A few minutes later, they were headed for the western edge of the ranch. It soon became apparent Bonnie didn't care for the sedate pace they were holding to. "Which way are we headed?"

Wade gestured toward some pines in the distance. "Over there."

"I think Bonnie wants to run."

"You okay with that?"

She nodded. "I think I have my saddle legs." She snickered. "If not, you can come back and get me." She gave Bonnie a light touch with her heel and loosened the reins, leaning forward in the saddle. The horse took off like a shot and Tori laughed at the sheer exhilaration of riding again.

♡

An hour later, they reached the summit at Walker Pass. Wade watched Tori dismount and walk to the edge of the small plateau without saying word.

He was spellbound as she drank in the beauty of the valley below and the snow-capped mountains in the distance. She closed her eyes, inhaled and exhaled, then turned and smiled.

That radiant smile shook him to his core and stole the breath from his lungs.

"Thank you for bringing me here," she said softly, "I thought the ranch was the most beautiful spot in the world... until now."

"I'm glad you like it."

What a dumbass thing to say. But he could not, for the life of him think of anything else.

"Like it? I *love* it! It's magnificent." She spread her arms wide, obviously taking it all in. "I don't have the words to describe it."

Wade laughed. "I think this is the first time I've seen you at a loss for words."

She arched a brow and smiled. "Well, miracles do happen, you know." She moved to a large boulder and sat. Her horse followed a step behind, then stopped to munch the scattered grass. "What's over there?" She pointed to the left corner of the valley.

He got off his horse and let the reins trail knowing the gelding wouldn't wander far and sat beside her. "An old game trail hunters have turned into a road of sorts for four-wheelers. Follow it south, maybe a mile or so, and it meets up with four-oh-six which takes you back to town. And over there just behind those rocks," he pointed to an area off to the left, "is the start of that trail. You follow it down to an old line shack we don't use anymore. Well, hunters use it from time to time. Wanna check it out?"

"Another time." She turned toward the valley again. "I think I'd like to just sit here for now." Tori glanced toward him then quickly looked forward, the ever-present blush tinging her cheeks a lovely shade of pink.

He loved—and hated—those blushes, for they conjured instant fantasies of what she might be thinking. His body, always on a low simmer around her, reacted.

Their resting place was narrow but flat, so they touched shoulder to knees. Wade could smell strawberry scented shampoo, mixed with the pleasant smell of horse and leather. Desire percolated through him and he tamped it down. Again. His heartrate kicked up a notch, and his groin tightened. *Again.*

Tori shivered, whether from the early winter chill or something else, he didn't know.

"Cold?" he rasped.

"A little. I thought my jacket was enough."

Without taking time to think about it, he put his arm around her and pulled her against him. "Want mine?"

She tensed, then snuggled closer, shaking her head. "This is good."

Every inch of him craved her.

His pulse stumbled, then settled into a too-fast rhythm. Contentment flowed through him like whiskey, calming his soul.

This moment in time, he truly knew peace, no worries, no troubles…only this.

Only her.

Chapter Thirteen

"So, you get laid yet?" Sasha's question caught Tori unprepared.

She coughed and sputtered the coffee she tried to sip.

"Good grief, Sass, what the hell kind of question is that?"

"I take it the answer is no. Dang, girlfriend, what're you waiting for? It's been almost a month!"

She prayed for patience. "How are things in Houston?"

"Fine. Change the subject; but you know as well as I do you're wasting valuable time. And things are good. Still no sign of Rico. Hopefully he's in a shallow grave somewhere."

She started to protest the blunt statement but knew it would fall on deaf ears. Besides, she hoped the same thing. "How's every little thing these days? Anything new with Jonathan?" Jonathan Walsh was Sasha's latest steady and appeared to be the real deal.

After a short pause, her friend whispered, "He's moving in this weekend."

"Wow! That's great news….isn't it?"

Sasha, never at a loss for words, took a long time to reply, which threw up a red flag for Tori. "It *is* great news, right, Sass?"

"What if I'm making a mistake?" Her usually enthusiastic voice lacked certainty. "This is such a huge step. I'm crazy about him, I don't deny it. But what if he's using me? What if he doesn't feel the same way I do?"

She talked tough, but when it came down to it, Sassy was as vulnerable and unsure as most women where relationships were concerned.

"Do you love him?"

After a slight pause, she replied, "God help me, I do."

No one could doubt they were head over heels for each other with just one look at them together. Tori envied her friend more than she'd ever know. "Then it's the right step. You'll see. He's as crazy about you as you are about him."

"I hope so. I'd hate to know I spent all that money at Victoria's Secret for nothing."

Her deadpan comment made Tori laugh. "Girl you just won't do."

"Yeah, well at least one of us is getting some. You should to try it sometime. Does wonders for your attitude."

"My attitude is just fine, thank you very much."

"Any snow yet? Wade said it would start soon."

"When did you talk to Wade?"

"This morning. I called but you were out in the barn or something. We chatted a bit." She made a tsk-tsk sound. "I can see you rolling your eyes from here. I didn't say anything to embarrass you."

Tori grimaced thinking of all the things she *could've* said to him. "I'm not rolling my eyes…what did you talk about?" She pinched the bridge of her nose to stay focused.

"Nothing in particular, the weather, how you like the mountains; stuff in general, nothing in particular."

"Uh-huh."

"I don't see how you do it."

"Do what?"

"Listen to him speak and not jump his bones." She heaved a dramatic sigh. "I do believe I could come just listening to him talk. But don't tell Jonathan. He might not appreciate that."

"Sasha!"

Her exclamation was met by a peal of laughter. "Don't tell me it doesn't wind your stem, girlfriend, cuz I'd have to call you a liar."

She pinched her nose again. *Time to change the subject.*

"No snow yet. Wade said we should be getting some in the next week or so."

"Halleluiah! You'll get some next week!"

Tori snorted. "What am I going to do with you?"

"Make me proud, girlfriend, make me proud."

"I'm sorry, Sassy, I have to go. Wade just rode up and I need to get supper on the table."

"Call me when you get some. And I don't mean snow. Oh, I might've mentioned your love of whipped cream and chocolate syrup."

The line went dead before she could muster a response.

She stared at the phone for a moment and heat crept up her neck. She dreaded facing him now since she had no idea what Sasha might have told him, because, unfortunately, it could be anything.

She loved her best friend, quirks and all, and could not have survived the last two years without her.

Turning, she saw Wade walk up to the porch. Though he was wet and dirty, it did nothing to lessen his effect on her heart rate which skipped and fluttered like a school girls.

Somehow during the last four weeks, despite numerous self-talks about role-playing and keeping things in perspective, Tori had done the one thing she swore she'd never do. Found someone she could love.

She watched his face as he poured water in the basin; whatever was on his mind made him smile, and she longed to be the reason for it.

Calling herself seven kinds of a fool, Tori went to his room for dry boots and a towel.

♡

Wade kicked mud from his boots before he stepped onto the back porch, disgusted that once again he'd lost the trail he was following when the storm hit. He'd spotted the tracks again near the place where Isaac and Karen's Jeep went over the edge. It still pissed him off that Sheriff Wallace thought it was an accident. It wasn't. What about the damn boot prints? No one around here wore fancy soled hiking boots; they wore cowboy boots. And the wearer had a problem; he drug his right leg a little when he walked. Not much, just enough to smear his print.

No doubt about it. He was back; but why?

He doused his face with cold water to clear his head. Nothing to be done about it now. Tori would have supper on the table soon and he needed to get cleaned up.

Thoughts of her made him smile despite his troubles. His routine the last four weeks hadn't changed much. Except for the time he spent with her. Sporadic at first, he began to devise ways for them to be alone. He told himself it was because he wanted to get to know the real person and not the actress playing a part. Kisses notwithstanding, the fact was he enjoyed her company.

No, it was more than that, more even than simple friendship.

Nor was it just a sexual attraction though Lord knows it was off the charts for him. It was her. Everything about her. The way she hummed along with a song on the radio, the way she smiled, the tender way she dealt with Cody and the extra pains she went to caring for his mother topped a long list of *I likes*.

He toed off his sodden boots as his sister came to the back door. He still had difficulty believing she used crutches now and not the depressing wheelchair.

"Thought I heard you come up." She scowled at his soiled appearance. "You best not come in the house like that."

"What'd you have me do? Strip out here?"

"I bet she wouldn't mind if you did."

"Sheila!"

"I think she likes you," She sat on the step beside him, pulling her sweater tighter. "And you like her."

"What are you? Twelve?" His exasperation with his sister made him sound gruff.

"You like her."

Wade lowered his voice. "We have a business arrangement, nothing more."

"Yeah, right. Explains why you two sneak off behind the barn every chance you get."

"We talk."

"Of course."

"We have an agreement." Wade gritted his teeth. She was

like a dog with a bone.

"Uh-huh. So, you're saying she's nothing more than a business partner?"

"Exactly."

"Cody saw you kissing the other night."

He jerked his head around and sputtered.

Sheila nudged him with her shoulder and laughed.

Any further comments were silenced by Tori's appearance at the door. She held out dry boots and towel. "I saw you ride up and thought you'd need these. Oh, and a man named Douglas called earlier. He's supposed to be here later tonight."

Sheila scrambled to her feet. "Doug is coming? Wade, why didn't you tell me! My goodness! I have to go change." She turned and headed for the door, maneuvering the crutches with ease. "What time is he coming? Did he say?"

"I'm sorry. I don't know. Hank took the call. But I understood it might be late, maybe nine or ten. He a friend of yours?" She smiled as Sheila adjusted her crutches again.

"He's an old army buddy of Wade's. He drops in from time to time for a visit."

Wade grunted and pulled off his other boot. "And she immediately starts acting like a love-struck teenager. Please try to behave this time."

"Doug doesn't mind how I behave, so why should you?"

She hurried off to get ready leaving him alone with Tori who looked everywhere but *at* him.

Did I do something wrong?

"You don't just need dry boots, you need a bath."

He glanced down at his muddy jeans. "Yeah, I guess I do."

"You have time before supper."

"Okay. I can take a hint." He was about to put on the dry

boots when she stopped him.

"You aren't coming in the house like that are you?"

It'd been a long day and Douglas coming meant a long night as well. His patience ran low. "Like what?"

"You're soaking wet and covered in mud. You'll leave a trail all through the house."

"Well, what would you have me do? Strip on the porch and walk buck naked through the house?"

Her eyes whipped to his and the pink tinge to her cheeks was enchanting. But Tori never gave give up without a fight.

"Well," she said as though considering his statement, "it's an option, but sending you to the utility room to change into a robe might be a better plan, and it would keep the mess down."

Her reference to having to clean up after him was disconcerting though, in truth, she did every day. She now did the laundry and straightened the house as well as most of the cooking. She even did little things for the hands like baking a cake or a pan of biscuits.

In short, she behaved like a rancher's wife, and he liked it. And he hated it. The idea of her leaving was so distressing to him he refused to let it enter his mind. This past week, she had breakfast on the table by the time he was up and he found himself looking forward to each new day as never before.

They hadn't *talked* again since that night in the den but they did spend more time together.

"Yeah, well, that's probably a better idea."

"Although," She cast a quick glance at him, "your idea did have certain merits."

He froze for a moment. *You think that idea has merit, I have another one that's better.* "You've been around Sheila too long." He moved toward the door. "You're starting to think like her."

"Wait!"

"Now what?"

"Take off your jacket and shirt. Just leave your pants on till you get inside."

Another remark like that and I'll have you naked on the floor with me. "You're determined to have me strip aren't you?" His comment brought a brighter flush to face and he grinned. "I told you you've been around Sheila too long."

"Stop your yapping and do as you're told. I'll get your robe. Leave your stuff out here. I'll take care of it later."

He chuckled and shrugged out of his jacket, admiring the sway of her hips as she went back inside, discretely adjusting himself. *Damn, her ass looks good in jeans.*

"She's sure got a mind of her own," said Hank as he stepped around the corner, "If I was you, I wouldn't argue much. Lessen' of course you was countin' on makin' up later."

Wade ignored the jibe and accompanying wink. "I thought you were fixing tack in the barn?"

"I smelled bread a bakin' earlier so came by to check it out."

"I'll bet you got the first taste, too, didn't you?"

"Well, now, can I help it if I happened to be in the right place at the right time?" He stood up straighter and snorted. "'sides, she was tryin' somethin' new and asked me if I'd sample and tell her if it was good enough for you."

"And was it?"

"Well, the first loaf was a might yeasty."

"You ate a whole loaf?"

"Naw…Cody and Sheila ate some. Me and Miz O'Conner

helped, too."

The O'Conner's and Hank had been friends for more than forty years. Mr. O'Conner had died ten years ago, and a couple of years back, they began *dating* as they called it. It was obvious to anyone who saw them together, they were happily in love. He was envious of them for a time; but not since Tori had entered his life.

The door opened and she stood there, hands planted on curvaceous hips. "Are you going to take all day?"

"Better get a move on, boy, a woman don't like to be kept waitin.'"

"Hank," She looked toward the foreman. "I saw an old tub in the barn the other day. Would you please bring it around and leave it on the porch?"

"Yes, 'em, sure will. Guess you want me to put his clothes in it, huh?"

"If you don't mind. And fill it with water, please."

"Will do." Hank stepped off the porch. "I'm headed to town tomorrow, Miz Tori. I got your list if you need to add somethin' to it."

"Thank you, Hank. I can't think of anything right now."

"Add some chocolate syrup and Redi-Whip topping, the kind in the spray can with the red top," Wade said.

A sudden gasp had them both staring at her.

"Tori? Is something wrong?"

"N-no, no it's fine. I …its fine."

"I'll put 'em on the list, ma'am." Hank touched the brim of his hat and ambled toward the barn.

Wade stared at her shocked expression, all the more puzzling because of the flood of red accompanying it. *What the hell is up with that?* Immediately, his thoughts took a nose dive as images of what someone with a graphic imagination and a perpetual state of arousal—like him—might do with whipped topping and chocolate syrup. To Tori.

When their eyes met, lust blindsided him.

For the tiniest fraction of a second, a spark flashed in those captivating eyes. Desire? Maybe. Their relationship really defied description. She worked for him, sure, but it was more than that. They were friends, too, but…had friendship changed into something more? They danced around the attraction but it was it there, getting stronger every day.

He didn't miss how those hazelnut eyes followed the track of the towel as he dried his chest, the slight parting of her lips as she licked them. And the blush that deepened when he caught her looking.

And what about that other kiss?

She turned and hurried into the kitchen. "There's a trash bag on the floor for you to leave your pants on."

He left his boots and shirt on the porch as instructed and entered the utility room to change, trying to get his mind off Tori and what turmoil she inflicted on him with just a smile and twist of her hips.

He forced himself to think about Doug's appearance and if it was a friendly visit or something else. *Maybe he had news on Isaac's killer? No, he would have called. Probably just wants to see Sheila.*

He spotted Tori at the sink and his thoughts once again spun into chaos. Did she care about him? Did he imagine the look of desire he saw?

"Wade? Is everything all right?" Her soft-spoken question broke through his somber musings.

"What?"

"Are you okay? You seem so troubled."

"Just have a lot on mind today."

"Does it have anything to do with this Douglas fella?"

She asked him in the beginning to trust her, and he did; he wanted to share everything with her…but he couldn't. Not when she'd soon be gone. His chest constricted, and anxiety pooled in his belly.

"No," he lied, "it doesn't."

She recognized the lie so he turned away to avoid seeing the hurt that would be visible in her eyes.

"Wade."

He stopped but couldn't face her.

She stood behind him, her hand a gentle weight on his arm. Her strength and goodness radiated through him, soothed him as only she could.

"I know something's troubling you," she said softly, "and it's not just your mother. I've seen you walking around till all hours of the night, riding the hills every day. I don't know what you're looking for or if I can help you find it. But I can listen. You don't have to do it alone." She turned and busied herself checking food on the stove. "You have just enough time to bathe before supper."

He stood in the middle of the kitchen and debated his next move. No doubt his silence hurt her, but he couldn't afford to get any closer. The thought of her leaving was unbearable.

Their initial exhibitions for his mother were strained, but as time wore on, he found himself looking forward to each hour or so in the evening. Though her condition steadily deteriorated, she truly seemed to brighten when they were there. The more she enjoyed their performance, the more they put into it.

At first.

The last couple of weeks, the subject of how to improve their performances never came up. Instead, Tori talked about Texas, her family and friends, her nursing career. The few questions she did ask of him were casual; she never pried or got personal. She waited for him to open up but he put it off.

She was going to leave him. He tried not to care but did so anyway. The idea she might not care for him was almost too much to bear. So, he let her do most of the talking. Her honesty and bluntness were sometimes disconcerting but he found he liked that, too.

Tori and Cody were very close and he now called her *Aunt Tori*. She always had some amusing story to tell about his antics and he enjoyed the way her eyes sparkled when she did. They needed each other so he was thankful she was the one who answered the ad.

In spite of all his statements to the contrary, he was in love with her but worried she still grieved over the loss of her husband. She did tell him once she wasn't ready, but, there were times, like on the porch just now, when he thought she was. So, he wouldn't give any more of himself than he had to.

But...

He moved to where she sliced fresh bread for supper, boots in his hands. "I think everyone, including Major, already tasted that, which, by the way, smells delicious. Can I have one slice to tide me over till supper?"

She selected one. "Butter and honey?"

"Please." He smiled. She remembered his fondness for that mixture on warm bread.

She slathered on butter, added honey, then folded it in

half and handed it to him.

He looked at the bread, then down at his hands. "I seem to have my hands full." He didn't miss the quick admiring glance at his chest through the open vee of his robe before she looked up, and his body vibrated with unrequited desire.

Her eyes darted from his lips to his chest and finally, met his gaze, her cheeks crimson. After a slight hesitation, she lifted the bread to his mouth.

He leaned forward and took a generous bite.

"Mmmmmm…" He savored the yeasty tang before chewing and swallowing. His heart skipped a beat when he noticed she was focused on his mouth, her own parting in a silent "oh" when his tongue slid over his bottom lip to capture the savory mixture lingering there. Her hand appeared frozen in place and he saw a golden stream sliding down the back of her index finger. He bent lower and licked the trail of creamy sweetness then took the finger in his mouth and sucked gently.

Her gasp told him she was as shocked as he.

But she didn't pull back.

Their eyes locked as he continued to hold the finger hostage with gentle pressure. He took his time pulling back and took the remaining piece of bread in his mouth, lapping up all the tasty garnish in the process, never breaking eye contact.

"Your lips are the only thing that taste any sweeter." The huskiness of his voice spoke volumes. "I can't wait to taste them again."

She licked her lips, focused on his, each breath a short huff.

He wasn't the only one at this party. He felt it down to his toes.

So, he did what any red-blooded male would do.

He kissed her. Not the hot, tongue-thrusting, possessive kind he wanted to, but more like the soft, think-about-me-tonight kind.

And she kissed him back.

A flashfire of need coursed through him but held it in check—barely, and stepped back.

She smoothed down the front of her apron. "I have to take Miss Willie's supper in."

Those soft spoken words held a note of longing he didn't miss.

He needed to let her go before he did something foolish like toss her over his shoulder and carry her off to bed.

Cody bounced into the kitchen. "Aunt Tori, Miss Willie wants to eat."

"Almost ready." She sighed and finished setting up the tray.

"Why are you in your bathrobe?" The child stood in front of his uncle.

"Got caught in the rain. Have to shower before Aunt Tori will let me eat."

"Is she gonna wash your hair like she does mine?"

His innocent question brought a new fantasy—and more discomfort. *I wish.*

A quick knock on the door and Hank entered. "You ain't got that shower yet, boy? Suppers gonna get cold."

"Uh, yeah."

Cody grinned. "Did ya kiss her again?"

"None of your business, young man," chided Wade. "Go wash up. Supper's almost ready."

He glanced Tori's way. He inadvertently embarrassed her.

Oblivious to their distress, Hank grinned and headed for the cabinet holding the dinner dishes. "I'll see to it the table is set, Miz Tori. You go ahead and take care of Miz Willie." He winked and whispered to Wade. "You best make it cold shower, I think."

Chapter Fourteen

"How about a little more soup, Miss Willie?" Tori held the spoon over the bowl. "You've hardly eaten anything today."

"I'm not very hungry. The soup was delicious, though."

Tori set the bowl aside and moved the portable table out of the way before smoothing the covers on the bed. "Can I get you anything? Maybe read some more?"

"No, thank you." She paused for a shaky breath, then placed a fragile hand over Tori's. "You have done so much for me already. I can't thank you enough."

Tori pulled on all her reserves to maintain a calm, professional façade. "I love my job. I get to meet the most wonderful people." She smiled and lightly pressed the old woman's hand. "Like you."

A light tap on the door announced Sheila's entrance. "How are you tonight, Mother?" She placed a quick kiss on Miss Willie's brow, "Did you eat well?"

"Some." Taking in Sheila's stylish dress, she smiled. "You look lovely, my dear. Are we having company tonight?"

"We were. Douglas just called. He's not coming until tomorrow."

"I'm sorry."

"Oh, well, there's always tomorrow." She laughed. "Lord, I sound like Scarlett O'Hara." She placed one hand dramatically against her forehead, the other stretched behind her. "I can't think about that now," she purred. "I must think about it tomorrow. Because, tomorrow is— another day."

Miss Willie made a feeble attempt at applause. "You should've been an actress, dear. You do have a flare for the dramatic."

Sheila sat on the edge of the bed and brushed an errant curl from the older woman's forehead. "I would never leave here. Who would take care of…?"

"Who will take care of me, right?"

"Yes. No. I mean…"

Miss Willie reached for her hand. "It's okay, baby. I understand." She wheezed and continued. "Did you get everything completed?"

"Yes, ma'am." Sheila nodded, eyes downcast. "Everything is taken care of."

Miss Willie tugged at Sheila's hand. "I know this is hard for you, dear, but your brother wouldn't do it, and it had to be done."

"I know." Sheila glanced toward Tori. "Mother wanted certain things taken care of for her…her…"

"Funeral, Sheila," Miss Willie's voice was soft and gentle. "The word is funeral. Say it."

"She wanted her—funeral—arranged ahead of time."

Tori swallowed hard and struggled to keep her game face on. Hearing Miss Willie be so matter-of-fact about her impending death bothered her. *She is such a special person. I'm going to miss her so much.*

"I've had a very good life, and few regrets." Miss Willie

smiled and continued. "I have no fear of dying, but I do worry about you." She looked at Tori. "Wade has someone to help him over the rough days ahead."

Tori couldn't meet her steady gaze and busied herself cleaning up the supper tray.

"You're back to Jake Simpson, aren't you?" Sheila heaved a sigh and continued. "I don't love him. Besides, how do you know Douglas isn't the one for me?"

"I want you to be happy, sweetheart. That's all."

"And I will be. Rest assured." Shelia stood and placed another kiss on Miss Willie's cheek. "I better get changed. No use wearing this high dollar outfit if he isn't going to be here to see it. Good night, Mother. I love you."

"I love you, too, sweetheart. Good night."

Wade met Sheila at the door.

"Gotta go change."

"Yeah, no use wasting a fancy outfit on family, huh?" He smiled and dodged when she punched at his shoulder.

"There you are, Wade," Miss Willie smiled at him, "Where have you been?"

"Had to take a shower." He kissed her forehead. "Got a little dirty today and Tori made me take a bath 'fore she'd let me in the house."

Tori couldn't look at him without seeing him naked in the shower or the incident in the kitchen. And the kiss. Her body still quivered with need. It took maximum concentration to keep up the playful banter he'd started. "A little dirty? You were caked in mud and wanted to just go waltzing through the house."

He sat on the edge of the bed and glanced at the barely touched dinner. "Made me strip on the porch."

She slapped at his shoulder, unable to stop the heat creeping up her neck. "I did not."

He picked up the pudding in the dish and took a bite. "Well, almost stripped. She did let me have a robe." He grinned and asked. "You didn't peek, did you?"

"You're incorrigible!"

A rusty laugh came from the woman on the bed. "Do I need to referee?"

Wade laughed and took another bite of pudding.

"It does my heart good to see you two together." Miss Willie smiled. "To know you won't be alone when I'm gone."

Although Wade never said it out loud, Tori's instinct said it troubled him to hear his mother speak of her approaching death.

He placed the spoon on the tray and looked around. "Want me to turn the radio up? I know you like the music."

"We have to talk about it, son. It's not going to go away."

He looked away, didn't move.

Miss Willie's piercing hazel eyes fixed on her. "I can't tell you what having you here has meant to me. Not just because you have taken such good care of me, but because you put the smile back in my son's eyes. A smile I thought I would never see again."

Tori's stomach rolled. *It isn't real; it's all a lie. But I want it to be real.*

She had to take a breath before she could speak. "Please, don't exert yourself, Miss Willie," she said softly, "you need to rest."

"I'll have…eternity to…rest. This can't wait." Her eyes slid closed.

"Ma?"

The anguish on his face tore her apart.

Tori reached over and placed a hand in his. He clutched it so tight she almost cried out.

Miss Willie opened her eyes. "I know this is hard for you both," she whispered, "You, Wade, because you are my son and Tori because you love us both."

She pushed the tray table away without letting go of Wade's hand and caressed Miss Willie's cheek. "You are a very special lady. I will always treasure the time we spent together."

"You lost…a husband…and child as I did. You know what grief can do. Please…don't let it…happen to my son. Promise me…you won't…let it happen. I'll be happy…with Jacob and Isaac." The speech had cost her much and she was exhausted when it ended.

"Ma, please," begged Wade, "Don't tire yourself out."

"Promise me," she whispered.

Tori's vision blurred, and she couldn't stop the tears that flowed. "I promise, Miss Willie. I promise."

"Good," she mouthed and closed her eyes.

"Tori?" Wade's voice quivered with emotion.

She swiped at the tears streaming down her face. "She's weak and tires easily. She's resting."

His grip had tightened during the last exchange and now loosened allowing blood to again reach all her fingers. The tingling was annoying but she made no effort to pull free. He needed her strength and *she* needed to be close to him.

This room was the center of her world where she was free to express all the things she kept hidden; she teased and smiled and pretended to be in love.

Only, she no longer pretended. God how she loved him! But it was one-sided; he merely played a part, but so convincingly sometimes she actually considered he might love her as well. *Does he care at all? Is it all just pretend? There's an attraction, but is there more?*

Those questions caused many a sleepless night of late as she struggled to keep things on an even keel. But, here in this room, she hid nothing. She said and did whatever a woman in love would and no one was the wiser. However, time grew short. Soon…too soon, the charade would end. She had no way of knowing how long she had, so she took advantage of every opportunity and prayed maybe, maybe, he would realize it was not pretend after all.

Maybe she should just quit stalling and take a chance?

But what if he didn't feel the same?

There was no mistaking the look of desire in his eyes from time to time, but what did it mean? What if it was just an itch he needed scratched and anyone would do…like Eddie?

"Is that Vince Gill?" Miss Willie's low voice broke through her thoughts.

"I thought you were asleep," Tori said.

"Is it him?"

"Yes," said Wade, "it is."

"Turn it up."

He turned the dial. "How's that?"

"More. I love his voice."

He cranked the volume up a little more. "So does Tori. I bet she knows the words to every song he sings."

Why would he say that? Well, she did have a propensity for singing along with radio when she thought no one was around. Obviously someone had been.

He returned to his mother's bedside and looked at Tori. "Do you know this one?"

Tori nodded. "*I Still Believe in You.* One of my favorites."

"Sing it for me?"

"I can't carry a tune in a bucket."

"You sound pretty good in the shower."

Her face burned. "I didn't know you could hear me."

He smiled and placed a hand on her shoulder. "I'm sorry; I didn't mean to embarrass you." He glanced at his mother. "Isn't she cute when she blushes?"

Tori sputtered but coherent words wouldn't come. *If Miss Willie weren't here… Cute my ass!* Her face seared all the way to her hairline.

"Care to dance?"

"What?"

"Dance with me."

Tori's heart pounded. She'd be so close to him. After the incident in the kitchen, her libido was a live wire arcing through her. "What about supper? The others -"

"Are all big enough to take care of themselves. Shelia will help Cody." He pulled her hand. "So dance with me."

Wade stood with his back to his mother, brows furrowed, eyes filled with a pain he made no effort to hide from her. He adored his mother and watching her fade away a little more each day had to be pure torture for him.

The dance would be nothing more than a momentary distraction. He was trying to cope but couldn't do it alone.

He needed her.

She needed him to need her.

"I'd be delighted, Sir Wade." Tori executed a deep curtsy and stepped into his arms.His hand trembled as he pulled her close, and they moved in unison to the melodic words floating across the room; words about love and apology.

His hold tightened as Vince sang about forgiveness and need.

Is he trying to tell me something? Or is my over-active imagination saying what I want to hear?

The song ended all too soon, yet he continued to hold her close. At last, he pulled back, gave a silent *thank you* before he turned to his mother.

She was fast asleep, a slight smile gracing her face.

"Good night, Mother." He kissed her cheek. "I love you." He left the room without another look to Tori.

She stared at the door for several moments before she returned to her patient. She made sure all was in order before heading for the kitchen.

Sheila was trying to coax Cody into eating his supper. "Come on, big guy." She placed a piece of chicken fried venison on his plate. "It's your favorite."

"I'm not hungry." The tiny voice was barely audible.

"Cody?" Tori touched the back of her fingers to his forehead, "are you sick?"

"No, ma'am." His shook his head, blue eyes shining with unshed tears.

"Then why won't you eat?"

He ducked his head. "Today's Mommy's birthday. It's on the calendar. I made her a present."

She looked at Wade who nodded, then back to Cody. "What kind of present?"

He looked at Tori; his bottom lip trembled.

"I colored a picture. But I can't give it to her cause she died." As he spoke, tears spilled down his chubby cheeks.

She wiped his face with her thumb. "Of course you can, sweetie."

"How?" he sniffed, "She died."

"Her body may not be here, but her spirit still lives right here." She rested a hand over his heart. "And I know she's up in Heaven right now with a ginormous smile on her face because you remembered what today was and colored her a picture."

"She is?"

She nodded and wiped his face with a napkin. "When we lose someone we love, it hurts. A lot. And it takes a long time for that hurt to go away. But, as long as we remember them, keep them close in our hearts, they never really leave us."

"Do you still remember Joey?"

She flinched. "How do you know about him?"

"I heard Aunt Sheila and Uncle Wade talking 'fore you got here." His blue eyes searched hers. "Do you still remember him?"

She took a steadying breath. "A mother never forgets a son, no matter what. Even though your Mom isn't here, she still loves you very much and wants you to be happy."

"I miss her." His lips trembled and fresh tears threatened to spill. "I didn't want her to die! And now Miss Willie's gonna die, too!"

"I know, baby, I know, but you still have Uncle Wade and _"

"And you," He turned and reached for her. "I have you, too." He wrapped his tiny arms around her neck and hugged. "Promise me you won't ever leave me! Promise me!"

Wade sat beside Cody and rubbed his back. "I know this is tough, sport, but it will be get better."

Sheila patted his arm and said nothing.

Tori's throat constricted to the point no sound escaped. Cody's tears were her undoing and she pulled him close. She couldn't bear to leave him, but couldn't stay, either.

Everything is such a mess!

At last, she pulled away and wiped his face again with the napkin. "Where is the picture you drew for your mom?"

"In my room."

"Why don't you get it and we'll put it right there on the refrigerator so she will always know where it is."

Cody smiled. "Okay."

She placed him on the floor and before he bounded off to his room, he brightened. "Know what I just thought about?"

She shook her head, unable to speak.

"Since you're takin' care of me for her, maybe she's takin' care of Joey for you." He sprinted off to his room for the picture.

She couldn't move; simply stood there and watched him race down the hall.

"Tori? Are you Okay?" Sheila's voice sounded far away.

Tori swallowed several times before any sound would emit, keeping tears at bay by sheer force of will but she couldn't hide the tremble in her voice. "I better find a magnet for the picture."

"I'll get one." Wade dug through the junk drawer near the sink.

Cody returned with a paper clutched in his hand. "Here it is." He handed it to Tori. "Do you think she'll like it?"

She smiled at the childish stick figure drawing of what appeared to be a man and woman and a smaller figure she assumed to be Cody. "I know she will. Mother's love things like this."

"Did Joey draw pictures for you?"

Her heart pounded and her breath caught. "Yes. I still

have them."

She handed the sheet to Wade. "Where do you think we should put it?"

"Right on the front," chirped Cody.

"Okay," said Wade. "But how about up higher so it won't get knocked off when Major comes running through?"

"Okay."

She held the picture while Wade placed magnets at each corner. When they finished, she stepped back to look at it. "My, it is a lovely picture." Looking upward, she smiled, "Happy Birthday, Karen."

Cody took Tori's hand. "Happy Birthday, Mommy." He looked toward the ceiling, too. "I love you."

She regarded the cherubic face so full of trust and her heart ached for him. *I can't leave; I can't stay. Oh God! What am I going to do?*

Wade pulled her against him, providing much needed strength. "We'd better eat before everything gets cold."

"Wait," said Cody, "Can I say something else?"

Tori nodded, chaos ruling her emotions, afraid to speak.

Cody bowed his head, gnawed his lower lip as though in thought, then looked toward the ceiling again. "Mommy and Daddy...I really miss you, but Aunt Tori is taking real good care of me." He paused, then turned his eyes upward again. "So if you see her little boy, his name is Joey, would you take care of him for her, please?"

Tori pressed a hand to her mouth to stifle the soft cry that choked her.

Wade pulled her tighter against him, and placed his lips against her forehead.

Eyes throbbing with unshed tears, she slowly pulled away

from Wade and bent to hug Cody close. "Thank you."

"I'm ready to eat now." He cast a final look upward then went to his place at the table.

Tori noted both Sheila and Hank dabbed their eyes and neither spoke as they sat down. She took a shuddering breath, and took her place beside Cody. She went through the motions of eating but little made it past the lump in her throat. Twice she caught Wade watching her, his expression unreadable.

Sheila tried to make small talk but gave up when she got little response.

Hank was silent until he finished eating. "Miz Tori," he said as he got up to leave, "I put the tub on the porch and his clothes is in it. I'll rinse 'em out good so don't you worry none 'bout 'em."

"Thank you, Hank. Aren't you going to eat dessert? It's chocolate cake?"

"A fine meal as usual, ma'am, but I don't think I can eat cake right now." He stopped at the back door. "You're one of the finest people God ever put on this earth. Wade's one lucky man." He turned and walked out, closing the door softly behind him.

"I second that," said Sheila, "We're lucky to have you here."

Tori nodded to acknowledge their remarks, and stared at her barely touched plate. The nights' events had taken their toll in spades. If she spoke at all, the control she clung to so frantically would shatter.

"Can I have cake now, please?" Cody asked, "I ate all my supper."

"I'll get it." Wade stood and dished out the dessert to his nephew.

The remainder of the meal was completed in silence

broken only by Cody's exclamation that he loved chocolate cake.

Tori began to gather up the dishes.

"I'll do it," said Wade. "Why don't you turn in?

"I'll do it," insisted Sheila, "Both of you should turn in."

Tori stood but didn't speak, jaw clamped tight in an effort to keep flood gates of anguish from breaking free. She placed the dish she held on the table and left the room.

She made it to the sanctuary of her room before the dam burst and the tears choking her all evening flowed without restraint.

Chapter Fifteen

WADE LOOKED AT THE CLOCK. AGAIN. *Twelve-thirty.* Thirty minutes later than the last time he looked. Still, sleep eluded him. For once, he was glad Douglas hadn't arrive on time. He couldn't deal with another problem right now.

Images of Tori filled his mind. The taste of her kisses; the feel of her in his arms as they danced; the touch of her hand as she supported him at his mother's side.

Most of all, he remembered the unchecked pain he'd glimpsed when Cody begged her not to leave. That heart wrenching sight would haunt him forever.

The muffled sobs escaping though her closed bedroom door shredded his heart and he cursed himself with each one.

I never should've agreed to this. I should've sent her back to Houston at the airport like I planned.

But he hadn't. Now he couldn't.

He was in love with her. *When the hell had that happened?* Tori had captured him heart and soul and he couldn't bear the thought of living without her.

She might not love him but she did care for him. There was no doubt she loved Cody. *Did she still love Eddie? Was she ready to move on?*

He turned on his side and punched his pillow as thunder rolled in the distance. The storm from this afternoon raged on with a vengeance, a fitting metaphor for his current state of mind.

"Noooooo!"

At the sound of Cody's cry, he bounded from the bed and reached his door behind Tori. They entered the boy's room together and Wade flipped on the light.

"Don't let him get me!"

"Who, sport?" asked Wade as they sat on the edge of the small bed.

"The bad man! He hurt Mommy and Daddy!"

Wade's heart nearly stopped. Cody remembered something about the accident. After all this time, he *finally* remembered something. *I knew it!*

Tori took the boy in her arms and rocked him. "Shhh, sweetie, no one is after you. You had a bad dream. That's all."

He pushed away and looked at Wade. "I saw him. He's gonna get me!"

He took a deep breath and placed a hand on the boys' arm. "No one is going to hurt you, sport. No one. You're safe here. It was just a bad dream."

"See, sweetie." She brushed the dark hair from his forehead. "You're awake. We're here and we won't let anything happen to you, okay?"

"Can I sleep with you?"

His McBride Blue eyes, locked with Tori's and even Wade saw how he implored.

"Well, um, of course."

"And Uncle Wade, too."

Wade looked at her and Tori's uncertainty made him

stutter. "Well, I -"

"You have to." cried the frightened child. "He'll get me!"

"No he won't," said Wade, "I won't let him."

"But what if you're not there when he comes?"

"Cody," Tori pulled his chin up to face her. "I don't think we can all fit on my bed. How about I lay here with you till you go back to sleep?"

"Uncle Wade has a big bed. We could fit there."

Wade didn't know what to do. Tori wouldn't look at him and Cody was terrified.

Shit.

"Okay, sport," he said at last, "just this once." Before Tori could protest, he picked up his charge and headed across the hall to his room and placed him on the bed.

"I have to go potty." Cody jumped down and headed for the bathroom.

Tori leaned against the doorway, arms folded across her chest. She bit down on her lower lip, her eyes red-rimmed and swollen.

Another reminder of the agony she endured for his sake. *I'm the reason she's suffering now.*

"I'm sorry, Tori. I didn't know what else to do." He lifted his hands then dropped them to his sides. "I know this is asking a lot, especially tonight…but, well, maybe you could stay till he's asleep? I won't, I mean…." Uncertainty stole his words. He waited. He had no choice. His heart skipped a beat for every second she remained silent. He didn't have the guts to hope she'd say yes.

She pushed away from the door and walked toward him, eyes downcast. "Joey hated storms."

She stopped an arm's length away, her voice so soft he

had difficulty hearing her. "He used to crawl in bed with me." She looked up, the pain she tried so hard to hide poured free. "I miss him so much, Wade," she whispered, "so much."

He didn't stop to think, just wrapped her in his arms and pulled her to him. "I'm so sorry, Tori. So sorry."

She made no move to pull away and he realized this time *she* needed *him*; needed his comfort and support. He rubbed her back and placed a kiss on the top of her head.

She pressed her cheek against his bare torso, the wetness of a tear burning a hole in his heart as her arms circled his waist and she clung to him. Her shaky breath tickled the hairs on his chest and her body shivered.

"You look like Mommy and Daddy," Cody said. "Always hugging and stuff."

"What's wrong with that?" asked Wade.

"Nothin', I guess." He nestled under the covers. "Daddy said grown-ups do it all the time."

Tori's soft snort was warm on his skin.

He rubbed her back again, relishing the feel of her in his arms. "He did, huh?"

"Uh-huh. He said I'll do it, too, when I get married."

Wade rested his chin on top of her head, not ready to release her. "Won't be anytime soon, will it?"

"No silly. I'm only six!"

Wade smiled at his exasperated expression. *God how I love that kid.*

Tori turned toward the child and smiled, her arms still wrapped around Wade's waist. "It'll happen before you know it."

"I have to go to school, first."

"Okay." Wade said. "You can go to school first."

"Are you gonna stand there all night?" The youngster yawned and snuggled deeper under the covers. "I'm sleepy."

Wade looked at Tori and she gave him a half-hearted smile, then eased away from him and climbed in the king sized bed beside Cody.

Wade reached for the light switch.

"No!" cried Cody, "leave it on."

Wade ran his fingers through his hair. *I'm being punished for sure. First Tori, then this, now the lights on. What next?*

"Cody?" Her calm voice even soothed him. "It will be really hard for us to go to sleep with the light on."

"But the bad man -"

"The bad man was just a dream. We would never let anyone hurt you. You know that, right?"

"Uh-huh."

"Then let Uncle Wade turn off the lights."

He considered it a moment then mumbled, "You have to turn 'em on if he comes back."

"Deal." A quick glance at Wade, she nodded. "Okay, lights off."

Wade flipped the switch and headed for the bed but stubbed his toe on a chair in the process. "Dammit!"

"Wade!" Her scold didn't hold much anger. "Watch your language."

Cody held the covers back for his uncle to get in bed. "You're funny, Uncle Wade."

"I'll show you who's funny." He tickle-attacked the child.

Cody laughed and thrashed about. "Aunt Tori! Make him stop!"

"Stop nothing! Little boys who wake me up in the middle of the night get tickled!" She joined in the melee until the youngster begged to be allowed to go sleep.

"Alright, sport," Wade said, "no more tickling. But if you start snoring, then man are you gonna get it!" He goosed him once more for emphasis and Cody squealed in delight.

"I won't snore! I promise!"

"Good. Now go to sleep." He pulled the covers up over them and stretched out beside his nephew.

"Uncle Wade?"

"What?"

"I love you."

His heart swelled with pride. "I love you, too, sport."

The child snuggled under the covers and pulled Tori's left hand across his chest and then placed Wade's hand on top as though building a barrier between him and the ghosts haunting him. Content at last, he whispered, "I love you Aunt Tori."

"I love you, too, sweetie."

Wade didn't miss the catch in her voice when she replied.

In no time at all, Cody drifted off to sleep, the silence broken by the gentle snore of the child between them.

Tori's warmth radiated from under his hand and wrapped itself around him. Instead of the arrangement being awkward, Wade rested for the first time in months.

Her soft cries woke him around two a.m.; she called Joey's name and begged him to forgive her for not saving him. Wade moved to her side of the bed and cradled her in his arms, whispering everything would be all right, his own heart sharing her pain. She whimpered softly and he pulled her tighter against him, kissing a tear from her cheek. "I love you, baby." He whispered. "I'm so sorry I made you suffer."

Wade continued to hold her, whispered he'd make all this up to her; and then prayed he'd be able to keep his promise.

After a while, she relaxed and fell into a peaceful slumber. It wasn't long until he joined her.

♡

He woke with a start when she slid her hand across his chest, fingers curling into the thick mat. It took a moment for the sleep haze to fade and for him to realize they were alone, and Tori lay wrapped in his arms. Her head rested on his shoulder, her right hand on his chest. She shifted from time to time, but always toward him as though to meld into him. He groaned at his intense discomfort as he tried to keep his body- one part in particular—from responding to her movements.

She murmured in her sleep and he stroked her bare arm; the pebbly texture of goose bumps eliciting fantasies of what might've prompted them.

She wants a friend, not a lover. A friend, not a lover. He silently repeated the mantra but his aching arousal persistently disagreed.

More than once he stifled a response as she slid her hand over his chest or rubbed her cheek against his bare nipple. He told himself she reacted to her dreams and had no interest in him as a lover—unless, of course, the dream was about him *as* a lover, and, well, that would change things.

She rubbed her leg over his, molded herself to his body and exhaled a long sigh that to him, sounded like a moan of pleasure. All his rational self-talk about what she did and didn't want went to straight to hell.

At this moment, her knee rested much too close to his lower half, the thin fabric of his boxers the only barrier as he struggled to keep his traitorous body in check. She wore no bra under her shirt and Wade tried, mostly in vain, not to think about panties. She moved again and her knee rolled slowly across his groin.

A flash of potent desire ripped through him. He hissed in a breath through clenched teeth as she rubbed her cheek against his super sensitive nipple.

Tori murmured something unintelligible and her tongue brushed his bare skin as she licked her lips.

"Hot damn and holy hell," he whispered and pulled her closer and, with willpower he didn't know he possessed, got himself under control.

This is gonna be a lot harder than I thought.

He grimaced at his accidental pun while his body pulsated with tightly controlled hunger.

Chapter Sixteen

The dreams were collage of images past and present. Eddie and Joey were there one minute, their smiles radiant, then gone in a blinding flash. She called and searched the darkness for them in vain.

She saw Joey, heard him cry, but when she reached for him, he wasn't there. On some level, she understood it wasn't real, but remained locked in the clutches of the nightmare. She cried, tasted the salty tears, the unbearable pain of loss again, while consciousness alluded her.

From somewhere deep within her dream-shrouded darkness, the husky timbre of Wade's voice broke through. His whispered words soothed her troubled mind, the warmth of his touch on her skin melted the coldness surrounding her soul, and encased her in a cozy, secure cocoon.

The heart-wrenching visions soon morphed into other more pleasurable ones; she was in bed with Wade—no, Cody; no, wait both of them.

Of course, he had a bad dream and had asked to sleep in my bed. But Wade is here too...isn't he?

Bogged down in the nowhere land between sleep and awareness, she remained nestled in the cloak of sensed protection. The pain of last night forgotten; the disquiet engulfing her gave way to peaceful slumber filled with delightful fantasies she reveled in. She enjoyed the cover's raspy smoothness against her cheek and palm when she shifted, and it moved, too, forming itself to her body, from the top of her head to the tips of her toes. Velvet tentacles caressed her arm and burned her skin wherever they touched

Tori moaned as the Dream Weaver worked his magic, and her muddled brain created images which made her breath catch; Wade on the porch, shirtless and dragging the towel across his remarkable chest; the kiss in the moonlight, the bread incident in the kitchen, and finally, him in bed, his finger crooked in open invitation to join him.

She forced her way to the edge of her dream world, to wake up and end the exquisite torture her mind inflicted on her body.

In those first few moments of alertness, several facts congealed at once; it was well past daylight, she lay splayed across his chest like a patchwork quilt, her knee a heartbeat away from his groin.

And he was awake.

His breath was even; hers ragged. She could feel his heart beat steady and strong under her hand which contrasted with the rapid pace of her own. Despite the coolness in the room, perspiration formed on her upper lip, and she couldn't quite get enough air as her body responded to his gentle embrace, the way their legs entwined, the warmth of his bare chest on her cheek and the musky man-scent emanating from him. Her brain shouted for her to get up, but her body refused to cooperate, the heady pull of his masculinity hypnotic.

She pushed against his chest in an effort to extricate

herself. Wade made no effort to release her so she resumed her previous position.

"Sleep well?" His throaty voice vibrated through her cheek as she lay against him and her nipples puckered.

"…Yes." She struggled for air as calloused yet gentle fingers moved in lazy circles on her arm sending shivers of delight through her.

"Me, too." He rested his hand on her arm. "You had a bad dream."

"I…" Her sharp intake of breath sounded more like a gasp. "Um, it's late…"

"I know."

She tried again. "I—we really should get up."

"Uh-huh."

Regardless of what she said, she had no desire to move. It felt good to be here, to be *held* like this. No matter if out of pity or guilt or whatever it was on his part, for her, it felt *right* to be in his arms and, he didn't appear inclined to let her go.

It was Wade's sexy, gentle voice that ended the tortured dreams, his warmth and closeness comforted her and resurrected feelings she thought long buried and forgotten.

And she wanted him.

Now.

Bad.

But he didn't want her; at least not in the forever-and-ever way she wanted him; more like the here-and-now version as evidenced by the growing bulge skimming her knee. True, they had become close over the last few weeks; maybe even be considered good friends; or friends with benefits at some point, but that's all they were.

Wasn't it?

Her mind drifted back to the scene in the kitchen and her pulse jumped. *Did he care or did he just have an itch to scratch?* Her heart told her that wasn't the case, it couldn't be. But how did he *really* feel about her?

Desire pulsed through her body like hot lava, something she never felt with Eddie. Guilt warred with that longing. *I can't. It's not right.*

Sasha suddenly appeared in her mind's eye. Tori could almost hear her friend scolding her and encouraging her to go after what she wanted.

Oh my God! Wouldn't you have a field day with this! She smiled.

"You find waking up in bed with me amusing?"

She heard the smile in his voice. "Actually, Sasha crossed my mind."

"Oh, so *she* would find being in bed with me amusing?"

She sniffed. *You have no idea.* "Not going there."

His fingers continued their assault on her nerves and she shivered. Her nipples tightened even more; started to tingle.

Wade pulled the covers up higher and brought his hand back to rest on her arm.

Damn! Doesn't he know what this is doing to me?

Getting up didn't even hit the top twenty-five of what she wanted to do at the moment. Tori languished in his embrace, savoring the long-dormant desire vibrating through her, threatening to rob her of clear thought. It had been so long. *Too long.* She should move. *Now.*

"We should get up."

"Why?"

Wade's response surprised her to the point she had no reply so she automatically repeated his question. "Why?"

He chuckled. "That's my question. Come up with your own."

Unfortunately, her brain could only focus on one consistent thought—the light brush of his growing member against her knee. She wanted to press against it, slide her knee over the length of it and see what happened. *Like I don't know.*

She wanted to. Desperately. But she didn't.

"I'm sorry about last night," she said at last, "I guess yesterday…got to me."

He tightened his hold, brushing against her breast in the process which kicked her already hyperactive libido into overdrive.

He had to know what he did to her but still he made no move on her.

Is it me? Am I undesirable like Eddie said?

Or, is he waiting for me to make the first move?

"I'm the one who's sorry," His voice was soft and tender. "You've been good to me—to us—and I took advantage of you."

Surprised, she pushed up on her elbow, her hand on his chest for balance. "What do you mean?"

He cast his gaze at the ceiling for several moments before he looked at her. "This has been a mess from the beginning, but you took in all in stride. I knew it would be hard for you but didn't dwell on it because it suited my needs." His deep blue eyes held hers hostage.

Her stomach contracted and her body flushed with heat.

"I never thought about how it might affect you. It wasn't until last night I realized what torture this must be for you." He brought his hand up and cupped her chin. "I'm sorry I've hurt you, Tori…so very sorry. I never should have agreed to this."

His sincerity broke through the last barrier around her heart, startling her with its revelation: She loved him with every fiber of her being.

She tried to keep those emotions from showing in her voice. "I knew what I was getting into. Well, almost knew, so you've nothing to be sorry for."

"You cried half the night."

She looked away, the image of sweet Cody asking his mother to look after Joey forever imprinted on her mind. "I'm sorry I distressed you, Wade." She gave him a timid smile. "But…well, sometimes, crying is medicine, too."

He didn't answer; just looked at her, his steady gaze intense.

In a heartbeat, everything changed.

She wanted to look away but couldn't. Her mind screamed for her to leave immediately but her body had its own agenda and urged her lower…lower…until her lips brushed his.

The *blitzkrieg* of emotions raging through her both astounded and thrilled. A taste was not nearly enough. She kissed him again, at first hesitant, then eager, hungry.

Wade's response was passionate, bone-melting and left her breathless. His arms encircled her waist and pulled her on top of him, the evidence of his desire pressed against her cleft.

She took his lower lip between her teeth and tugged. His groan made her bolder. She opened her mouth and licked his lips.

He plundered her mouth with deep, sweeping stokes of his tongue, branding her forever as his. He pulled the hem of her sleepshirt up and cupped her bottom, pressing her cleft against him, and held her there as his tongue pushed against hers in a sensual battle that left them trembling and gasping for air.

In a single move, he rolled her onto her back and hovered over her.

"Are you sure about this?" he asked, his voice gruff. "Because I sure as hell am." He drew in a ragged breath, "So if you're in doubt, tell me now."

"I—"

A knock on the door stopped her reply.

"Wade?" Sheila's voice carried through the closed door. "Doug's here."

The door swung open and Cody bounded in with Sheila in close pursuit, her movements hampered by the crutch.

"Are you gonna sleep all day?" he asked as he jumped on the edge of the bed. "I been up a long time."

"I'm sorry," said Sheila, eyes averted, "Didn't know he was behind me."

Wade rolled off her and lay on his side, his arm across her waist, his left leg still covered hers, apparently as speechless as she.

"Come here, Cody. Now." Sheila's voice brooked no opposition. "They're awake. Leave them alone."

He crawled across the bed and sat by Tori's pillow, his pudgy fingers pushing the hair from her face. "Joey's okay."

"What?"

"He's ok. Mommy's taking care of him. She said so."

"She did?"

"Uh-huh. I was sad when you cried. But Mommy said they were happy in Heaven, and her and Daddy are taking care of him for you."

"She told you?"

"Uh-huh, I heard her."

"I—thank you." Her words quaked with emotion and tears hovered near the surface.

"That's great, Sport." Wade patted him on the arm. "Now get a move on. We'll be along in a minute."

"Come on, Cody," said Sheila. "Now."

"Alright. I'm coming." He slid off the bed and headed for the door.

"I told Doug to wait in the den." Sheila said over her shoulder.

"Fine."

Tori bolted from the bed the moment they were alone.

Wade grabbed her arm before she escaped. "Tori?"

She couldn't look at him, she floundered in embarrassment and wanted to die on the spot. "I have to go."

"Not like this."

"Please…"

"I know you're embarrassed and I'm sorry about that. But, the fact is, I'm not sorry for what was happening."

She struggled to speak and failed, merely sat there, half on the bed, half off, Wade's hand still on her arm. She sucked in a breath. "I have to check on Miss Willie."

He sighed, released her arm and she stood to go.

"Tori."

She stopped but did not turn around.

"I'm not sorry for what was happening. Are you?"

She was drowning in humiliation. And she had no one to blame but herself. She started it.

"Are you sorry?" he persisted.

She didn't turn around. Couldn't.

Her anguished "No, I'm not." Followed her to the haven of her bedroom.

Chapter Seventeen

WADE MARCHED DOWN THE HALL TOWARD THE den, his mood foul at best. The shock on Tori's face when Cody burst in undid him.

He caused her to suffer. Again.

He humiliated her. Again.

Would he never learn? More importantly, would she ever forgive him?

He found Doug staring out the window when he entered the room and shut the door.

"About time you got up." Doug stuck out his hand. "Since when do you sleep in?"

Wade ignored the question and extended his hand. "What have you found out?"

Doug frowned at his retort then shook his hand. He then passed Wade a file from his briefcase and waited in silence for him to skim the contents.

"You think this is the guy?" Wade tapped the top photo paper clipped to the inside of the folder.

"One of them. Bad boy wanna-be named Benito Gomez. Other one is his boss, Rico Morales. Been on their trail for months. Lost 'em in Colorado. Spotted Benito in Helena about a month ago. Wherever he is, Rico isn't far behind.

Sources have him in this area though don't have an exact location. My gut tells me I'm close."

"What do they want here? We're in the middle of nowhere."

"Drugs. Word is they're looking for a back door into Canada."

"And you think Isaac was on to them?"

"Looks like it to me. He called about two weeks before the accident. Said he found some suspicious stuff up near Eagles Nest. Wanted me to check it out." He paused. "I wasn't fast enough."

Wade looked at his friend. "It's not your fault." He raked his hands through his hair, and tossed the folder on the table. "Dammit it all! Why didn't he tell me? I could have helped. Done *something*!"

"He knew you had your hands full with the ranch and your mother. Besides, he didn't want to bother you with what he thought might be a wild goose chase."

Wade paced in front of the window. "He should have told me. Maybe if he had…" He placed his hands on the sill, head bent.

"It's not your fault, either, dude. And if he had, maybe you'd both be dead. Then where would your family be?"

Several heartbeats passed before Wade straightened and spun around, hands on his hips. "At least Cody survived the crash."

"Has he remembered anything more about the accident?"

"No. Up until last night, all he remembered is they went over the edge."

"What happened last night?" Doug stood straighter, eyes focused on his friend.

"He had a nightmare about *the bad man* who hurt his parents." Wade paused to get control. *Cody saw the man who killed my brother.* "He was so upset I didn't question him about it. But I will today." He paced in front of the fireplace, so on edge he was ready to explode. First Cody, then the *almost* moment with Tori. He needed something to take his mind away from that. "What about Sheila's accident? Do you think they're connected?"

Doug hesitated.

Wade heaved a heavy sigh. "Look, I know you're DEA and I'm just a rancher from Montana, but I need to know. Is my family in danger?"

"I only know as soon as I came around asking questions, she gets run off the road. I leave, nothing more happens."

Wade puffed out a breath. "I found tracks similar to the ones found where they went over yesterday, before the storm hit."

"Where?"

"Not far from the accident site. They're probably all gone now."

"Maybe, maybe not. How soon can we take a look?"

"Whenever you're ready."

"No time like the present."

Sheila hobbled in, stalling their exit. "You're not leaving already are you? You just got here."

"No," Wade answered, "we're going for a ride. We'll be back for supper."

"Oh."

Wade smiled at his sister's obvious disappointment. "Did you need something?"

She gave him her best *leave-me-the-hell-alone look.* "Is

there anything special you'd like for supper? I mean, you are our guest, after all."

"No, nothing special, except maybe your company?"

She beamed. "You got it. Wade, Mother's awake. Why don't you go see her before you leave?"

He grinned at her ruse to be alone with his friend. "Yeah, good idea. Coming, Doug?"

"Uh…I'll be along in a minute."

Wade winked and left the room, closing the door behind him. Doug liked Sheila and that pleased him, despite how he teased her.

When he reached his mother's door, he knocked and waited for permission to enter. Her gentle "Come in, Wade," made him smile.

"How'd you know it was me?" He stopped short when he saw Tori adjusting her blankets but quickly recovered. "Do you have x-ray vision?" He bent and kissed her.

"I know your step. So does Tori. She heard you first."

She glanced at him then looked away. "You have a distinctive step."

Miss Willie looked at them both. "What's wrong?"

"What makes you think something is wrong?" asked Wade.

"You always go right to Tori and kiss her hello or ask her how her day is going. Today neither one of you looks at the other."

"It's nothing, Miss Willie," Tori patted her arm. "Really."

"Have you had a fight?"

His mother's question caught him off guard and he hesitated. "What makes you think we've had a fight?"

"Because I'm not stupid."

"We haven't had a fight."

"Then what's the matter?"

"It's nothing. I promise," added Tori, "don't go worrying yourself."

"If it's nothing, why are you avoiding looking at each other?"

"Mother," Wade began, "We—"

"Sit down." Miss Willie patted the edges of the bed. "Both of you." When they complied, she continued. "No one knows better than us how fragile life is; how fast it can be snatched away from you." She paused. "It's vital to let those we love know how we feel every chance we get." Her breathing grew labored as she continued. "Because...in the blink of an eye they can be...taken from you, leaving you with a bunch of unspoken I-love-yous that….choke the very life from you."

"Mother, please."

"Not finished, Thomas Wade." A smiled tugged at the corner of her mouth. "When I am, you can talk." She looked at Tori for a long moment before she spoke, each word taking its toll on her energy reserves. "This is...first time... since you came...I haven't seen you smile when Wade walked in." She closed her eyes and strained for air.

"Mother?" Wade's heart skipped a beat. He knew her time grew short, but he wasn't ready. Not yet.

"Miss Willie?" Tori clasped her fragile hand and leaned forward. "Are you all right?"

She opened her eyes. "I'm sorry if….frightened you...so much to say, so little time."

"Mother, please. Don't exert yourself."

"Are you breaking up?" she asked softly, her eyes on Wade.

"What?"

"Are you breaking up?"

"Of course not. It's nothing like that," stammered Wade, "We um, we…left something unfinished."

She looked at Tori. "Is that right?"

"Umm, yes. Unfinished business…I mean conversation."

"You are…so right for each other… breaks my heart to… see you this way."

"Miss Willie," said Tori, "please don't -"

"Don't let pride or fear….or anything ….keep you apart." Each breath became more like a ragged gasp.

Wade hated seeing his mother so distressed. His mind raced to come up with a way to change the subject.

"Everything will be fine, Miss Willie." Tori's calm assertion brought his gaze to her face. "As soon as Wade admits I was right."

Wade, clueless about her plan, played along, trusting her completely to find a way out this mess. "Oh, so, I was wrong?" He kept his voice light, forced smile in place.

"Well, I'm glad you're seeing things my way."

Immediately, he thought of her poised over him, her lips touching his, tentative, exploring, then exploding with passion. He rallied the most sinful smile he could, eyes locked with hers, his voice dropped to a low, sexy drawl. "Well, your…idea certainly had merit. But mine did, too."

The fire in her eyes confirmed she understood he referred to their all too brief encounter this morning. "Maybe we were both right," she said at last, her cheeks a fiery red.

"Then, if you're…both right," Miss Willie said, "No reason you…can't kiss and make up, is there?"

Wade looked at his mother's sly smile and his retort died

on his tongue.

She looked at Tori. "Is there?"

"No, um, I guess not."

"Well?" She looked from one to the other and waited.

When he looked at Tori, memories of this morning flashed through his mind; her body pressed against his, her kisses…God, her kisses…the taste still lingered on his tongue. He knew if he kissed her now, her effect on him would manifest itself in a very embarrassing fashion. But he'd do it, not to satisfy his mother, but because he craved the feel of his lips on hers once more. He prayed he could still maintain a smidgen of control over his one-track-mind body.

Yeah. And maybe pigs will fly today.

"I, well, um," Tori stammered, her face a new shade of crimson.

Wade felt a nudge in order and leaned toward her. "I'm willing to call it a draw if you are."

"Um, okay, yes, I guess."

"You *guess*? You could at least act little bit enthused about this," he teased, "I might end up with a complex or something."

Her scowl was more like a grimace. "Well, how am I supposed to act with your mother right here?"

Her exasperation gave him a twinge of guilt he chose to ignore.

He wanted to kiss her.

And she wanted him to despite protests about his mother.

He saw it in her eyes as she looked at his mouth and licked her lips.

Oh yeah.

Probably just hormones or something; after all, her

husband died two years ago, and he'd known from the beginning she hadn't dated yet. But regardless of what prompted those feelings, they were there. He tasted them; he ached for them.

And he wanted her.

All of her.

For now, he'd settle for a kiss.

"Don't mind me," Miss Willie smiled and closed her eyes. "Won't even look."

Tori snorted at her patient, "You needn't try and look so innocent."

"Want you to make up. That's all."

Wade reached for her hand. "Well? Are we making up or not?"

"Fine. Let's get this over with."

"Ouch!" He slapped a hand over his heart." "Could you at least *pretend* to enjoy it?"

She leaned toward him, cheeks flaming, face firmly set.

I'm so dead later.

He smirked as he bent across his mother to meet Tori in the middle.

Manifestations be damned.

He'd show her what the hell a make-up kiss was all about.

Chapter Eighteen

You can do this; a kiss to make a dying woman happy. You don't even have to like it.

But she would like it. She could pretend she didn't want it, but she did. And him.

A few months ago, she'd believed love was a one shot deal. It was both frightening and exciting to find that was not the case. Fear and anxiety clawed through her. Tori loved him with a potentially heart-breaking passion and didn't know what to do about it.

No matter how Wade felt—or didn't feel about her—it appeared he wanted her, because dammit it all, she was here and more than willing. Pride should've stopped her from going further, but just the thought of kissing him again made her drunk with happiness. Her body begged for his kisses, refused to consider rejecting them.

She leaned forward, her body sizzled.

Lord, have mercy.

The moment their lips touched, she lost all coherent thought.

He kissed her, a teasing, tantalizing lip lock that made her crave more.

She considered resistance, but eagerly opened her mouth

to allow him entry.

He cupped her neck, his thumb caressing her jaw line, down her throat.

She brought her hand up and grabbed his wrist but made no effort to stop him.

He deepened the kiss, his tongue skimmed hers, withdrew and returned, the action so sensual it set her body aflame, every nerve alive and igniting at once.

His mouth should be registered as a lethal weapon.

Wade pulled back and rested his forehead against hers, but didn't release his hold on her neck. "I'm sorry."

His whispered apology went straight to her heart. "I know."

"Things just -"

"Got complicated?"

"Yeah. Complicated."

She gave a shaky sigh. "We're getting pretty good at complicated, huh?"

His smile made her knees weak. "Yeah, we are."

"Much better," Miss Willie whispered, "I -" A spasm of pain caught her and she twisted, clinching her jaw against it in obvious agony.

"Tori?" Wade's panic-filled question said it all as he grabbed his mother's hand.

"Hang on Miss Willie, hang on." She reached for the syringe to prepare the injection.

"No drugs, not yet."

"Mother, please."

"Won't be long." Eyes shut, mouth clamped tight against the pain, she waited.

Tori set the medication aside and took her other hand.

"Try and take deep breaths, Miss Willie, let 'em out slow. Good. Good. One more time. Good, girl."

"Wade?"

"I'm here, Ma, I'm here."

"I….love you."

"I love you, too."

"I'm not…afraid…to die."

"…I know."

"Don't…be afraid for me." Her words came out on a long sigh.

Tori saw the torment in his eyes and said a silent prayer for him. Time grew short and Wade would soon need her more than ever. And Cody. *Oh God. Cody.*

"Tori?"

"I'm here, Miss Willie."

"Thank you for being here…for me." She struggled to get the words out.

"I love being here. And I love you so very much." Her fragile fingers were ice cold in Tori's hand.

She continued to talk softly to her patient, coaxing her to relax past the pain, told her how much she loved her and cherished their time together.

Miss Willie blew out a ragged breath. "Wow…a pretty good….one."

"Can I get you anything?"

"Some water please."

Tori filled the glass from the bedside pitcher and helped her drink.

"How much longer?" the soft spoken question was unexpected.

She heard it many times from patients. Sometimes they

wanted the truth; sometimes they wanted a lie. She always instinctively knew which answer to give. Until now.

"I—I don't know."

"But you have… an opinion?"

Tori gazed into Miss Willie's eyes. *How do I tell her? I love her like my own mother and she'll be gone within a month. Probably less.*

"Please," the older woman pleaded. "Need to know."

She glanced at Wade who continued to watch his mother. He didn't want to hear what she would say, but he must.

"It's hard to say." Her voice broke. "Your cancer is very aggressive. A month…or so… I wish I could do more, but…"

"Everything…happens for a reason." Miss Willie squeezed her hand. "We don't always understand." She paused for strength and whispered. "So…angry…with God for taking my Jacob, then Isaac and Karen."

"You should rest now, Ma." Wade took her hand and pulled it to his chest. "You can—"

"No." She looked at Tori. "You understand, don't you?"

"Yes. It was…hard for me when Joey and Eddie died."

"You lost your family…so He gave you mine…because He knew you… would be needed here." Her words were halting, the exertion to speak wrenching the energy from her.

Tori stared, trying to comprehend her meaning.

"He closed a door but…"

"Opened a window." Wade whispered.

Miss Willie nodded, glanced at Wade. "I want to see you married."

"What?" He sat up straight and looked at his mother.

"Want to see you get married." The statement reverberated in the room.

Tori looked at Wade.

The confusion on his face confirmed it: this *complication* hadn't occurred to him, either.

"Well, we, um, haven't discussed it, have we?" Tori stumbled over the words.

"Uh, no. We were so focused on other things we haven't given it much thought."

"Next week."

Their simultaneous "What?" would've been funny if the situation wasn't so serious.

"Friday will be my last birthday. Wonderful present to see my son marry the…woman he loves." It took her several breaths to get out the long statement which ended on a soft sigh.

The *'my last birthday'* statement hindered on blackmail but Tori immediately felt ashamed. It *would* be her last birthday.

Now what do we do?

Wade caught her eye, silently asking for a clue as to their next move.

Crap. Not what I expected today. "We'll see, Miss Willie," Tori said at last, "You rest now."

"Haven't asked her, have you?" She directed the question to Wade, her eyes narrowed.

"What?"

"Just assumed she will."

"We haven't discussed specifics." Wade said.

"Had to ask your father," she said with a smile, "or you might not be here."

"You asked Dad to marry you?" Wade's voice registered his surprise. "Why? How?"

Miss Willie sighed again and closed her eyes. "So handsome. Girls flocked around him…best dancer, too." She paused as though lost in a cherished memory. "Fell in love first time I saw him." She opened her eyes and looked at them in turn. "Much like you."

Tori struggled to remain expressionless.

A smile played across Miss Willie's face. "Sarah Lou had…eyes for him, too. Did all she could to come between us." She stopped and took a ragged breath. "But I won. Sent note to meet me." Her strength was obviously fading, and she rested a couple of breaths. "Our special place. Packed a picnic…some of Grandpa's cider."

"You got him drunk?" Wade's eyebrows rose along with his voice.

Miss Willie scowled at her son. "No. Convinced him… we should marry, and the rest…is history." Her voice ended on a stronger note.

Wade stared, brows pulled together, his voice skeptical. "I had no idea. What did you say to him?"

She patted his hand and smiled. "Told the truth. Said I loved him …with all my heart… would love him forever. Then I asked him to marry me."

"What did he say?"

"Isn't it obvious?"

"No, I mean how did -"

The entrance of Douglas and Sheila cut short his question.

Tori's mind raced.

What's Eddie's DEA partner doing here? Is he undercover? What the hell's going on? Mind choked with questions, her anxiety level reached critical mass when he didn't immediately acknowledge her until Wade introduced them.

"Doug, this is Tori Morgan. Tori, this is Douglas Willis, Doug for short. An old friend of the family."

She extended her hand. "I've um, heard a lot about you—Doug. It's nice to meet you."

"Same here…Ms. Morgan."

A million questions flooded her mind as she looked from Doug to Wade. *What will Wade tell Doug about our arrangement? Will he keep our secret?* The uncertainties added to the emotional turmoil turning her world on its ear. *What a day, and it's not even noon yet.*

Doug headed to Miss Willie's bedside. "How are you today, Beautiful?" He kissed her forehead. "I sure have missed you."

"How are you, Doug? It is so…nice to…see you again, isn't it, Sheila?" she asked with a smile.

"Mother." Sheila's voice shot up an octave.

Wade rose to his feet. "Mother, Doug and I have some work to do. We'll be back later."

"Okay, dear, but think about what I said."

Wade nodded, looked at Tori. "We should be back by supper."

"Tori cooks all the time," blurted Sheila, "I'll do supper tonight."

"Beautiful and cooks, too," Doug grinned. "I can't wait."

"Don't be too eager, Doug. I've tasted her cooking."

"Wade, be nice." Tori felt some of the tension ease by the playful banter. "Don't listen to him, Doug. Sheila's a very good cook."

"I'm not as good as Tori, but I'm learning."

Wade hesitated.

"Surely you don't …plan to leave …bride-to-be without a goodbye kiss?" Miss Willie's halting question stopped him in his tracks.

Tori zoned in on the look of shock on Doug's face but it disappeared in the blink of an eye. Her own face flamed as Wade came around the bed.

He gave her a quick peck on the cheek and turned to leave.

"You call that a kiss?"

Wade scowled at Sheila's remark then turned back to Tori.

"Yeah, you call that a kiss?" she repeated with a mischievous smile.

He gave a low growl and pulled her to him. She grabbed his shoulders for balance.

"How's this?" he asked as he brushed her lips with his. "Or this?" He kissed her again, harder this time, sliding his hands down her hips and pulled her against him.

When at last he pulled back, he grinned. "Well? Any better?"

It took a moment to find her voice. The man did know how to kiss. "Much better." Despite her annoyance at the display, she did egg him on so couldn't fault him for acting on her retort. But, she never gave up without a fight, either. She stood on her tip toes to whisper in his ear, "Remember, though, paybacks are hell."

He let out a laugh and stepped back. "I look forward to it."

Sheila looked at Tori after they left. "Oh my goodness! I can't believe I said I'd cook for him tonight. What's wrong with me?" She wrung her hands as she stood beside her mother's bed.

"You're a very good cook," Tori said, "But if you like, I'll give you a hand. We can get together later and decide what to fix."

"Thank you." Sheila hobbled to her mother and sat on the edge of the bed, down to one crutch now. "Can I get anything for you, Mother? Maybe read to you a bit?"

"No, dear, thank you. I'm pretty tired. Think I'll just nap a bit."

"Okay." She kissed her forehead. "Rest easy. I'll be back later."

As Sheila stood, Miss Willie spoke again, "I love you so much, Sheila. You're a good daughter."

She didn't bother to hide the tears spilling down her cheeks. "I love you, too." She bent over and gave her an awkward hug. "I'm going to miss you so much."

"Only be a thought away, always."

"But it won't be—"

"Only a thought away. No matter where you are, I'll be there with you."

Tori stepped away, stood by the window, suddenly feeling like an intruder. Pulling back the curtain, she saw Wade and Doug had mounted horses in front of the barn.

He sit's that big stallion like he was born to a saddle. He presents an image of strength and masculinity, but he has such a tender side as well. She saw it when he spoke with his mother, played with Cody, or tended to Shadow. More than once she wished she were that silly horse, so Wade would rub his hands over her body, croon softly to her.

And then he did. This morning.

And she wanted it again.

Soon.

She watched as he sat talking with Hank and two other hands, remembering their earlier encounter, his azure eyes smoldering with suppressed passion, his body pressed against hers, his breath ragged as he struggled for control.

She closed her eyes. She wouldn't leave him. Not now. Even if he didn't love her, he wanted her. Tori understood physical attraction soon faded. It had with Eddie almost from the beginning, despite her attempts to make herself exciting and attractive to him.

Sasha insisted all men weren't so shallow, but she remained un-convinced especially since many of the women she worked with said similar things.

She thought she understood about love, truly believed she loved Eddie, but as she watched Wade now, she knew whatever feelings she had for Eddie didn't compare to the powerful, all-consuming love she had for Wade and she tried to ignore the gnawing guilt as this realization washed over her.

Doug said something and Wade smiled. She smiled, too. Seeing him happy made her happy. He talked a moment longer to Hank and then looked toward her as though he knew she watched him. As their eyes met, she experienced the now familiar rush of excitement. With a slight tip of his head, they rode off.

"Oh my God! You're in love with him."

Tori jumped and found Sheila watching her.

"What? Who?"

"You're in love with Wade." Sheila grabbed her in a clumsy embrace hampered by the crutch. "How wonderful!"

She tried to back away. "I don't know what you're talking

about." She cast a cautious glance toward where Miss Willie was fast asleep. "We have a business deal; nothing more."

Sheila stepped back and leaned on the crutch. "Oh, so this morning was—what? Part of the deal?"

Tori's face grew warm. No doubt glowed a bright scarlet. "Nothing happened! It …we… nothing happened."

"Too bad. It'd do you both some good."

Her patience thinned. "Sheila."

"Well, it would. Does Wade know?"

"Know what?"

"That you're in love with him?"

"Sheila, please."

"He doesn't have a clue, does he?"

A shudder ran through her. She could no longer deny it. Her careless lapse in covering her feelings sprung the trap and now she lay caught in the jaws of truth.

Maybe it's just as well. I need someone to talk to about this and Sasha isn't here.

"No," she said at last, "he doesn't."

"Why haven't you told him?"

"Because …"

"Has he said he doesn't care for you?"

"Well, no, but…"

"Then how do you know?"

Left with no answer, she kept silent.

"You're the best thing that's ever happened to him. I can see it; Mother sees it, hell the whole damn ranch can see it."

"Sheila, please. Keep your voice down." Tori suddenly regretted her choice of confidants. Sheila was as outspoken and blunt as Sasha.

Lowering her voice, Sheila pleaded her case. "I've seen

the way you two are together; it's like two people with one mind. You pass him something at dinner he hasn't asked for, you help him work with Shadow and neither one of you say a word. Every night you bring him coffee in the den when he's working on the books—"

"We've talked a lot," she insisted, "We share some of the same interests. We're friends."

"Well, if this morning is any indication of how friends act I *so* want me one of those."

Oh, God, what have I started?

"Cody had a nightmare."

"I know. He told me."

Tori looked out the window and remained silent.

"You deserve to be happy, you know." Sheila's voice softened. "So does Wade." She stepped closer and put a hand on Tori's shoulder. "When Isaac and Karen died, Wade stopped smiling. He lost interest in everything. He didn't care about the ranch or us or anything. He stayed drunk for days. If it hadn't been for Hank, the place would've gone under. Then Mother's conditioned worsened and I got hurt." She took an audible breath. "Then you came along. I don't think he realizes how much he's changed. But I do. And it's all because of you."

"I've taken some of the load off him, that's all. It doesn't mean anything."

"He watches you when you're not looking."

"What?" Her gaze collided with her other patient.

Sheila smiled. "Like yesterday, for instance."

Tori thought hard but nothing came to mind.

"You were walking out to the barn to take Shadow her evening apple, with Major right on your heels."

"He kept walking between my legs, almost tripped me."

"So you chased him."

She smiled at the memory. "And then he chased me."

"Until you tripped and he jumped all over you."

Her smile broadened. "He likes to wrestle."

"Wade watched you from the corner of the house, grinning from ear to ear. I'd bet my last dollar he would've given anything to have been his dog right then."

She tended to sense when Wade was near, even if she didn't see him. It disconcerted her to know he'd watch and she not be aware.

"Doesn't prove anything, Sheila."

"Well, what did this morning prove?"

If possible, her faced turned even more scarlet than before. "I told you, nothing happened. I haven't…it was…"

"Was what?"

"Nothing."

"But it might've been something."

Yes. Something wonderful.

Tori strode toward the bed, ending the troubling conversation. "She asleep?"

"Yeah, she tires so easy now."

"As soon as I put this stuff away, we'll work on your therapy and talk about supper."

"He's worth fighting for, Tori, and he needs you."

She froze but couldn't face Sheila.

"And you need him. Everybody seems to know it but the two of you. Someone needs to get through to you both."

Tori gathered her courage and faced Wade's sister. "Whatever happens or doesn't happen, it has to come from Wade, of his own volition. It can't be any other way."

A reluctant nod and Tori knew she would not interfere.

"It's almost time isn't it?" Sheila looked at her mother, and her eyes filled with tears.

Tori noted her patient's pale, drawn features, the shallow, ragged breaths and nodded, unable to say the words.

"We can never repay you for what you have done for her." Her voice cracked.

Tori bobbed her head, words lodged in her throat.

Sheila bent to kiss her mother. "I love you," she murmured before leaving the room.

Tori placed the emptied syringe of pain medication in the Sharps container and finished her documentation. She locked everything up in the bedside table.

She went through this ritual each time she left, primarily because of Cody's natural curiosity, but also because she liked things all neat, tidy and in order.

Certainly doesn't describe my life right now. It can't get any more disorderly.

As the door closed behind her, she heard the unmistakable voice of Lucy Tate in the foyer and chided herself for speaking too soon.

Chapter Nineteen

T HE LATE AFTERNOON SUN DIPPED BEHIND THE distant mountains as Tori wandered around the yard. Her thin sweater inadequate for the increasing coolness, she rubbed both her arms as she walked, reminding herself again that October in Montana was a lot colder than Houston. Hank had said this morning it would snow again any day now and she made a mental note to keep a heavier coat by the back door. She considered going back for one now but had no desire to deal with Lucy again.

She'd known all along the red-head spelled trouble, but now thought, she may have underestimated her.

The calls had started about a week ago and all said the same thing, *go home or you'll be sorry*, then silence. Tori imagined Lucy somehow involved but since she couldn't prove it, said nothing. Her arrival today had started with more hurtful remarks and pointed innuendoes so she did her best to avoid her.

The last straw had come earlier today when she announced her plan to take Cody back with her and make a *real* home for him with *family*. Certain this was yet another ploy to get to Wade, she ignored her and decided to speak with him about it as soon as he returned.

Sheila, on the other hand, had long since reached the end of her rope and told Lucy flat out to go to hell.

Undaunted, Lucy laughed and said, "Oh, been there, done that," and walked away.

Tori had barely managed to grab the vase before Sheila threw it.

I have to keep a clear head and make sure Lucy doesn't follow through with this idiotic plan. She took several calming breaths. The situation called for a clear head.

How far will Lucy go to get Wade? How far will I go to stop her?

No brainer. She would lay down her life for them.

What if Sheila's right and Wade does love me? No, that's too big a stretch. We get along well enough, and sometimes communicate without words but what does that prove?

The questions piled up and answers remained hidden.

Shadow whinnied as she entered the barn and walked to her stall.

"Hey, girl." Tori rubbed the out-stretched nose. "How are we feeling today?" Tori loved the smell of the barn because it brought such fond memories of her grandparents' farm.

The mare neighed and stamped her foot as though chastising her for being late.

"Now you know I have to take care of Miss Willie first." She reached in her pocket and pulled out an apple and some sugar cubes. "And you-know-who is back." She offered the sugar and dropped the apple back in her pocket. "Here, see if this will sweeten your disposition." The horse feasted on treat and enjoyed the rubdown. "What am I going to do, girl? What on earth do I do?"

Shadow, aptly named with her solid black body, tossed

her head and stomped her foot, then shifted her weight from side to side.

"What's wrong, girl? You're not ready for that baby are you? I think it's a bit early." She opened the door to the stall and walked in, keeping her voice soft, rubbing her hands over the mare's swollen middle.

The mare scraped her hoof on the straw laden floor and swished her tail, the coarse fibers raked across Tori's face.

"Oh, this is the thanks I get for bringing you apples and sugar cubes, huh?" She smiled and continued her cursory exam. "I don't know, kiddo, maybe. I know you're miserable, but it won't be long now."

She patted the horse again, climbed on top of the gate and sat on the small ledge. Her rear smarted from the uncomfortable seat so she stepped down and grabbed a saddle blanket from the wall, folded it over the top rail and perched on top of it, twisting a little so her back rested against the corner post. Shadow moved closer and nudged her lap.

"Feeling a little neglected, are we?" She pulled the apple from her pocket and sliced it with her small pocket knife. "I know the feeling; pregnant, big as a barrel and no one to rub your feet; or in your case, your ears."

Shadow nickered as though in agreement and Tori laughed. "I know what you mean. I couldn't see my feet after five months. No, it's true. I even spent the last two flat on my back in bed, but it'll be worth it. You'll see. The first time you set eyes on that spindly-legged, clumsy-footed colt, you'll forget all about this."

The horse scraped her hoof on the ground.

"Oh yes you will. When Joey was born—" She stopped short and pushed the memory back in its corner with much effort, the pain still too hard to bear. "Well, you'll see."

She closed her eyes and continued rubbing the horse's head. She had felt a certain affinity for her four-legged friend from the beginning, and chalked it up to her genuine love of animals.

A lot of her childhood was spent on her grandparent's farm, surrounded by a variety of four-legged beasts, and as a shy, gangly teen, preferred them to people most of the time. She met Eddie there the summer she turned sixteen. The reckless nineteen year old grandson of their neighbor, she'd fallen hard for the Prince Charming of her dreams. Blinded by inexperienced love, they'd married as soon as she graduated high school, much against the wishes of her family. A true romantic, she'd imagined a perfect life together.

It'd taken her a long time to realize perfection didn't exist.

Eddie couldn't be faithful. She never understood why and the marriage floundered on shaky ground. Even now, she didn't blame him; maybe because he'd died, maybe because they shared blame for the difficulties they faced.

Oh, what the hell. Stop reliving the past. Get on with the present.

She sighed and allowed her mind to roam free, uninhibited hoping answers to her many questions would magically appear. Instead, the images popping in made her pulse quicken and her heart race. Her whole body ached with a longing that shocked her. She sat up straighter. "Well, hell. What a lousy idea."

"What was?"

She jumped and would have fallen backward off the gate if Wade hadn't caught her.

"Dammit, Wade," she spewed as he placed her feet on the

ground. "You scared the hell outta me."

"Sorry, I thought you heard me ride up."

"Well, I didn't," she snapped glancing at his brown stallion, Gizmo, calmly standing beside him. "How long have you been standing there?"

"Not long." He grinned. "What was a lousy idea?"

She ignored the question. "When was the last time the vet checked on Shadow?"

"Not lately. Why?"

"I don't know, she's pretty restless today and I'm halfway certain she had a contraction earlier."

"She's not due for another couple of weeks."

"I know."

"I'll have Doc Green come by and check her out."

"Okay. Sure you haven't misjudged the time?"

He smiled and her heart jumped. *There should be a law against a man having such a raw, sensual voice and a seductive smile to boot.*

"No, I didn't miss it, but I'll give him a call."

She nodded. Shadow neighed and nudged her hand. "What's the matter, girl? You jealous?" She patted the head pressing forward and pulled out another lump of sugar. "Okay, but this is the last one. And don't try your poor-pitiful-me look, either. It won't work."

Wade pulled Gizmo into the adjacent stall and pulled off the saddle.

After the mare finished her last treat, Tori gave her a final pat on the head and joined him. She picked up the burlap sack on the wall and wiped the beautiful stallion down. They worked in quiet unison, following unspoken commands until the horse had been rubbed, fed and watered.

Not until they were almost finished did she recall her conversation with Sheila this morning. She'd never considered the possibility of two people being so in tune they could work as one, but she and Wade did it all the time. Second nature now, she didn't notice when it happened. She concluded love on her part accounted for the bond, but what embodied his? How was she to know his true feelings?

Does he really care?

If she came right out and asked and he said the former, she'd be devastated; if she said nothing and he cared, she'd be devastated.

Damned if I do and damned if I don't.

"Wanna talk about it?" asked Wade, watching her over the horse's back.

"About what?"

"Whatever it is putting a scowl on your face."

"You mean aside from the fact that Lucy's back and mean as ever?"

"Crap. When?"

"Right after you left this morning."

"Great." He ran his fingers through his hair and sighed. "Perfect ending to a perfect day."

"Wanna talk about it?"

"I asked first." Wade smirked.

"So you did."

He patted the horse's rump and came around to her. "Is it about this morning? Are you still upset with me?"

She shook her head without looking at him. "No."

The early winter chill wasn't what caused her to shiver. *I have to tell him about Lucy. I don't want to—I can't- leave. But what if he doesn't want me to stay?*

"When are you going to learn?"

"What?" She rubbed her arms.

"To wear a jacket." He removed his own and placed it around her shoulders. "This ain't Texas."

"Well, I did remember. Just didn't want to have to see Lucy to get one."

"You'd rather freeze than deal with Lucy?" Wade chuckled.

Tori snorted. "Wouldn't you?"

"Yeah, I guess I would." He stepped out of the stall and waited for her to exit before shutting and barring the gate. He started toward the entrance and turned when she didn't follow.

She scrutinized at him for a long moment. "What's going on Wade?"

His expression changed with his thoughts and she decided whatever he hid from her had something to do with Doug's sudden appearance.

He walked to her and placed his hands on her shoulders. "Will you tell me what's bothering you as well?"

"…Yes."

"Not here". He took her by the arm. "Come on."

He led her behind the barn taking a roundabout route to the cabin no doubt to keep prying eyes from seeing where they went.

Once inside, he started a fire in the fireplace while she paced and worried about what Doug may have told him. Eddie and Doug had partnered on several cases and spent a lot of time together over the years. She suspected he knew about Eddie's affairs, but what had Eddie told Doug about *her*?

Insecurity engulfing her, she pulled Wade's jacket tighter around her, imagining his arms held her. She hadn't realized until lately how much she missed being held. She'd grown up in a family of huggers and enjoyed those shows of affection. Eddie, however, hadn't and she'd finally given up trying to make him so. She'd given up on pretty much everything until she got pregnant with Joey. He became her whole world and when he died, she had nothing left.

Then Wade walked into her life with Cody. If she lost them now, she wouldn't have the strength to fight anymore.

But she had strength now, and she'd fight for what she wanted.

She inhaled, savoring the gamy mixture of sweat and horse and man permeating the coat he'd wrapped her in. The fire crackled and sputtered to life casting a warm glow over the tiny room, making shadows dance along the walls.

It didn't matter that her back was to him; she could feel when he came to stand behind her.

"Want me to light a lamp?" Wade asked.

"No. Yes…whatever."

Neither moved.

"Where's Doug?"

"With Sheila."

Another long pause ensued.

"Who goes first?" There was a hint of a smile in his voice.

"Lucy wants to take him away."

"What?" Wade grabbed her shoulders, twisting her around.

"I'm sorry, I didn't mean to blurt it out, it's just that I've been so upset—"

His fingers bit into her shoulders. "What do you mean by take him away?"

She took a steadying breath and related the day's events. She could tell by the set of his jaw, Lucy would play hell taking

Cody away from him.

But what if she does?

"And she said she talked with a lawyer and he thinks she shouldn't have any problem getting custody." The words came out in a torrent, so fast she couldn't be certain exactly what she'd said.

"Cody's not going anywhere," he said firmly.

"I-I can't bear to lose him, Wade."

"I told you." Wade rubbed his hands down her arms. "He's not going anywhere."

"I'll take good care of him. I-I don't want to leave." She whispered, afraid of what he might say.

"You can't stay."

She couldn't breathe, wasn't certain her heart continued to beat.

He wanted her to leave.

Oh, my God! What a fool I am to think he would want me. He doesn't care.

"Of c-course." She stumbled back until she hit the little table in the center of the room.

"No. No…I didn't mean that the way it sounded." Wade reached for her. "Please hear me out."

She nodded, emotions in chaos, unable to utter a sound.

"I met Doug in the Army. I didn't know until today you knew him as well."

She tried to keep her voice level. "I knew him as JD, Eddie's DEA contact and sometimes partner. They'd just started a new case when Eddie died."

"I know."

"Does Sheila know? About Doug, I mean?"

"Yes."

She made herself look at him, saw the uncertainty and concern he tried to hide. "It's not a friendly visit, is it?"

"No."

"So…"

He shook his head. "I don't know. It's possible the people responsible for Isaac's death may be back."

She waited for him to continue.

"Doug thinks Isaac may have stumbled onto the beginnings of a drug route to Canada. He called to ask Doug check it out, but before he got here…" Wade's voice broke. "I had no idea."

"You're not to blame."

He paused and turned to the fire. "I never believed it was an accident. Shit didn't add up." He inhaled deeply. "Cody was in the Jeep when it went over the edge."

Her concerns were immediately forgotten. "What? Oh my God!" She looked at him for a moment. "The bad man? You think Cody knows something?"

Wade nodded. "I haven't had a chance to talk to him yet. I wanted him to have time to get over it."

He threw his hat on the bed, raked his fingers through his hair. "This is so fricking complicated." He took a breath. "Doug isn't sure but it's possible they may be responsible for Sheila's accident as well. I'm not convinced, but I suppose it's possible."

"Oh no! Are Cody and Sheila in danger?"

"I don't think so. But you may be."

"Me? Why on earth would I be in danger?"

Wade trapped her with his eyes, face hard as stone. "Because he thinks Rico Morales and Benito Gomez might be involved. And they're hiding around here."

Chapter Twenty

TORI SWAYED, AND EVEN IN THE MUTED LIGHT OF THE cabin, Wade saw the color drain from her face. He reached to steady her.

"Wh-what? Are you sure? It can't be true."

"Yes. Maybe."

"Oh, God, no." Her knees folded.

He grabbed her around the waist to keep her from sinking to the floor. An old bed in the corner provided the only place to sit so he led her there. Wade didn't know what to do.

She shook all over and looked so devastated. He couldn't stand it; he pulled her in his arms and held tightly.

"Rico. Here," Tori whispered, "It can't be. The nightmare…is b-back."

Wade held her and mouthed words of comfort he hoped to be true. "You're safe, Tori, he won't hurt you again. I promise."

"How do you know it's him?"

He related what he knew about how Rico and Benito had come to be here and what they suspected. As he spoke, he continued to hold her until the trembles eased, then stopped.

She sat on the edge of the bed, her feet curled under her, her body molded against him.

"You may be in danger if he finds out you're here."

"What about Cody. And Lucy?" Her voice quivered and she chewed her lower lip.

"She knows better than to try and take him away."

Tori pulled back to look him at him, her eyes reflecting the fear and anxiety he tried to hide from her. "She's obsessed with you, Wade. She'd do anything to get you. Even use Cody."

"I don't know. She's weird but…"

"What about the phone calls?"

"What calls?" He clenched his jaw as she relayed the calls that began last week.

"It's a man's voice. There is something familiar about it but I can't place it. And it sounded, like, I don't know, like maybe he was trying to disguise it, like with a rag or something."

"But you think Lucy may be behind them?"

"Frankly, I wouldn't put anything past her. I've thought about it a lot. She could have gotten someone to make the calls to frighten me. It's the only explanation that makes sense."

Wade's next thought made his blood run cold. "Could it be Rico or Benito?"

Her gasp told him she never considered it. But then, she didn't know until now they might be around.

"Could it be either of them, Tori?"

"No. I don't know. Oh, God, Wade…"

Her silence tortured his soul. "All right," His firm voice brooked no opposition. "Until this matter is taken care of, you are not to leave the ranch alone. No rides, or walks or anything without me, Hank or Doug. Understood?"

She nodded, then rose and walked to the fireplace, arms outstretched toward the heat.

"Do you think I'm the reason they're here?"

Wade didn't know how to tell her. "I don't know." He stood next to her. "There may be another party involved. I found some tracks leading back toward the ranch; it's possible someone is watching the place."

"You mean someone here might be—could be spying on us?"

"I don't know. The tracks were washed out by the storm. It may be nothing. There's a lot of activity around here getting ready for winter."

"But who could it be," she stammered, "You said these men have been with you a long time."

"A couple came on this year."

"I haven't talked about what happened in Houston to anyone but you and Sheila. How would someone know about it or make a connection to me?"

"No clue at the moment. I suppose its possible Cody may have said something, hell, maybe they googled you." He ran his fingers through his hair as he talked. "All I know is until this thing is settled, I want you somewhere safe."

She went back to the bed and sat down. "I won't leave, Wade. I can't leave."

He took a seat beside her. "You could be in danger."

"What about Cody? I promised not to leave."

"I'll think of something."

"No." Tori sat still, hands gripping her knees, her face set. "I won't leave him, Wade. He's just a baby. He won't understand. I can't leave him."

"Ok," he said at last, "But you don't go anywhere alone. And I want to know about any more calls, anything suspicious."

"What about Lucy's latest scheme?"

"Let me worry about Lucy."

She gave him a shaky smile, "Oh, so *now* you're gonna worry about her."

"Well, I'll admit maybe I underestimated her some."

"Some?" Her annoyance flared, her words sharp. "Did you ever hear of *Fatal Attraction*, Wade?" She shook her head. "She's crazy and dangerous."

"Granted she is, well, crazy." Wade crossed his arms, "But I just can't see her as dangerous. But, to be on the safe side, stay away from her as much as you can. I'll see if I can get her out of here tonight."

Tori shuddered, and her face paled. "I don't trust her, Wade. Please be careful."

The moment their eyes met, the full force of the attraction between them ignited. He tried to block it but failed miserably. *She wanted him but was there more? Or did her dead husband still own her heart? How would he know for sure?*

"Wade?" She looked down at her tightly clasped hands. "What if we had a way to stop Lucy once and for all? Would you do it?"

Surely she doesn't mean -? "What are you saying?"

She paced in front of the fire. "As long as you're, well, available Lucy's going to be a problem, right?"

"In theory, yes."

"What if you weren't available anymore? Officially, I mean."

He watched her as she moved closer, hands shoved in her pockets. "She keeps saying he needs a home; a mother and father specifically. What if we gave him that? What if we got married?"

Wade stared, not believing his ears.

Did she just ask me to marry her?

His mind raced to comprehend what she said while his heart kicked into overdrive. *She wants to marry me.* He tried to focus on the words flowing in a torrent of unrestrained urgency.

"I'll do whatever it takes to make a good home for him—and you, *us*. I have my own money. I don't have anything back in Houston to speak of. I mean my family is there and all, but well, I don't want to go back." Her hands waved about as she talked, phrases pouring out on top of each other. "I'm no spring chicken, but then neither are you. And Lucy does seem to be the only other prospect right now." She started to pace again.

Wade listened in stunned amazement as she continued her declamation with hardly a breath.

"I'm a good cook, you said so yourself. I'm a hard worker; I can be entertaining if necessary. I'm not demanding and wouldn't expect you to, you know, to do anything you didn't want to."

She's listing her qualifications to be a wife; like a shopping list. What the hell?

He stared. Couldn't utter a sound if someone put a gun to his head.

Tori, on the other hand, had plenty to say. Sentences continued to spill out so fast he had trouble following them all.

But one thing stood out crystal clear; *she asked me to marry her.*

"On the down side, I can be moody, but, then so can you; and I do seem to have a tendency to be hard headed about some things." She sucked in a breath. "But the biggest thing, or one of them, is, well, I may not be able to have another child. It's a rather complicated story, but that's the gist of it." She stopped in front of him, her eyes bright, her chin quivered as she waited for his response.

He stood. "Let me see if I understand this correctly," he said with exaggerated calmness, ignoring the turbulence in the pit of his stomach. "You think we should get married so Cody will have—what—a home? He'll have that regardless."

"Of course he will. I know he will."

"What about love?"

"What?"

She looked like a kid with her hand caught in the cookie jar and he forced himself not to smile.

She wants to marry me.

"I thought all women believed love a prerequisite for marriage?" He watched her face for any sign to indicate what she might be thinking but saw nothing.

Maybe there is more to this proposal than she is saying. An interesting turn of events.

"It's been my experience," she said after a long pause, "um, love is, well, somewhat overrated."

"Overrated?" His head snapped back and he arched an eyebrow.

She nodded. "I think it's more important for two people to respect each other."

He took his time replying. "I see. So…a marriage of convenience based on respect… nothing else?"

Tori averted her gaze. "I can't deny there is a certain… attraction between us. This morning is proof enough, but it's been my experience that, well, such attraction is overrated, too and doesn't last."

Wade chose his next words with great care. Whatever prompted that statement meant a lot to her. Her proposition meant the world to him. "So…love and sex are overrated and a marriage of convenience based on respect is preferable?"

Shoulders squared, she tilted her head to look him in the eye.

He stared down at luscious, full lips, a pertly up-turned nose and chocolate brown eyes that shimmered with doubt and anticipation.

"Yes," she said at last, "it is."

He found himself cursing a dead man he never met for making her believe such rot. Doug had told him about their rocky marriage, how Eddie bragged about sleeping around; how hard she struggled to keep it together, the miscarriages and the agony she'd gone through before Joey was born.

Then the murders and what she'd endured afterwards.

He longed to hold her, to tell her he wasn't like that, and he loved her and would never hurt her. But he didn't. She wanted respect, and he would make sure she received it. Among other things.

"So, would this marriage be in name only or what?" he asked.

Head bowed, she pulled her hands from her pockets, pushed them back. "That will be up to you. I meant what I said. I will do whatever it takes to make a good home for us. I'm thirty-three, I've been married but well, I know I'm not very…um…exciting, so I'll understand if you don't want to…"

Her eyes remained lowered and it took all his will power not to pull her to him and tell her he wanted her now and forever, and he'd make love to her anytime, anywhere.

Still, he waited.

"What makes you think you're not exciting?" Even as he asked the question, he knew the answer. Eddie. *The bastard.*

"Fine, you want it spelled out? I'll spell it out."

Tori's sudden burst of anger caught him by surprise. His stomach muscles clinched, this whole conversation must be pure torture for her and he kept adding to the pile.

"Tori—"

"I couldn't keep my husband interested so he went to other women. Surely Doug told you…" She shivered. "I tried. I read books, but I wasn't—I didn't…."

Way to go, asshole. Kick her when she's down.

He grabbed her arms and refused to release her when she tried to get away. "Look at me. Please." It took a couple of tries but she managed to face him, pride no doubt the chain keeping her in control. "I don't know why Eddie ran around, but I'd bet my last dollar it wasn't because you weren't exciting in bed."

"What? Why would you say such a thing? You barely know me."

"The woman who kissed me this morning, the woman I held in my arms is exciting and passionate. Her lips teased like this." He grazed her lips with his, savoring the tremble it elicited. "Her hands caressed like this." He pushed the jacket from her shoulders and slid his hands down her back to her rear, and squeezed. "And she makes my blood boil with just a smile."

She chewed her lower lip. "But is it enough to keep two people together? Can it stand the test of time?"

He grinned in spite of the seriousness of the conversation. "I think it could stand on its own right now."

"I'm serious, Wade."

This time he didn't try to stop her when she pulled away and stared at the fire.

"I can't deny that well, I'm…attracted to you…sexually…and it appears the feeling is…somewhat mutual. But, once the new wears off and it's gone, there has to be something else, some shared interests…something."

"Respect?" *Sonofabitch sure did a number on you. I'd kill 'em myself if he weren't already dead.*

"Yes, respect." She met his gaze. "Respect for the other person, for things they hold dear…friendship if you will."

"Friendship?" *I'll give you anything you ask of me.*

"We get along well enough, we…enjoy each other's company and we both love Cody and want him to be happy."

"What about us? Don't we deserve to be happy, too?"

She puffed out a breath. "Yes, we do. And I would do everything within my power to make you happy. I know you don't love me, but you like me. And should the time come when you wanted out, we would end it like we started—as friends who want nothing but happiness for each other."

Don't love you? My God I adore you. It didn't escape his notice she'd never mentioned herself or her feelings for him. "What about you, Tori? What if you wanted out?"

Her smile was pensive. "Well, unless Prince Charming rides up on a white stallion to whisk me away to the Magic Kingdom, I reckon I'll be here…as long as you want me." She looked down, then back to the fire.

He moved behind her and resisted the temptation to touch her. '*I love you, Tori,*' hung on the tip of his tongue along with '*I want you beside me now and forever,*' but he said nothing. He had to know how she felt about him. Did she seek a way to gain back the son she lost or a way to be with someone she cared for?

She continued to stare into the fire, the gleam of unshed tears crowding the corner of her eye.

"You still haven't told me what's in this for you."

With visible effort, she made herself look at him. "Cody needs me and I need him."

Wade took a step back. "So, I'm nothing more than a means to an end then?" He tried to keep the hurt from showing in his voice, but thinking she cared nothing for him ripped his heart to shreds. "That's all I am to you?"

She jerked up straighter, mouth gaping. "No! Wade, I care about you. You know that."

"I only know what you tell me." He paused, his heart in pieces at the thought she cared nothing for him. "And what you've said is you want Cody and are willing to sacrifice yourself to have him."

Chapter Twenty-One

Tori stared. *Was he upset at my confession to be near Cody? I can't tell him I want to be near him as well. Or can I?*

Things happened so fast she hadn't fully absorbed the fact she asked *him* to marry *her*.

Is there no end to the humiliation I'm willing to endure for the sake of being with him?

"I'm not sacrificing myself. I would get something, too."

"Such as?"

"A husband who respects me, is intelligent, handsome—"

"You think I'm handsome?" He smiled, pleasure evident in the grin he wore. "You never told me that."

"You never asked."

"So, I have to ask specific questions to get specific answers?"

"Well I—"

"Do you—could you—love me?"

She stared at the fire, heart pounding so hard the sound echoed in her ears and obscured all other sound.

If I say no, I'm lying. If I say yes, I'm setting myself up to be hurt. I have no pride left. What's one more step down this road of mortification?

"Tori?"

"It would be easy to love you, Wade." The crack in her voice evident, she didn't breathe or turn around; couldn't bear to see what he might be thinking.

The silence drug on so long her heart ached with dread.

Oh God…he doesn't want me.

"One condition."

His tone was different, not hard, not soft…different.

She spun around and saw the corners of his mouth curled up in a sexy smirk. Her stomach clinched tight.

"You'll do it?"

"I will, but under one condition."

He spoke so mater-of-fact she was afraid what his *one condition* might be.

"Okay."

"We are the only ones who know the particulars of our arrangement. It will be a marriage in every sense of the word."

She blinked twice and nodded, trying to make sense of what he said.

"So, do we shake on this deal or what?" A jaunty cock of his head accompanied his outstretched hand.

She shifted from one foot to the other, hands jammed in her pockets. "I—I don't know…"

"Or…"

He stepped closer, reached out and traced her lips with his thumb.

Frissons of desire exploded through her.

"We could pick up where we left off this morning." The smoldering look in his azure eyes leaving no doubt what option he preferred. "Well?"

Her breath hitched. "Well what?"

His thumb continued it sensual assault. "Care to finish what you started?"

She jerked her hands out of her pockets and rubbed them on her hips. *What if I do something wrong? What if I truly lack lovemaking skills?* Her shaky self-confidence crumbled. His censure would be unbearable. "I—it's been a while." Eyes averted, her voice trembled, but his gaze was unrelenting.

He tilted her chin until she faced him. "Then we'll take it slow." He kissed the open palm of her hand. "I like it slow."

She shivered, sucked in a breath.

He traced the life line with his tongue. "You set the pace. You say stop, we stop."

She grabbed a handful of his shirt for balance.

"Just so you know...I for one don't believe lovemaking comes from a book or a movie. It comes from here." He brought her hand down and placed it over his heart, its rapid thump pulsed under the skin. "And here." He brought it up to touch his head, then back to his mouth where he caressed it again with his tongue. "Is there anything..." He took her index finger in his mouth and sucked gently, his tongue circling its tip... "*Anything...*" He took her middle finger into his mouth.

In. Out. In. Out.

"You'd like to do right now?" His tone, seductive on a good day, bordered on illegal.

Her knees wobbled like Jell-O, desire verged on physical pain intensified by the sexy rasp of his voice, the slide of his tongue pinging off nerves too long dormant.

Holy mother of pearl! Sassy was right...

"Well, is there?"

"I want you." She couldn't control the quiver in her voice.

"Tell me what you like."

He rested her hands on his chest, holding them in place with his own. "It's about mutual pleasure, baby, it's not one sided." He kissed her on the nose. "You first." He held her gaze and whispered, "Make love to me, Tori."

She reveled in the passion ablaze in his eyes.

In a heartbeat, uncertainty vanished, replaced by overwhelming hunger. She slid her hands up his chest, around his neck and tugged. Their lips met; lightly at first, a timid, yet electrifying skim. She leaned into him, his growing arousal twitched in response.

His powerful arms were taut as a bowstring when he pulled her against him all the while letting her control the kiss. Her tongue probed his mouth, exploring, seeking.

He met each parry with thrusts of his own that triggered waves of sensual pleasure. His arms trembled, a low groan rumbled in his throat.

He trailed a path of wet kisses from her lips, to her throat, and back up again. Muscular hands gripped her hips, pulled her against his erection.

She whimpered as one hand skimmed her breast, its tip puckered in response and she froze.

"Come on, baby." He ground out the words. "Don't think....do."

She fingered the buttons on his shirt. "Can I take this off?"

"Be my guest." He dropped his hands and waited.

She fumbled with the buttons, pulled it free of his jeans and tossed it aside. He shrugged out of the thermal undershirt as she tugged and it soon joined his shirt on floor.

Empowered by potent need, she ran her fingers through

the dense curls on his chest, brushing the tight nipples, enjoying his gasp of pleasure when she placed feathery kisses on each.

She stepped back, amazed at the rampant hunger burning in his eyes and pulled a blanket from the bed. She spread it on the floor in front of the fireplace and motioned for him to lie down.

He lay on his back, hands clasped behind his head. Waiting.

Without warning, old doubts and fears tried to surface and she hesitated.

"What would you like to do next?" He made a low noise in his throat, his pupils darkened until they appeared black in the muted light.

She nibbled her lower lip, then bent and removed her boots and socks. Tori stood, memorizing what she saw… brawny arms supported his head, cobalt eyes no longer hooded but open with blatant desire, sensuous lips parted, his tongue tracing his lower lip, the broad expanse of his chest that rose and fell with each jerky breath, the dark hair a trail pulling her gaze lower… lower where the evidence of his own desire grew.

She knelt, pulling off his boots and socks then reached for his jeans. One by one, she unfastened the buttons, liking his reaction—a gasp and jerk—when she touched him as she pulled the Levis past his hips. His jeans topped the pile of discarded clothing. She shrugged out of her sweater and tossed it on the bed, then fingered the front clasp of her bra.

Wade's eyes locked on her hands, his chest motionless as he watched.

With deliberate slowness, she stood and fumbled with

the belt, unbuttoned her jeans.

She fingered the zipper.

He licked his lips and gulped a mouthful of air as she eased it down. She heard his breath catch when she wiggled and slid them past her rear, kicking them aside.

Clad only in a bra and panties, she waited, noted the way he twitched, hands gripping a handful of quilt. She knelt between his legs, hands on his thighs and slid them back and forth, easing upward and in until they hovered over his arousal.

He groaned and reached for her.

"Not yet."

He lay back and clutched the quilt again, a low growl coming from his throat.

At her light caress he sucked in air, arched up.

She took his hands and laced their fingers together as she leaned forward to trail kisses from his navel, up his chest, across rigid nipples. With each feathery touch he groaned and she felt every tremble rocking his body as he reacted to her ministrations.

"Aaaagh….Tori…."

Her knee swept his groin as she moved up his body. "I've dreamed of this," she whispered, placing delicate kisses on his face, down his neck, then south again across his chest. She paused over his straining erection and skimmed it with her cheek.

He sucked in a breath, bowed upward.

Their remaining clothing joined the expanding heap.

Naked, she bent low and ran her tongue up the firm flesh, across the tip and down again before taking him in her mouth

"Lord, Tori, you're killing me!" He made a half-hearted effort to pull her up but she pushed his hands away and continued her sensual assault.

With a strangled moan, he pulled her up and over him in one fluid move. His lips crushed hers, their passions exploded and the need to touch and be touched was uncontrollable.

She couldn't get enough of the feel of his body; she stroked his back, felt the muscles flex as his hands explored her breasts, her hips and back up again. She matched each fiery stroke, their mutual sounds of pleasure echoing through the tiny cabin. She whimpered and squirmed as he suckled each nipple, kneading the peak with his teeth and tongue until she cried out.

His hand left a fire trail as it slid its way downward.

She didn't breathe when his fingers slid through her dark curls to caress the sensitive nub hidden inside. Back bowed, she whimpered when he coupled those moves with a hard suckle at her breast while calloused fingers slid against her femininity that pulsated and tingled in response.

Hands tangled in his hair, she tugged as his kisses, hot as liquid fire, seared the center of her passion. She gasped and pulled harder when his tongue slid over the sensitive nub again and again until she begged for an end to his exquisite torture.

"Wade!"

He moved up her body, anchored her with a passionate kiss before entering her with one hard thrust, her body ready for his, her ardor a match to his own.

He propelled himself forward, over and over, bringing about new sensations, taking her higher and higher. Hands slid over slick skin adding to the sensations. Gasping for air, she hovered on the brink.

Wrapping her legs around his waist, she clutched at his back, his hips, raked her fingers up and down his back in sensual abandon, her body thrumming with incredible sensations.

His thrusts came harder, faster, his muscles tensed and she sensed it building, growing stronger and teetered on the precipice with him…waiting for it.

He swallowed her cry with a kiss as they reached the crest together, overwhelmed by waves of pleasure when their bodies convulsed as one in a shattering explosion.

Neither moved for long moments, their heavy breathing the only sound in the room. Wade's arms quivered as he tried to hold himself upright, obviously not ready to break the link that bound them together. Finally, he rolled onto his back and pulled her into his arms, her head on his chest.

She heard the hard pound of his heart over the roar in her ears as her own heart struggled to regain a normal rhythm. Her body hummed with the remnants of pleasure. "I never knew it could be like this." She flinched *Oh damn! I said that out loud!*

Wade tightened his hold, but didn't comment.

Curiosity urged her to continue. "…umm… is it…always like this?"

He laughed; the low, throaty sound vibrated through her cheek. "I don't think I've been asked that before."

"I'm sorry, it's just…" She cursed the rush of heat creeping up her face.

"What?"

She hesitated, but couldn't stop the confession that poured out. "Eddie was the only one…it was never like this."

He rose on his elbow and tilted her chin up so she'd have to look at him. "You get out of lovemaking what you put into it." The edges of his mouth curled up in a satisfied smile. "And you put in a lot."

"Did I…" *Oh God! He's going to think I want a critique.* "I mean -"

He placed a finger over her lips, "You talk too much." He leaned over and kissed her.

No question about it. She had never, ever, been *truly* kissed. Until now.

"Wade…" She caught herself before blurting out the I-love-you resting on the tip of her tongue.

He pulled back and whispered. "My turn."

She quivered with bone-melting desire as he pressed hot, open-mouthed kisses on her sensitive flesh, muscles tensed in anticipation. Gentle, weathered hands caressed her body, deftly stroked and kneaded until she feared she might perish from absolute, sensual ecstasy. Her body arched to meet each caress, alive as never before; his touch electric.

He sought her most sensitive place and pressed his mouth to it, rolled the tight bud with his tongue, making her writhe and squirm until her body exploded, his name a cry from her lips.

He moved back up her body, entered her slowly; withdrew and entered again; each one harder, faster than the last, and, gasping for air, brought them to the brink again, hovered a moment, then crashed to the other side in a shuddering crescendo of pleasure.

Afterwards, cradled in his arms, she enjoyed the sensation of his body against hers; hidden feelings too close to the surface.

Why can't I ask how he truly feels? Is it only sex or does that passion express a deeper emotion?

A timid knock on the door broke the spell.

"Boss! It's Hank. You in there?"

"Don't let him come in." She grabbed at the blanket for cover.

"Yeah, Hank. What is it?"

"It's Shadow. She's tryin' to foal and it's a breach. She's in a bad way."

Wade jumped to his feet, scrambled for his clothes. "I'll be right there."

"I'm coming, too." Tori struggled to find her things in the room's semi-darkness, her own concerns forgotten.

"OK, but hurry. Better take my jacket. Unless you'd rather go get one from Lucy."

She threw his sock at him and continued to dress in a rush.

Wade reached for the door's handle, stopped and turned to her. Without a word, he bent and pressed a tender kiss to her lips, then smiled and opened it to the cool night air, dotted with winter's first snowflakes.

Chapter Twenty-Two

They reached the barn and found Hank and two hands inside trying to help the struggling mare. Sheila and Doug stood off to the side.

"I can't get 'em turned, Boss," said Hank, "he's a big 'un."

"Here," Tori threw Wade's coat on the gate. "Let me try. My hands are smaller." She quickly knelt behind the horse. "I delivered my first colt when I was fifteen." She inspected the mare. "Besides horses, babies, the principle is the same."

Wade beamed with pride as he watched her take control of the situation.

"Hank, get over here and keep her legs still. Don't let her kick." Several tense moments later, she looked at Wade. "We got bigger problems."

Wade squatted down beside her. "What do you mean?"

"Twins."

"What? Doc never mentioned twins."

"Are you sure, Miz Tori," Hank poked his head over Wade's shoulder. "Doc Green never said nothin' 'bout twins."

"I'm sure. I can feel them both. I need to get one moved back some or we're in big trouble."

"Damn." Wade ran his fingers through his hair. "Do you think you can do it?"

"I don't know, there isn't much room. Maybe if I can push one back. Wade, push on the outside….easy does it….good…good….no—more from the bottom….okay… good….keep her legs still, Hank."

"I'm tryin', Ma'am. Barney, get over here."

"I think he's moving," she whispered. "Easy, Wade, not too hard…I think we got it!"

No sooner were the words out than a hoof appeared followed by the nose, then the rest of the body. She made no attempt to avoid the sticky mess that followed, instead working to assist the next colt's delivery. "Wade, is he breathing?"

"Not yet." Wade continued to rub the colt trying to stimulate her to breathe. "Barney," he ordered, "get a bucket of cold water and throw on her."

Anxious moments passed before the little filly jerked and took her first breath. More long minutes later, the second foal joined his sister on the ground.

When at last she gave the all clear, everyone moved away as Shadow turned to sniff the new arrivals.

Tori's smile was radiant and Wade's chest filled with pride. *I'm the luckiest man alive.*

"Oh, Wade, they're beautiful. Look at them. Black as night. Just like Shadow."

"They're so small." said Sheila, "Will they be alright?"

"It's not unusual with twins for one or both to be small," said Tori. "Same for humans."

He appreciated the fact she didn't mention the odds of both colts surviving were slim.

"The fact they both made it this far is a good sign. I think it's like one in ten thousand births are twins."

Wade moved to her side and pulled a piece of straw from

her hair. "Once again," He grinned, "You've outdone yourself."

The way she blushed and looked down instead of at him, he knew she understood he referenced their encounter in the cabin.

"I've been slimed." Tori held her hands out, palm side down.

"So you have." Wade moved behind her and wrapped his arms around her waist. "And may I say you never looked lovelier."

She rewarded him with a dazzling smile and leaned against him.

Wade got down to business. "Hank, get heat lamps in here and make sure there's fresh hay and extra feed and water. Find blankets for the colts for when Shadow is done. Barney?"

"Yes, sir?"

"Keep trying to get Doc Green. I want him here as soon as possible to check them out."

Wade glanced at Doug who tilted his head toward Tori and smiled. The search for Rico's trail was fruitless, but their long conversations on the current status of Wade's love-life were not. Before he knew it, he admitted to being in love with her.

Doug had spent the remainder of the day trying to convince him to tell her. Wade wasn't sure the time was right. But tonight, although she never spoke the actual words, he saw it in her eyes as they made love; felt it in every touch, every kiss.

She said '*it would be easy to love you*'.

"Douglas, my boy, what are you doing Friday?"

"Friday?"

"Yeah, Friday, you know, the day after Thursday and before Saturday?"

"Not sure. Why?"

"I thought you might want to be best man at my wedding." He tightened his arms around her. "Tori has decided to make an honest man out of me."

♡

Everyone talked at once and Tori had difficulty keeping up with what was said.

"How wonderful!" Sheila gushed at them in turn. "Mother will be thrilled."

"Yippee." Cody clapped his hands, "can I be the ring boy, Aunt Tori? I did it before."

"'Bout dang time!" said Hank as he handed a rag to her. "Here ya go, Miz Tori. You can wash up at the sink yonder."

"Thank you, Hank." .

When she finished, Doug reached for her hands. "I think you are a very brave woman to take on the job of keeping Wade in line." He kissed her lightly on the cheek. "And I can't think of anyone more deserving of happiness than you," he whispered.

"Oh, goodness." Sheila counted off a to-do list on her fingers, "We have less than a week to plan this out, we need flowers, a cake, and a dress, gotta have a dress—"

"Whoa, there, Sheila." Tori held her palms flat and high, "don't make a big deal out of this. All we need is a preacher or JP or—"

"Oh, please, please, don't cheat me out of planning a wedding. My brother is marrying the woman of his dreams. Please, let me have a wedding."

Tori smiled as brother and sister argued. *I don't care what we do or how we do it.*

"You can plan your own one day," said Wade, "we don't need a big shindig."

"Waaaade… I promise it won't be a big deal," she pleaded, her hands folded as if in prayer. "Just us, a few friends. Mrs. O'Conner can do the cake, and I'll get some flowers from town. We'll do it in the den; pa-leeease"

Wade looked at Tori, brows raised in question.

She hesitated then nodded toward Sheila. "How can I say no to such a pitiful face?"

"Yes!" She clapped her hands together. "I promise I won't go overboard."

"Overboard on what?"

Everyone turned as Lucy entered the barn.

Tori stiffened. She'd forgotten Lucy was still here.

"What's going on?" She fixed her eyes on Wade.

"Uncle Wade is gettin' married and I get to be the ring boy!" Cody announced. His child like innocence caused more than one to smile.

But not the red-head.

"Married? To her?" Lucy pointed a shaking finger at Tori, her green eyes blazed fire, body rigid with fury.

Tori's eyes widened in fright. *Oh my God! She has totally lost it!*

Wade moved forward and placed his arm around Tori. "Yes, Lucy, to *Tori.*"

"Over my dead body." Lucy spit the bitter words out one at a time.

"What a pleasant thought."

"Sheila." Wade's firm command silenced any further comment from his sister.

"What about me? Us?"

"There never was an *us*, Lucy, how many times do I—"

"You bastard! You tell me you love me, get me in bed…"

Tori jerked like someone hit her in the stomach and stepped away from him. "You slept with her?" A tortured whisper was all she could manage.

"No! Dammit! Sheila, take Cody in the house."

"What's wrong?" Cody's confusion made his face crinkle but he took Sheila's hand. "Why is Aunt Lucy mad?"

"Come on. Let's go set the table for supper." Shelia said.

"But why is Aunt Lucy mad at Uncle Wade?" Cody insisted.

"Cody. Let's go." said Sheila. "Now."

At a look from Wade, their audience plodded outside. He turned to Lucy. "I don't know where you got this notion but that's all it is— a silly notion. Nothing ever happened between us."

"Liar!" Lucy's face contorted, anger pulsating off her in waves. "We made love all night. You said you loved me."

Wade tensed, his eyes narrowed. "Nothing happened and you know it."

"You can't marry her. You love *me*."

"No, I don't."

Tori had never heard that deadly tone from Wade. She felt the tenseness in the arm around her waist, could feel the fury he controlled.

"You have to marry *me*." She took a step toward them, her eyes wide and dangerous. "I'm pregnant!"

"If you're really pregnant, which I seriously doubt, I'm not the father and you know it."

She took another step forward and Tori flinched at the

look in her eyes. *Madness, evil madness.*

"I didn't come this far to lose you now." Her voice turned cold and hard. "You think I don't know what you're trying to do? You think I don't know how you poisoned him against me?"

"Lucy, I—"

Before Tori could react, Lucy's hand struck her cheek with a stinging blow that brought tears to her eyes. "You lying bitch! You'll pay for this!"

Wade tried to grab Lucy's arm but she stepped away.

"Bastard!" she shouted then ran out of the barn. "I'll see you in hell!"

Tori remained glued to the spot, face still hurting, eyes blurred. There was little doubt the woman hovered on the edge of reality, madness glimmering in her eyes as she fled the barn.

But what if she were pregnant? The thought was unbearable.

"Is she carrying your child, Wade?" She held her breath. If she did, Tori would die of a broken heart on the spot.

"I don't think so."

"What's that supposed to mean?" She folded her arms over her chest.

He placed his hands on his hips, then shoved them in his front pockets. "A month or so after Isaac and Karen died I went off the deep end; neck deep in guilt, grief. Lucy came over one night with a bottle of booze. I'd already been hitting it pretty heavy. I woke up the next day to find her walking out of my shower."

She stared, waiting for the rest. "And?"

"That's all I remember. I was drunk and sick with grief,

but not so drunk I would sleep with her. Hell, I don't even like her!"

"But it's possible?"

"I guess it's possible but—"

"And she might be carrying your child."

"You know how babies get made!" Wade's voice radiated tension as he fought for control. "I wasn't in any condition to fill the bill. And even if I was, she is the last woman in the world I'd want to be with."

She thought back over the last few weeks and had to admit he displayed no interest whatsoever in Lucy, even went out of his way to avoid her. But, Eddie had affairs then acted like he never met them.

He's not like Eddie. Is he?

"I didn't sleep with her, Tori." His eyes pleaded for understanding.

"But you aren't sure, are you? She could be carrying your child."

"Lucy can't have kids," said Sheila from the doorway.

"Stay out of this Sheila." Wade barked.

"Lucy can't have kids," Sheila repeated.

"How do you know that?" Tori hugged herself, the urge to scream and cry a crushing weight on her. *Lucy might be carrying Wade's child.*

"Karen told me last year. It's why Lucy always hung around them. She even told me Lucy sometimes pretended Cody belonged to her, even tried to get him to call her Mama Lucy instead of Aunt."

"Are you sure about this, Sheila?" Wade's voice cracked with force of the emotions he held in check. "You're not, you wouldn't…"

"Oh for heaven's sake, Wade! Do you think I'd lie?"

"Well, I know how you feel about her."

"Big effin deal! So does half the state of Montana. But I'm not a liar."

"Sheila." Tori tried to speak in calm, even tones. "Why can't she have kids?"

"She had cyst problems all through high school and ended up having one ovary removed. Her first year in college, she had some kind of weird pregnancy. I'm not sure of all the particulars, but she ended up losing the baby and had to have a hysterectomy."

Wade looked at Tori, brows knitted together.

"She can't have kids."

Sheila shifted the crutch under her arm. "Which means she lied about being pregnant."

"But what about…" Tori stopped.

"I don't believe for one minute he slept with her. Not because he's my brother, either. He can't stand her. None of us can. Hell, even Karen didn't like her much and they were sisters."

"I appreciate your loyalty, Sheila, but—"

"No buts. Good, bad or otherwise, whatever happened before you met is ancient history. What matters now is you love each other." Sheila hesitated then murmured, "You do love him, don't you?"

Tori looked at her, then back to him, emotions churning like waves in a hurricane. *What if he doesn't love me? What if Lucy is carrying his child?*

Heart on a platter, she prepared to hand it to him, knowing the gift may very well be one-sided.

Chapter Twenty-Three

WADE WATCHED TORI'S FACE, READING HER thoughts as though she spoke them out loud. He wanted her to believe him, to trust him, but would her experience with Eddie prevent her from ever trusting anyone—him included—again?

His heart ached with the need to make her understand, for her to believe he loved her and would never hurt her, but words were useless now. He waited as she considered Sheila's question *you do love him, don't you?*

His whole world hinged on her answer.

"I -"

"Wade!" shouted Doug from the porch, "Come quick! It's Miss Willie!"

Wade saw the color drain from Tori's face and his heart sank. *Oh God. It was time.* She sprinted for the door and he followed as Sheila struggled to keep up.

Wade's heart thundered as he reached the porch and headed to his mother's room. *Please, God, please not now.*

Tori raced past him and entered first.

Doug sat on the edge of the bed, holding Miss Willie's hand, speaking softly to her.

"What happened?" Tori asked as she assessed her patient.

"I'm not sure." Doug's voice radiated his concern. "Lucy came running through the kitchen yelling obscenities about you and Wade. Sheila couldn't stand it and went back to see what happened. I saw Lucy leave as I came in." He paused and looked at them, his expression radiated concern. "I don't know what she told your mother, but she told *me* we'd all be sorry."

Wade's heart lurched when he saw his mother, so weak it took all her energy to breathe.

"Wade?" Her raspy whisper tore at his heart.

When she looked at him, he just knew.

Time had run out.

"I'm here, Mother." Wade sat on the edge of her bed and gently took her hand in his, its icy feel confirming his worst fear.

"Tori?"

"I'm here, Miss Willie," she replied, "I'm here." She stood beside Wade and smoothed the hair from her face. "Are you in any pain?"

"…heart hurts."

"Your heart hurts?" Tori grabbed the stethoscope from the bedside table.

Panic washed over Wade. *She's having a heart attack?* "Tori, please. Do something."

"I don't understand, Miss Willie. Is it chest pain?"

"Not see you…married."

"What?" She spoke so softly Wade didn't understand what she said.

"No wedding…"

Wade and Tori looked at each other, comprehending her meaning at the same time. She would die before they were married.

"Lucy…said Friday."

"Yes, ma'am." He rubbed her frail hand. "Tori said we'd been semi-engaged long enough and we set the date for Friday, your birthday, just like you wanted."

She smiled but didn't open her eyes, "She did?"

"Yes, I did." Tori wiped her face with a cool rag. "I thought if I waited for him to set a date, I might have to wait a long time."

A tiny smile curved the corners of her mouth. "Good girl."

"Hang in there, Mother." Tears trailed down Sheila's cheeks. "Only a few more days."

"Not be there."

"No! Please, Mother, not yet." She sat on the edge of the bed, and clutched her mother's hand.

"No more time…..be there…in spirit."

"I can't get married if you aren't there." Wade made an instant decision, praying the love his gut said Tori felt for him would override her concern about the past. "So I guess we have to do it now."

"What?" Tori's head jerked up and she fixed him with troubled eyes. "Now?"

"Yes." He reached for her hand. "I don't need a preacher to tell me I'm married. We'll do a wedding, right here, right now."

"But, Wade, It won't be legal."

"Do you love me, Tori?" he whispered, his heart filled with a heady mixture of hope and fear.

Her eyes shimmered with unshed tears. "Oh, Wade," she whispered at last, "I do love you."

Wade released the breath he held, exultation raced

through him. *She loves me.* His hands trembled as he reached for hers. "And I love you. More than I can say." He brought the back of one hand to his mouth and kissed it. "Nothing else matters."

He turned to his mother. "I can't wait till Friday to make Tori my wife so we're going to get married now."

Miss Willie struggled to open her eyes. "Can't see."

Wade held her while Tori raised the head of the bed, then lowered her back, adjusting her pillow until she was comfortable.

"How's that?" his soon-to-be wife asked.

"Good," she whispered.

"Sheila, Doug" Wade pointed. "Y'all are the witnesses."

"What about me? I wanted to be the ring boy?" Cody's tone was petulant and Wade had to smile.

"We don't have a ring, we'll—"

"Use mine." His mother nodded toward to the dresser, seemingly too weak to lift a finger. "Jewelry box."

Cody ran and grabbed the designated box and brought it to the bed.

"Miss Willie," said Tori, "I can't—"

Sheila placed a hand on Tori's should and squeezed. "I'd love for you to wear Mama's ring."

Wade suspected his love may be torn about what to do, but he also knew she loved him, so he pushed forward. "We'll use hers until we get our own." He found the single gold band in the box and gave it to his charge. "Hold this till I ask for it."

"Wade," said Miss Willie, "Jacob's ring…use it."

He hesitated then dug through the box for his father's wedding band and handed it to the boy as well.

Taking the rings in his chubby hands, Cody stood

proudly at Wade's side and waited.

He heard others enter the room and glanced up to see Mrs. O'Conner and Hank standing beside the bed.

"You're just in time." He took Tori's hands in his and smiled. "I knew the moment I met you, Victoria Morgan, you were trouble with big brown eyes. You came rushing into my life like a whirlwind. I wasn't prepared for your honesty, your bluntness, your sense of humor. I told myself you couldn't be for real; there had to be a hidden side of you. I finally realized I was the one hiding something. I was afraid to tell you how much I loved you, afraid you didn't feel the same, so afraid of losing you."

"Oh, Wade."

"Give me the ring, Cody."

His nephew passed the ring to Wade who placed it on her finger, not surprised it was a perfect fit.

After all, destiny and fate worked together to make this happen.

"With this ring, I thee wed. I promise to respect you always, to love you unconditionally, be at your side in sickness and health, good times and bad, till death do us part." He paused and when Tori didn't respond, he grinned. "Your turn."

Her smile was radiant as she regarded him with eyes so full of love the breath caught in his throat.

"I thought I knew about love, and believed the lucky ones got one shot at it. I was convinced I'd never experience it again. Then I met you. I felt…*something*…the first time I heard your voice. And when we met…" She took a breath. "Wow. Those feelings grew stronger every day until I can't remember not loving you. I was so afraid you didn't return my love I almost blew it. I don't care what happened in the past. I know you love me…nothing else in the world matters."

She held out her hand for the ring and slipped it on his finger. "With this ring, I thee wed. I promise to love you and respect you always, obey you—most of the time, be at your side always, through good times and bad, in sickness and health, til death do us part."

"Then," said Wade, his voice quivering, "by the power of the love we share, I now pronounce us husband and wife."

He sealed the declaration with a tender kiss, relishing the feel of her lips on his. He'd never be happier than at this moment in time.

He turned to his mother. "Well, what do you…..Ma?"

No one had to tell him she was gone.

Chapter Twenty-Four

A THIN BLANKET OF SNOW COVERED THE GROUND AS the small funeral procession made its way from the cemetery back to the house. Located on a small knoll behind and to the right of the little cabin, it overlooked the valley below and the mountains in the distance.

Tori spent the previous night helping groom and dress Miss Willie. Reverend Parker, a close family friend, presided over the brief ceremony.

While Wade, Hank and two other hands completed the burial process, she went about preparing a meal.

Cody remained glued to her side as he had since Miss Willie died three days ago. She understood his insecurity. He had lost so much in his short life he needed to know they were there for him; he even slept with her and Wade at night.

Distraught over his mother's death, intimacy would have to wait. Still, she missed having him to herself, even for a short time, and longed to feel the passion he ignited in the cabin, to feel him inside her again. The time would come, and Tori called herself selfish for being impatient, but it didn't alter the desire to savor those feelings again.

Cody tugged on her sleeve. "Aunt Tori?"

"What is it, sweetie?"

"Will you send me away?"

She knelt in front of him, hands on his shoulders. "Of course not, Cody. We would never send you away. Why on earth would you think that?"

"Aunt Lucy said you only wanted me cause Joey died," he whispered. "And when you and Uncle Wade have a baby you'll send me to go live with her."

She hugged him close. "Oh Cody, we would never send you away. We love you and will never, ever do that." She pulled back to look at him. "When did you talk with Aunt Lucy?"

He looked at the floor. "I ain't 'posed to tell."

"When did you talk with her, Cody? Has she been here?"

He shook his head.

"Did she call on the phone?"

"She'll be mad if I tell."

Tori tried another tactic. "Sweetie, Aunt Lucy is, well, not herself. She doesn't always mean the things she says."

The child glanced up, then back to the floor. "She said Uncle Wade is a bad man and hates her cause you told him lies about her."

A tremor rocked her while she fought for control. She brushed the hair from his anxious blue eyes, going all soft and loving. "I know this is all very hard for you to understand, but Aunt Lucy is—she's sick, and sometimes says things she thinks are true. But they're not. And it's very important that we know if she calls or comes by."

Cody hesitated, and hung his head. "She called last night. When you were fixing up Miss Willie."

"What else did she say?"

"That you'd be sorry you came here." He threw his arms

around her neck and held on tight. "I don't want nothing to happen to you!"

Tori held him and tried to reassure him. "Nothing's going to happen to me, sweetie, but I have to know what Aunt Lucy says if she calls. It's very important. Okay?"

"Yes, ma'am."

"Now, you'd better go get changed. Uncle Wade and the crew will be in soon and we'll eat dinner."

His smile was timid. "I love you, Aunt Tori."

Her breath caught and she had to swallow before she could reply. "I love you, too, sweetie."

Tori's mind worked overtime as she finished setting the food out. Lucy's call meant she still had an agenda, which wasn't really a surprise, but what on earth could it be?

She had said in the barn the night the twin foals were born, *I didn't come this far to lose you now.*

What on earth did she mean? She intended to ask Wade about it, but they never seemed to be alone. After Miss Willie's death, they had funeral preparations to make and at night, Cody to contend with. Her husband talked little about it and outwardly appeared to handle things, but sooner or later, there'd be a reaction.

"I'm sorry I left you with all this to do," Sheila said as she entered the kitchen, Doug at her side, his arm around her waist. "We were talking and I lost track of time."

Last night, Wade and Doug brought everyone up to speed on what they believed was taking place and how Rico and Benito may be involved.

Tori knew how Sheila felt about Doug and the feelings were mutual. She hoped another wedding might be on the horizon.

"Is there anything I can do?" Her new sister-in-law's haggard expression showed the strain of the last few days.

"No, I think it's all about ready."

"I'm sorry. I should have been helping."

"You don't owe me any apology. Besides, too many cooks spoil the stew." Tori's smile was weak.

"Especially if one of 'em is Sheila." Wade stood at the kitchen door, dusting snow from his coat.

"Stop teasing, Wade," admonished Tori. "She's a great cook."

"But my wife is the best."

She glowed with pride as he pulled her against his chest. "I don't think I'll ever live up to your expectations."

"You already have." He kissed the top of her head and moved toward the kitchen sink cranking on the faucet.

Tori looked down the hall where Cody had scampered off. She had to tell them before he came back. "Lucy's at it again."

Wade jerked around to face her, dripping water on the floor. "What do you mean?"

She relayed her conversation with Cody. "She's up to something, I just don't know what."

He grabbed a towel from the counter and dried his hands. "Have there been any more phone calls?"

"Not since the last one I told you about."

"What phone calls?" The question came from Doug and Sheila at the same time.

"Sorry, Doug, with everything going on, it slipped my mind." After his brief rundown, Wade turned to Tori, face etched with concern. "What I said the other day is even more important now. You go nowhere alone; neither does Cody."

Tori nodded and looked at Sheila as the little boy ambled into the kitchen. "Why don't you set the table; dinner's ready."

"I'll help," Doug said. "I'm starving."

"Me, too." Cody piped in as he moved to his seat at the table.

"Sport?" Wade squatted down beside him. "Aunt Tori told me about Aunt Lucy's phone call."

He ducked his head. "I'm sorry. Are you mad?"

"Of course not, sport. You know I wouldn't get mad about something like that. But it's very important you tell us when Aunt Lucy calls. Better yet, for now, if the phone rings, let one of us answer it, Okay?"

"I will. Promise."

Wade stood and looked at Tori. "Do I smell apple pie?"

"Just about to take them out of the oven."

She grabbed a couple of oven mitts and pulled out the first pie, placing it on the stovetop. "I made two since we have extra guests tonight." Tori added the second one to a trivet on the counter. "They may be too hot to eat, though. I was a little late getting them in the oven."

"There's no such thing as apple pie too hot to eat, right sport?"

"No sir! Not when it's Aunt Tori's."

Wade chuckled. His somber expression evaporated at the light banter and Tori gave a silent prayer of thanks.

A soft knock on the back door preceded the entrance of Hank, and the two hands, Allen and Roscoe, who'd helped complete the burial of Mrs. McBride. "Ma'am," said Hank, taking off his hat, "I brung the boys in like you asked."

The two men stood behind him, their uncertainty of what to do next obvious in their stiff stance and hats clutched in their hands. While Tori often cooked special things for them to eat, this was the first time they'd been invited inside.

"Thanks, Hank. Please, gentlemen, come in and make yourselves at home. You can sit on the bench there beside Cody. Wade, would you put their hats and coats in the hall, please?"

With Sheila's help, dinner was placed in the center of the table and Tori did her best to include the newcomer's in the conversation. By the time the meal ended, they were relaxed and joking with Hank and Wade.

"Well boys," said Hank, "it's time we get back to the bunkhouse." The foreman stood and faced Tori. "Thank you for supper, Ma'am. As usual, it was delicious."

"It sure was, Ma'am," said Roscoe and Allen almost in unison.

"Thank you. I'm glad you liked it. Wade, would you get their coats, please?" Tori walked toward the counter where remnants of the second pie rested. "I'll wrap this up for you. You might want a snack later."

Roscoe and Allen joined Hank by the back door as they waited for Wade, watching intently as Tori wrapped the pie in a towel.

Once they were gone, she reached for an empty dish on the table.

"I've got this," Sheila stood. "You've done enough for to-day. Doug will help me." She glanced his way. "Won't you?"

"Anything for you." He rose and grabbed a plate.

"Uncle Wade?" Cody's question had them all looking his way. "I'll be okay to sleep in my own bed tonight." He got up from the table and looked at Tori. "I already got my bear and put him in my room."

His comment caused Tori's stomach to flip. They'd finally be alone.

"Ok, sport. I'm glad to hear it. You snore like a train."

"I do not. But Aunt Tori does." He giggled with delight and bounded off down the hall.

"I snore?" Tori looked at Wade.

"Maybe a little." He winked and turned down the hallway. "I have some paperwork to finish."

♡

An hour later, Tori stood in the doorway of Wade's office and watched him. He stood with hands on his hips, gazing out the window toward the cemetery. He arched his back and flexed his shoulders. Although he went through the motions of normalcy during dinner, he must be spent.

With a deep sigh, her new husband turned and spotted her in the doorway. He nodded toward the cups in her hand. "One of those for me?"

She headed toward the cabinet in the corner. "Yes, but I'm thinking you might need something a little stronger." Tori added a healthy dose of his favorite whiskey to his cup and handed it to him.

She motioned for him to sit in the chair and moved behind him, swiveling it parallel to the desk. She set her cup on the desk and massaged his tense shoulders.

Wade leaned back and sighed. "I'll give you thirty minutes to stop."

Tori snickered. "I guess those massage classes I took are paying off."

"Uh-huh."

She worked on his tense neck muscles until they relaxed then moved to his left shoulder, pressing and rolling the muscle into submission while he sank deeper into his chair, head lolling back.

"Damn." His soft expletive equated to approval. His grip on the cup relaxed and liquid sloshed onto his thigh but he didn't seem to notice. "Better let me take that." Tori reached for the cup, her breast brushing his cheek.

His body tensed.

She placed the mug on the corner of the desk, stifling a soft moan when her nipple puckered in response.

He turned toward her, the stubble on his cheek scraping the sensitive nub. His eyes locked with hers, desire looming in the depths.

She placed a light kiss on his nose. "I'm not done yet."

Ten minutes later, Wade's tension hadn't dissipated, although at this point, for an entirely different reason.

"You're driving me crazy." A raspy groan punctuated his comment.

"Am I?" The question was followed by a hard press of her fingers on his bicep.

He spun around and she found herself sitting across his lap. He said nothing for several seconds, then closed his eyes and laid his head on her chest, arms surrounding her. "I love you."

Her heart swelled with love as she cradled him to her. "I love you, too. With all my heart."

They clung to each other in silence for a short time.

She knew the precise moment the mood changed.

He looked at her, his eyes dark and stormy. "You have on too many clothes."

Head cocked to one side, she grinned. "Maybe so, but running around naked is frowned upon in polite society."

His kiss was hard and demanding, leaving no doubt of what would happen next. He stood her up, then pulled her back down, straddling his lap, his arousal pressing against her cleft. Wade kissed her again, his fingers fumbling with the buttons of her blouse, exposing lace-clad breasts to his eager hands.

"Wade! We can't. Not here." Tori pushed back on his shoulders, eyes darting to the open doorway. "Someone might come in."

"Shit." He closed his eyes and rested his forehead on her chin. "You're right. Just give me a minute."

At last, he leaned back and buttoned her blouse with shaky fingers. She didn't bother to re-tuck it in the waistband of her slacks. They hurried hand in hand down the hall to their room.

Inside, she waited while he closed the door and placed a chair under the handle, no doubt to ensure no surprises this time. "Where were we?"

"I think you said I was driving you crazy." Tori's hands stroked his chest. She stood on her tiptoes and brushed her lips over his. "And I wondered what you planned to do about it."

"This." Wade pulled her hard against him, placing hot, open mouthed kisses on her lips, down her neck, the valley between her breasts. "And this," he whispered as he flicked his tongue across one taut nipple through the lacey barrier.

She whimpered and arched toward him when his teeth scraped across the tender flesh. "What else?" A small breathless whisper escaped parted lips.

"This." He unfastened the front clasp of the bra and tossed it aside, freeing her breasts from confinement. He pulled a turgid peak into his mouth, rolling it with his tongue.

Tori groaned when he skimmed the nub with his teeth before suckling vigorously, his hands sliding down her body, working the button on her jeans.

She jerked at his shirt, popping buttons in her haste to rid him of the barrier, moving to his belt.

He stepped back and they made quick work of shedding their clothes, coming back together for kisses filled with such tenderness, she might die of sheer bliss.

Wade pulled the covers back on the bed, and laid her on the cool sheets. When he joined her, the love shining in his eyes filled her with wonder.

His hands stroked her body, cupped her breasts as they made their way down until he reached the center of her pleasure. "And this." He kissed her again as his hand stoked the fire raging within. "And this." He poised over her, then entered her slowly, one agonizing inch at a time, pulled back and entered again; she couldn't get close enough to him, and her body craved more.

She arched up. "Waaaade."

"And this." He buried himself in her delicate softness bringing a new wave of pleasure. Their bodies moved as one as they hastened to satisfy the fierce hunger in the other, reaching the summit together with a mind-blowing intensity that left them gasping for air.

Cradled in his arms, Tori's heart swelled. She had it all again, a husband, a child, a beautiful life. Without warning, she shuddered, because she knew how fragile life was, how fast it could be swept away.

"Cold?" asked Wade, bringing the quilt up to cover them.

"No…I'm scared, Wade."

"Scared? Of what?"

"Losing this."

He braced himself up on his elbow to look at her. "What are you talking about?"

"Rico is out there, so is Lucy." She shuddered with the enormity of the danger still surrounding them. "They could destroy our life in the blink of an eye…like before."

"I promise you, baby, no one's going to hurt you again."

"Oh Wade, I couldn't bear it if something happened to you or Cody!" Fear and anguish filled her voice.

"Nothing is going to happen." He pulled her against him, his arousal pressing against her thigh.

Troubling thoughts of what might happen later were replaced by much more pleasant things happening now.

Chapter Twenty-Five

S PORADIC SNOW FELL FOR THE NEXT THREE DAYS. NOT the heavy, hip deep variety Tori expected, although Wade assured her that would come soon enough, more of a light dusting that put several inches on the ground with scattered drifts of a foot or more.

She stood at the kitchen window and admired the simple white blanket accented by dark spots that were horses and cows grazing in the distance and crisscrossed with wooden rail fences capped with white.

It surprised her to discover how much she liked the snow, watching it fall in big, flat flakes to accumulate on every surface it touched giving the landscape a softer, less rugged look. Hank told her this morning the big snows were maybe a couple of weeks away and she might change her mind about its beauty.

Her gaze dropped to the plain gold band, evidence of their spur-of-the-moment marriage. Well, sort of marriage. Wade had surprised her this morning when he'd said he realized she worried about the legitimacy of their union, even though in his eyes, they were forever man and wife. So, he called Reverend Parker who agreed to return next week to perform a simple ceremony.

His thoughtfulness made her love him even more, especially when he added he would ensure her parents and Sasha were here if she wanted. She'd given it some thought but declined, adding the unpredictable weather would make travel difficult at best and maybe they could plan a trip to Texas in the spring.

He kissed her and replied, "Anything for my beautiful wife," then proceeded to show her why she was the luckiest woman alive.

After one last look at the snow-capped mountains, Tori went back to the task of making fresh coffee, thoughts jumping to Lucy. There'd been no other calls since the one Cody had taken, but it wasn't over.

The only question being how and when the redhead would strike again.

"I can't believe you two are going out in this weather!"

Sheila's exclamation brought Tori's head around with a jerk and she watched Doug walk in followed by Sheila and Wade.

"We have to find out if in fact it's Rico and his henchman and where they are before the snow gets too heavy." Doug's face softened when he looked at her. "We won't be gone long."

"You can't be serious. There's too much snow. How in the world will you track them?" Tori's anxiety caused her to rush the question, stumbling over the words.

"The snow isn't bad right now and we shouldn't get anymore until later tonight or tomorrow morning. We know about where they were before the snow started, and what direction we think they are headed." Wade hurried to his new wife and placed his arms on her shoulders. "Plus, there are limited trails out and even fewer spots to wait out the snow and I know them all. We won't be out long. I'll be back before dark."

"But it's so cold." Tori bit her lip. She didn't want to be one those nagging, worrisome wife's, but she was concerned about him.

"I grew up in these mountains, with this weather." He slid his hands over her arms. "Don't worry, sweetheart, I'll be fine." He gave her a quick kiss. "There's no way in hell I'm letting anything or anyone, come between us again." He looked at Doug. "Ready?"

"Yeah. Gimmee a minute." Oblivious to onlookers, Doug pulled Sheila in his arms and kissed her. "Keep a warm spot for me?"

"If you're not back here by five thirty, I'm coming after you with a baseball bat." Sheila's retort held no anger.

"Ouch! I'll make sure I'm back by then." Doug chuckled and kissed her again.

The two men went out the door with Tori and Sheila following behind. They mounted the horses tethered near the steps, and turned as one to smile at the women huddled on the edge of the porch.

"Don't it make your heart sing?" asked Doug with wide grin. "Knowing two beautiful women can't wait for us to get home?"

"It ain't just my heart that's singing," said Wade as he winked at Tori. "Not just my heart at all."

With a last wave, they rode toward the distant mountains.

"Please be careful, Wade!" shouted Tori, "I love you."

If he heard her, he gave no notice as they kicked the

horses into a lope.

"What now?" asked Sheila.

"We wait," said Tori softly. "And pray."

♡

Two hours later Tori's restlessness sent her to the barn to check on Shadow and the new colts who, while improving, struggled daily.

Cody begged Hank to take him earlier and was no doubt still there. She loved how excited he got every time he saw the twins. Wade had told him he would let him help pick out a name and he took every opportunity to spend time with them so the names would be perfect.

She followed their tracks toward the barn. The temperature continued to drop as the front moved through and each breath formed a vaporous fog that floated in the frigid air. Intermittent clouds signaled more snow to come. She pulled the collar of her jacket up tight around her neck.

Please hold off until they get back.

Shadow's nervous whinny and hoof stomping drew her toward the back of the barn.

"Oh no. The babies." She hurried forward but froze when she rounded the edge of the stall.

Hank lay face down on the straw-covered floor.

"Oh my God, Hank!" She knelt beside him, jerked off her gloves and searched for a pulse. A slow, steady beat beneath her fingertips drew a frantic sigh of relief. "Thank God."

She completed a quick cursory exam, noting blood on the side of his head above his ear where a huge knot bulged. She shook his shoulder. "Hank…Hank? Can you hear me?"

He gave a soft moan and she gingerly rolled him onto his back. His eyes were closed and he struggled to open them.

"Hank? What happened?"

"…hit me—tried to—stop 'em."

"Who Hank? Who hit you?" Tori looked around. No one in the barn except them.

"…didn't see…other 'un."

"What other one?" Tori tried to remain calm but anxiety swirled around her and she could barely breathe.

Who would do such a thing? Were they still here? She cast another nervous look around the barn.

"…feller what hit me…took 'em."

She got lost in his rambles and couldn't make sense of what he was trying to say. "Okay. Someone hit you," she repeated patiently, "and there was someone you didn't see?"

"Uh-huh."

"And this someone took something?" She saw nothing out of place.

Then her heart lurched.

"Where's Cody? Hank! Where's Cody?"

"Took 'im. Tried to stop 'em…hit me."

"Wh-what? Someone took him?" Panic seized her. *Please God not again.*

Hank tried to nod but grimaced. "Took 'im."

"I have to get you to the house. Can you stand? Are you hurt anywhere else?"

"Help me up. Can walk."

Tori struggled to get the older man on his feet and headed toward the house. She shouted for Sheila before they hit the porch.

The door swung open and she hurried to help get the

wounded man up the steps. "Oh my God! What happened?"

Together, they managed to get him to the bench at the table. "Sheila, get the first aid kit from the pantry." Tori sat beside him, relying on her nurse training to remain composed though fear all but paralyzed her.

Her throat thickened with sobs she refused to yield to. *Cody was gone. Oh God, he was gone!* A heavy weight settled around her heart. *It was happening again.* She took the small first aid kit from her sister-in-law and tore through the contents. "Okay. One more time. You were in the barn; Cody was with you…"

Hank rotated his head back and forth as though trying to clear the cobwebs brought on by the blow he suffered. "We wuz standin' there watchin' 'em nurse. I heard a noise and turned; this feller hit me and grabbed for the boy. I tried to stop 'em, Miz Tori, I swear to God I tried." The misery in his voice undid her resolve.

"Someone took Cody? Oh my God! Someone took Cody?" Sheila's terrified voice did nothing to alleviate Tori's own growing anxiety which now reached critical mass.

"Yes. Evidently there were two men hiding in the barn. One of them hit Hank and the other grabbed Cody and took off." She patted his shoulder as she spoke, refusing to succumb to the terror clawing at her insides. She had to be strong. "You did all you could, Hank. It's not your fault. Did you know the man?"

"No." He shook his head and grimaced again. "Not from 'round here. I never seen the other one. The first feller said to keep the kids' mouth covered and get the hell outta there. He hit me again and knocked me out." Hank's shoulders slumped lower and he hung his head. "I shoulda stopped 'em,"

Tori had no time to comfort him. "Sheila, call the Sheriff's Office and tell them what happened. Tell them we need an EMT to check on Hank." She pulled out bandages, wipes and tape and worked on his injury.

Sheila returned and sat down beside Hank.

"The cut isn't bad." Tori looked at her frightened sister-in-law. "Finish cleaning it and put a bandage on it. I'm going outside to look around the barn, and see what I find. Don't let him go to sleep. Keep him awake; keep talking to him. I'll be back in a few minutes."

She grabbed a coat off the rack and ran out the back door. She spotted tracks by the gate beyond the wood pile nearest the door leading to the stalls. The slushy-muddy ground revealed activity by multiple feet, both human and horse and it took her several minutes to find tracks heading west.

She followed the trail a short distance and made a decision.

Ten minutes later, Bonnie was saddled and tied to the back porch. Tori ran inside to change, grab the rifle Wade insisted she carry and a few supplies.

Sheila jumped up as she entered the kitchen. "Sheriff's on his way but it'll be about half an hour before he can get here. Same for EMS. What are you doing?"

"Going after him."

"What!" Sheila grabbed her arm as she rushed by. "Are you nuts? You can't do that!"

"They will get too far ahead if we wait for the sheriff. And it will be dark in a couple of hours. We can't afford to waste any time." She held up her hand to stop further argument. "I'm going. Get another coat for Cody. He only wore a light-weight one this morning. And a change of clothes. I'm going to change and get my rifle." She headed down the hall to the bedroom, still issuing orders. "Tell the Sheriff there is a trail back behind the wood pile on the back side of the fence. Two horses which means he rode with one of them. They came in and rode out the same way. I'm going to follow the trail."

Minutes later, rifle in hand, extra rounds in her pocket, she returned to the kitchen.

"Tori, I don't think you should do this." Sheila wrung her hands. "You don't know the land, you might get lost, or the weather could turn; you might get hurt."

"I have to go. Cody's life could be at stake."

"Miss Sheila's right, ma'am." Hank's haggard face mirrored Sheila's concern. "You should wait on the Sheriff or Wade and Doug to get back. The weather is taking a turn for the worse; I can feel it."

"All the more reason for me to go now. Wade won't be back for hours. I can't wait that long. If the kidnappers aren't from around here," she avoided mentioning it might be Rico's men, "they may not be prepared for this weather, either which could put him in even more danger."

"I tried to reach the crew out on the south pasture where they're putting out hay," added Sheila, "but they must not have a good signal since it keeps going to voicemail."

"Have you tried to call Wade's cell?"

Sheila shook her head. "He didn't take it. I saw it on the hall table. I tried Doug's cell but again, no signal."

Dammit.

Wade hated cell phones, said they were useless in the mountains, which they were most of the time. "Okay. As soon as you get in touch with the boys, have one of them see if they can find Wade. Tell him the tracks lead away from the house, going west. I have no idea where they may be headed."

"Well, 'less they strike south toward town when they reach the back fence," said Hank, "it would be the old line shack or maybe a couple of old hunter cabins further up the mountain but I doubt it. I reckon it's more likely the line shack. It's closest to the old game trail that takes you back to the highway toward Helena."

"Do you mean the one south of Walker Pass?"

"Yes 'em. You been there before?"

"We rode near it the other day but didn't take the time to follow the trail. Wade did mention how to get to it. Tell me how to get there from the turn off on the trail toward Walker Pass, what do I need to look for? I don't know if they are headed there or not. I'm going to follow the trail and see where it leads. I'll use the shack for shelter if I have to."

Tori paid close attention to his instructions as she gathered food and water.

Hank shook his head, "Miz Tori, that's at least two hours in this weather for you."

"I'm so scared for you Tori." Sheila rubbed her hands on her thighs. "You don't know what it can be like this time of year."

"Cody is out there and I have to find him. Where's Wade's phone? Is the battery charged?"

Sheila grabbed the phone, checking the charge. "Crap! It's low, maybe half and will probably die trying to find a signal."

"Better than nothing. I'll leave it off to save power and try to use it to check in." She stuffed it in her pocket and checked the time. "It's four-thirty now; I'll try to check in every hour or so and let you know where I am providing I can get a signal. If not, well, we'll have to wait and see."

Sheila grabbed her arm. "Tori, please don't go!"

"I have to. Take care of Hank and get the sheriff and Wade out there as soon as you can."

Tori hurried to Bonnie, stowed the supplies in her saddle bags and took off, praying she wasn't making a mistake that may end up costing both her and Cody their lives.

Chapter Twenty-Six

TORI LOOKED AT HER WATCH; TWO HOURS HAD PASSED. *Damn.* The sky was almost hidden by the trees and ever increasing snow but she estimated she had about an hour or so of daylight left.

Twice she tried to use Wade's cell phone but the signal came and went. She'd opted for a short text, *line shack* hoping at some point it would make it through. She kept Bonnie to the side of the trail left by the kidnappers, and even wrapped in multiple layers with a heavy scarf and hat, she was chilled to the bone.

She worried about Cody having enough clothes on after finding one of his gloves and his scarf along the way. Whether by accident or design, it gave her hope. She estimated the shack couldn't be more than half a mile away now although the snow obscured some of the landmarks. She tried not to contemplate who else may be headed there as well.

Cold and fear for the child shook her to the core as she urged Bonnie forward. Approaching a slight bend in the trail, she saw something red on the ground; his other glove. She dismounted and grabbed it, holding it close to her heart for a moment then placed it in her saddle bag. She searched the area for anything else he might have left or lost, and tried to pick up their tracks again.

The erratic trail concerned her. *Were they lost or trying to throw off pursuit?* Her heart skipped. They were indeed headed for the shack, and like her, maybe had difficulty with landmarks in the snow; hence, the zig-zag approach. She went back to the horse, so cold she had difficulty moving.

Oh, God, what do I do? I need shelter but what if they're headed somewhere else? I could get lost following them. She rested her head against Bonnie's neck and swallowed hard to keep terror from consuming her. *Are you warm enough without your gloves and scarf? Have they hurt you?* And the biggest question of all—why did they take him in the first place?

With a silent prayer that it was the right decision, Tori remounted but stopped short when sounds drifted by on the wind.

There it was again. Someone arguing.

She dismounted, pulled the rifle from the scabbard and looped Bonnie's reins over a limb and trudged through the snow toward the sound.

♡

The trek through the mountains turned out to be an exercise in futility. A clear trail in the beginning soon became sporadic due to continued snowfall. Half an hour ago, they lost it altogether.

At this point, Wade knew it was fruitless to continue.

"It's no use," he told Doug at last, "we have to get back. Should let up some in a day or so and we can pick it up again. They can't get far. There are very few places to hole up."

"Dammit!" Doug slapped the reins against his leg, "I

don't like not knowing where the bastard is."

"Neither do I, but it's a safe bet he isn't going anywhere for a while."

With one last look toward the pass they thought Rico might have taken, they turned and headed back to the ranch. Thoughts of Tori waiting at home made him smile. Life was good.

"What the hell do you mean she went looking for them?" Wade's shout coupled with his scowl made Sheila take a step back.

"We tried to talk her out of it, but she was determined to follow them so they would not have too much of a head start."

"Son of a bitch!" He slammed his hat against the table and looked at Sheriff Wallace and the deputy who were talking to Hank. "How long has she been gone?"

"A couple of hours," said the sheriff. "I was delayed by a wreck on the highway. At this point, I think we need to wait for first light. It's almost dark and the snow is too heavy to track anything."

"It's all my fault." Hank hung his head and his scrawny shoulders stooped. "I shoulda stopped 'em from takin' the boy."

"You're not to blame for this, Hank." Wade took a breath. "You couldn't have stopped them from taking him." Wade looked at the EMT who stood beside Hank. "He gonna be okay?"

"Yeah, slight concussion but no other injuries. Probably have a headache for a couple of days."

The young man continued talking about what to watch for but Wade no longer heard him, his thoughts focused on his wife and Cody and how to find them. Doing nothing until morning wasn't going to work.

"Are you sure she planned to head for the line shack?" He stood at the kitchen window and looked toward the mountains, hidden now behind a thick curtain of falling snow.

"She was going to follow their trail. The shack and those old hunter cabins are the only shelter in the area." Sheila avoided her brother's harsh glare. "She said if it got late she would use the line shack for shelter."

Sheila's phone beeped indicating an incoming text. "It's from Tori!" Her voice rose and her eyes widened in excitement. "She's there!" She pushed the phone to Wade for him to read the short message, *'line shack'*.

He grunted and handed it back. "Wait…What time was it sent?"

She checked the data on the message. "A little over an hour ago. Why am I just now getting it?"

Wade ran his fingers through his hair. "I'm sure the weather had something to do with it. I'm guessing she had the phone off and on looking for a signal. I'm surprised you got it all. At least we know she is out of the weather."

"Could she have made it to the line shack in two hours—in this weather?"

The question from Doug made Wade's heart lurch because he knew the answer: Not very likely. She was not familiar with the area and knew nothing about tracking. With the continued snowfall, it was possible but doubtful she could reach the cabin in two hours.

"Okay. She wasn't there when she sent the message but headed that way and wanted us to know."

"But what if the kidnappers are there, too?" Sheila asked.

My deepest fear. There were few places to take shelter

from the storm. The chances of her being there alone were slim and none. "I can't wait until morning," Wade grabbed his hat and headed for the door. "I can't take the chance she won't have company when she gets there."

"No, Wade, you can't." Sheila cried. "It's a blizzard out there, near white out conditions."

"I know the area, she doesn't. And she doesn't know what she might be in store for. I have to go after her."

Doug grabbed his arm. "Sheila's right, Wade. This is not the time to try and be a hero."

"I can't sit here and do nothing!" His shout resounded in the small room, fear twisted his gut. "She is out there alone with Rico and God only knows who else with no protection!"

"She has her rifle and extra ammo," said Sheila, "and she took provisions for her and Cody."

"What the hell good will that be if she freezes to death?" Wade slung his hat across the kitchen. "I have to do something; I promised I would I protect her; I can't lose her, not now, not like this."

"We'll head out at first light or as soon as the snow stops. You know this is the best way to help her." Doug's assurance did little to assuage his anxiety.

"Doug's right, Wade," said the Sheriff, "This storm will last most of the night and visibility is already next to nothing. We'd be walking blind."

"Tori's smart and strong." Doug spoke with firm with conviction. "She knows to head for the shack and more than likely is already there. In the meantime, we'll keep trying to call your cell. Maybe we'll lucky and the call goes through."

They were right but waiting and doing nothing tortured him. "I'll wait till the snow stops or daybreak, whichever comes first. Sheriff, you and your deputy can stay in the bunkhouse tonight unless you want to try and make it back to town."

"Thanks, we'll take the bunkhouse. I'll radio the office and let them know. I have a search party ready to head out at first light. Can we get a couple of your broncs for me and my deputy?"

Wade nodded. "I'm going to check on the horses and make sure everything is ready for a quick departure."

Sheila moved to the counter and grabbed the empty coffee pot. "I'll get some coffee going and something for everyone to eat."

It would be a very long night.

Chapter Twenty-Seven

TORI FOLLOWED THE SOUND TO A SMALL BEND IN THE trail where a large overhanging boulder provided a hint of shelter from the snow. The line shack was thirty feet away.

She pulled the scarf tighter over her nose to keep her lungs from freezing with every breath of frigid air. A sudden surge of adrenalin raced through her when she spotted Cody with his back to the wind, arms folded and shoulders hunched.

A desperate urge to jump for joy almost caused her to blow her cover.

Two men stood beside her nephew, backs to the rock wall. The shorter one she recognized as Carl Franks, one of the new hands hired in the summer, the other man a stranger to her.

"I'm done taking shit from you Parker." Carl's angry voice rose with each word spoken. "I'm going inside."

Parker whirled, grabbed the ranch hand by the arm, and slammed him against the rock wall. He pressed his forearm across Carl's throat. "You ain't in charge of this party, cowboy, I am." His razor-sharp declaration radiated controlled anger. "You do *what* I say *when* I say."

Cody whirled to the men during the exchange, eyes wide in fright and whimpered. "I'm cold. I wanna go home."

Parker stepped away from the cowboy and stalked toward the boy. "Shut the hell up, kid."

Cody brought his head up a little and stared at Carl, his little chin quivered but he didn't cry. "Uncle Wade is gonna kick your butt when he gets here."

The ranch hand rubbed his throat and grumbled, avoiding eye contact with Parker. "Your boss ain't going like us not sticking to the plan."

"Couldn't be helped. Snow was coming, had to move." Parker looked at the sky and nodded. "Won't last long. We'll be out of here in the morning."

"Why can't we take the four-wheeler and keep going tonight?" grumbled Carl. "Wade's probably already on our tail."

Parker ignored his question. "You scared, cowboy?"

"Wade don't like to be crossed. And you took his kid. He's got to be pissed."

"*You* took the kid." His smile was cold and calculating. "I just hit the old man."

"Just the same," muttered Carl, "I'll feel better when we're outa here."

"Take care of the horses." Parker grabbed Cody's arm and started for the shack. "And bring more firewood back with you."

Carl blocked his path, fists clenched at his side. "I ain't your damn slave." He took a step forward. "I want my money now and I'm outta here."

"You'll get your money when the boss gets the kid. Not before." Parker was cold as the blizzard blowing in.

Carl stared at him, and Tori guessed from his tense

posture it wouldn't take much for him to pounce on the other man, size be damned. The standoff lasted less than a minute before he caved. "I'll take care of the horses."

"Don't forget more firewood."

Carl grabbed the horses' reins and headed toward the shed.

Parker shuffled toward the shack, favoring his right leg, dragging a reluctant Cody with him.

She waited until they were inside before she eased back to where she'd left Bonnie. A few minutes later, Carl came back, rounded the shed and grabbed an armful of wood before returning to the shack, head bent against the wind.

Tori stomped her feet in an effort to keep warm and considered the options, such as they were. *Carl mentioned four-wheelers? That would make getting out so much easier.*

She craned her neck as much as she dared and tried to find them to no avail. *They have to be on the other side of the shed.*

Going back to the ranch was out of the question. "We have to find shelter, Bonnie, and pray the opportunity presents itself to get out of this." Tori rubbed the horse's nose and waited, counting off ten minutes in her head before she led the mare to the back of the small shed, using the tree line for cover. The outside wall held an assortment of fencing supplies and chopped wood…and two ATV's covered by a heavy tarp.

A quick look under the tarp revealed no keys in either one. *Damn. They must have them. And this isn't the best place to stay but at least it is out of the wind and snow.* She looked inside the tiny building and another idea took hold.

Small and enclosed, it contained no heat, but it would be shelter from the elements. The other horses were munching feed, and a look around the semi darkness produced a bag of oats which she fed Bonnie. The water barrel was near the door and the top layer of ice already broken. It took several more minutes of searching to find something to water her horse with.

Satisfied there was nothing more to be done, Tori stood in the icy darkness and pondered the situation. Even with walls to break the wind, the place was glacial; she may very well freeze to death in here. The saddle blanket would be a good insulator, but she opted not to unsaddle her mount, for fear they might need a hasty retreat if she couldn't get one of the ATV keys. Even dressed in several layers, it wasn't enough to stop the incessant shivering and teeth chattering.

Two bales of hay near the far wall appeared to be her only option for warmth. Mind numb with cold, she moved forward and tried to focus on a plan to get them out of this mess.

"Well, well, well. Lookie here what I done found."

Chapter Twenty-Eight

TORI STUMBLED AND FELL TO HER KNEES AS SHE slogged through the snow toward the shack, Parker's pistol pressed to her back.

I am such a fool! I never even heard him walk in!

"Get up, dammit!"

She stumbled again on the bottom step, righted herself and made it to the door. Her hands were so cold she had trouble maneuvering the handle to get it open. Inside, Tori's eyes darted around and found Cody in front of the fireplace, arms stretched toward the growing warmth. "Cody!"

He turned, and she ran to him, dropped to her knees and hugged him to her chest.

"Aunt Tori!" He returned the hug, then pushed away and looked toward Parker. "You'll be sorry now. Uncle Wade is gonna kick your butt."

"Shut up, kid." Parker turned to Carl and growled, "Get some more wood."

Carl stared at him several heartbeats before storming out the door.

Cody looked behind her. "Where's Uncle Wade?"

"Don't worry, sweetie, he'll be here soon." Tori prayed it wasn't a lie. "Your hands are like ice." She rubbed them between her own, then nodded toward the fire. "Get closer to the fire." She urged her nephew forward and he obeyed, reaching toward the growing warmth.

"Who knows you're here?" Parker's sharp question made her jump.

"Everyone."

"Bullshit." His body language radiated anger, the gun an ominous reminder things could go from bad to worse in the blink of an eye. "McBride and his friend was gone. Nobody home but that old geezer, you, and his sister."

"I called the Sheriff as soon as I found Hank in the barn. He's no doubt on his way as we speak. And Wade called to say they were headed home right before I found Hank so we can expect him at any time as well." She hoped her lack of conviction did not show.

"You're lying. Cell service sucks up here. No way he called anybody."

"Doug has a satellite phone. Pretty high tech stuff." Again, Tori hoped nothing betrayed her. "He's a fed. Or didn't you know that?"

The shocked look on his face said he did not.

"Kidnapping is a federal crime."

Carl returned with another arm full of wood. "I ain't going back out there tonight. You want any more you can damn well get it yourself." He dumped the logs on the floor by the fireplace, never quite meeting Tori's gaze.

"Wade trusted you, and you betrayed him. I sure wouldn't want to be you when he gets here."

Carl ducked his head and sat on the floor near the fireplace.

Parker slid the pistol in his waistband and headed to the

small table where a camp stove, coffee pot and box of what appeared to be supplies sat. He picked up the coffee pot and set it back down. He looked at Tori. "Make some coffee," he snapped.

She opted to choose her battles for now. "Where do I get the water?" *And the poison?*

He nodded toward a bucket beside the fireplace. "There's snow melting in there."

In a few minutes the room filled with the enticing smell of brewing coffee. She filled a Styrofoam cup from the box then stood beside Cody, her back to the fire.

"Aunt Tori," he whispered, "when is Uncle Wade getting here?"

She placed an arm around his shoulders and brought him close, placing a soft kiss on his head. "I don't know, sweetie. Soon I'm sure."

He pulled on her jacket, urging her down. He cut his eyes toward Parker and murmured, "It's him."

"Who?"

"The bad man."

"Bad man?"

His eyes darted toward Parker who ignored them. "He pushed us off the road."

Fear hit her like icy water as realization dawned. *Parker killed Cody's parents?* "Are you sure?"

He nodded, and inched closer to her. "I saw him."

She hugged him to her side. "Just stay close to me. Uncle Wade will be here soon."

"Is Hank dead?"

"No, sweetie, he's fine. A little knot on his head is all."

The scared child lowered his head. "It's my fault. I wanted

to see the colts."

She tilted his chin up. "You are not to blame for this, Cody. None of it."

Tori remembered his recent nightmare; *the bad man was after him.* Did Parker know he had been in the car? She had to assume no since he didn't show any particular interest in Cody other than his *boss* wanted him. "Are you sure he's the man you saw?"

He nodded, face solemn.

Oh, God.

She blew out a breath. "Everything will be alright. Don't worry. Uncle Wade will be here soon."

"What's gonna happen?"

Parker's feral eyes made her skin crawl. *What's he thinking?* "I don't know. But I need you to be strong, okay? If I tell you to do something, you do it without question."

At his grave nod, she sipped her coffee and tried to sort things out. Carl and Parker kidnapped Cody for…someone, but who? Parker was apparently involved in the death of Cody's parents but why? And who on earth was *the boss* Carl referred to, and what did he want with Cody?

"Whatever it is you're thinking of doing you best forget it." Parker's brusque command bounced off the walls of the shanty, his fingers twitched near the butt of the gun anchored in the waist of his jeans.

"I'm not thinking of doing anything."

"Bullshit."

"I have to go to potty." Cody's announcement was strong despite the fear she knew he harbored.

"You see a bathroom in here?"

"I gotta go."

"Can I take him out back?" Tori asked.

"You think I'm stupid?" Parker's sneer punctuated the question.

Yes. Very; and you have no idea what's in store for you when Wade gets here.

"Unless you want a mess in here you need to let me take him out back."

"Carl!" Parker's sharp command made the other man jump. "Take the kid out back to piss."

"I want Aunt Tori to take me."

"I don't give a damn what you want." He barked at Carl. "Take the kid out to do his business and get back in here."

"I ain't takin' him nowhere." He pointed toward Tori. "Let her do it."

Parker stepped toward him, hand on the butt of his pistol. "I'm not telling you again." He pulled on the gun. "Take the kid outside."

The situation had the potential to get out of hand in a hurry.

"Look, he's just going on the porch. He doesn't need anyone to take him." She turned to him. "Do you, sweetie?"

"No, ma'am. I just gotta pee."

"It's much too cold for him to stay out long." She spoke calmly, refusing to let them see the fear percolating through her.

Parker hesitated. "Fine. The kid tries anything, I'll kill you first."

Cody started to cry. "I won't do nothin'. I promise. Please don't hurt her."

She wiped his tears with her thumb. "It's okay baby, he's just trying to scare you. He won't do anything. Go ahead and hurry back. It's freezing out there."

He looked at her then Parker, and paused at the door to glance back again before going outside, pulling the door closed behind him.

Tori continued to sip her coffee and waited for the other shoe to drop. Neither of the men spoke and their silence frightened her more than words.

Soon, the door opened and Cody returned going straight to the fireplace. "It's really cold out there."

"I know. Are you warm enough? I have more clothes in my saddle bags."

"My feet are cold. The snow got my pants and shoes wet."

"I have some dry clothes for him in my saddle bags. Can I go get them?" *And maybe my rifle?*

"No." Parker didn't even look up.

"His feet are freezing. He needs dry clothes."

"Shut the hell up!"

Tori persisted. "Look, he needs dry clothes or he'll get sick. Does your boss want that?"

He turned to Carl. "Go get the saddle bags off her horse," he snapped.

Carl sat on the floor near the fireplace, glowering. "I told you I ain't going back out there."

"Look," said Tori, again striving for peace, "I give you my word, I won't try anything. It's still snowing and there's no way I'm going anywhere without him."

"Shit." Parker set his cup down on the table. "Come on."

"Cody, you stay here by the fire. I'll be right back."

"But -"

She smoothed his hair back. *He'll need that haircut when we get back.* "Everything will be fine. I'll be right back."

Cody glanced at Carl and sat down on the other side of the fireplace.

Once outside, she looked at Parker. "You made those calls, didn't you?"

He jerked his head toward her, eyes narrowed. "What if I did?"

"Why? Who made you do it? What did they expect me to do?"

He glared in silence

She took a breath and asked the question uppermost in her mind, dreading the answer. "Do you work for Rico?"

"No."

"Rico Morales didn't tell you to make those calls? To kidnap Cody?"

"Didn't I just say I don't know him?"

"Then who—"

"No more questions." Parker pushed her toward the shed. "You'll find out soon enough."

If Rico isn't behind all this, who is?

"Move it!" His impatient command brought her back to the present as she lumbered through the ankle deep snow toward the shed, thankful the snow had ceased to fall.

He saw the rifle in the scabbard and immediately grabbed it. His sneer said he guessed what Tory had in mind.

She ignored him and pulled the saddle bags off Bonnie.

"Give it here." He rifled through the contents before passing them back to her.

She reached inside and pulled out two candy bars out, showing them to her captor, who nodded. She stuffed them in her pocket and touched the extra cartridges she grabbed on her way out of the house along with Wade's cell phone. *Maybe*

I can find a way to use them to my advantage.

The clouds had dissipated and a few stars poked their way through. Tori had no way of knowing how long the break in the weather would last and hoped it would be long enough for Wade to find them. Uncertainty and fear made her blood run cold as the wind that whipped through the tall ponderosa pines.

Once dressed in dry clothes, and candy bar eaten, Cody yawned and stretched. "I'm tired, Aunt Tori. Where can I sleep?"

"Just lay here in front of the fire so you'll stay warm. Put your head in my lap."

He obeyed and soon fell asleep while she stroked his thin shoulders, his back and baby soft hair. *Please God; don't take them away. Not again. Please. Not again.*

Carl dosed against the wall and Parker sat in the lone chair, rifle across his lap, merciless eyes fixed on her.

Hurry, Wade.

♡

Wade looked at his watch for the umpteenth time as he paced around the bedroom. *One a.m.* He stopped at the French doors and peered out.

Tori was out there with Cody.

He tried not to dwell on what they may be going through.

And here he stood; doing nothing. The impotent rage he felt toward whoever took his nephew and forced Tori into doing something so dangerous was enough to scare even him.

Doug better find the bastard first if he had any chance of surviving.

He clenched his fists and studied the distant mountains. The snow continued to fall, though not as heavy as before. He walked out onto the porch and looked up. The clouds were thinning. The snow would end soon. Forecast said no more for a couple of days, and the temps would linger above freezing. The wind, always a huge factor this time of year, would subside some tomorrow, but the cold would be intense.

He plunged his hands in his pockets and paced along the porch. Snow drifts were over two feet in places. Overall maybe ten to twelve inches covered the valley. There could be higher drifts in the mountains.

The area he hoped Tori took shelter in had lots of trees but on the north side of the mountains so it might be worse there. "God please let her be safe," he whispered, "Please let them both be safe."

He went back inside and lay down, not bothering to undress, knowing he should rest for the ordeal to come.

He threw is arm over his eyes and pleaded, "Hang on, baby…I'm coming."

Chapter Twenty-Nine

ADE WOKE TO THE DELICIOUS AROMA OF FRESH coffee and the smell of bacon frying. *Tori is making breakfast.* The smile died before it fully formed.

She was gone.

Alone, somewhere in the mountains with a monster on the loose. He glanced at the bedside clock—five a.m. He'd actually slept several hours. He threw off the quilt and headed to the kitchen.

Sheila met him in the hall. "I got another text. Not sure when she sent it but it said *we're safe.*'"

Doug sat at the table, a mug of coffee in his hand. "I think she made it to the line cabin and found it occupied. But at the time she sent that," he nodded toward Sheila's phone, "they were safe."

"Snow stopped about an hour or so ago," said Sheila, "I knew you would want to head out as soon as possible." His sister moved to the stove. "I already packed you some bacon and egg biscuits and a thermos of coffee."

"Thanks, Sis." Wade tried to smile but his heart wasn't in it.

"Should I call over to the bunkhouse and wake the Sheriff?"

"No. He needs to wait for the search party. They won't be here until after sunup. I can't wait any longer."

Doug put his mug in the sink. "Ready when you are."

Wade studied his friend, remembered other times they faced an unknown enemy side by side, each trusting his life to the other.

The stakes were higher now; other lives were involved but the trust never wavered.

He took the sack Sheila offered and nodded. "Let's ride."

♡

The rumble of heated conversation cut through the fog of restless sleep and Tori opened her eyes enough to see what was going on.

Cody slept curled up on the floor, her jacket lying over him, his arm a pillow. The room was chilly even though the fire still burned in the hearth; Carl and Parker argued in the corner.

"Why do I have to do it again?" whined Carl, "I marked the trail with the four wheeler yesterday."

Parker took a step toward him, fists clenched at his sides. "I said, get your ass down the trail to where it meets the road and make sure."

The standoff continued a moment longer before Carl conceded defeat. "I don't know who died and made you God, asshole." He grabbed his heavy coat and hat. "But when this is over, it's you and me."

He stomped out the door.

Parker barked at Tori. "I know you're awake so you might as well make some coffee."

She pushed herself from the floor and took a moment to stretch the kinks out of cramped muscles before adding more wood to the fire, the rumble of an ATV engine grabbing her attention.

She looked toward the door then back to her captor. "I'm guessing the guest you're expecting is the host of this party?"

Apparently, Parker wasn't a morning person because his only response was a glare and a grunt.

"Why are you doing this? Is it money? If it's money I can pay you more."

His eyes narrowed then he snorted. "You talk too much."

"You'll be lucky to get out of this alive. My husband was an Army Ranger. He knows how to kill slowly and make it hurt." *I hope.*

He flinched but quickly recovered. "You ain't married."

How the hell did he know that? Oh, Carl. "We married three days ago." *Well, sorta married.* "And he'll be looking for us by now. If you're smart, you'll be gone when he gets here."

He whirled around, savage eyes gleaming. "I said shut the hell up."

In the distance, the drone of an engine announced Carl's return. *Did he bring the boss with him?* Her hands shook as she sipped the coffee and tried to mentally prepare for whatever was to come next, fingers of her hand clutching three bullets she smuggled out of her coat pocket last night.

Oh God, give me strength.

♡

"Well," observed Doug, "smoke in the chimney means someone's there."

"Yeah…but who?" Wade kept his voice low, head down.

The front door opened and Carl Franks stepped onto the narrow porch. He glanced around the yard then ambled toward the back of the shed.

"You sonofabitch." Wade's whispered oath spoke volumes, his grip on the rifle in hands so tight the knuckles turned white.

"You know him?"

"Carl Franks. Hired him back in the summer."

Doug put a hand on his arm. "Easy does it, man. Easy does it."

"I swear to God if that bastard hurt one hair on their heads I'll kill him with my bare hands."

They heard an ATV crank up and watched it disappear down the trail.

"Where the hell is he going?" Doug looked at Wade. "What'd you think?"

"There's at least one other person inside. We saw three sets of tracks back there. And no way is Carl in this alone."

The DEA agent nodded, eyes moving to the shed. "One set of tracks must be Tori's. I'm gonna move around and check that out." He inched to his left, then turned back to Wade, one side of his mouth curled up. "Don't do anything I wouldn't do till I get back."

Wade kept his eyes on the shack, shoulders tight. "No promises, so hurry."

His buddy returned in record time. "Three horses in the barn; one of 'em is Bonnie, still saddled." He paused for a breath. "And there's another Ranger four-wheeler behind the shed. No key."

"You need a key?"

"Not since I was thirteen." He met Wade's worried eyes. "Get this…there's a lot of ATV traffic on the trail. Our guy's tracks aren't the first. Some are covered by the snow but it's easy to see there is more than one set."

"What'd you think it means?"

"Could be anything. They used it to bring supplies, someone else is involved, in and out traffic." Doug shook his head. "I'm thinking our guy is checking for someone or making sure the road is clear. Or both."

"Yeah, that would be my guess, too. Otherwise, they would have used the four-wheelers to get away by now. Why would she leave Bonnie saddled?" Wade mused out loud. "Were the others saddled?"

"No, only hers. Stalls are small with no gates. Bonnie's reins were looped around a post with enough slack she could reach hay on the floor and some water." Doug rubbed the stubble on his jaw. "My best guess is our girl put her in there at some point last night to get out of the weather and didn't plan on staying long."

Wade's stomach knotted. "And was caught."

"Yeah."

"I need to get a look inside before Carl comes back." Wade scanned the area he could see around the shack. "I'll use the tree line for cover and move around back. If I remember right, there's a small porch with a window on one side."

"Whippoorwill." Doug's reference to their danger alert signal originated in their Ranger days.

"Roger that." Wade was almost to the window when he heard the Whippoorwill call.

Chapter Thirty

A DARK-HAIRED MAN WADE DIDN'T KNOW STEPPED out onto the porch, and walked to the edge where he relieved himself before returning to the cabin.

Wade remained pressed against the wall until the man shut the door. He counted off two minutes then edged around where he could see inside the tiny window. The strange man had moved to the front window and looked out. Tori stood in front of the fireplace, sipping from a Styrofoam cup, Cody apparently asleep on the floor, her jacket over him. Relief rushed through him, making him weak-kneed. Thank God they appeared unhurt!

His wife chose that moment to glance his way and gasped when their gazes locked. She quickly looked down at her cup which sloshed hot liquid on her hands.

The stranger twisted around and Wade ducked out of sight.

He heard their voices inside, the man's raised in anger, Tori's shaky but clear.

"What's the matter with you?"

"I spilled hot coffee on my hand."

His reply was mumbled, and Wade missed it, but now he knew there was no one else in the room. He'd just made up his mind to rush in and take their captor out when he heard the Whippoorwill call again followed by a vehicle approaching.

Motor's different…Not the ATV. Shit. Someone else is joining the party.

Wade moved back to his spot at the edge of the shack and watched the Jeep as it pulled to a stop in front of the cabin. His heart rate escalated when the door opened and Lucy stepped out.

♡

Tori forced herself not to look back toward the window again for fear Parker would see Wade. *Thank God he's here!* She set her coffee down and wiped her hands on her jeans.

Cody still slept soundly a few feet away and she debated whether to wake him or not. She had no idea what Wade planned but he was right outside and she needed to be ready to move.

A car door slammed and she jumped.

Parker went to the door and pulled it open. "What the hell took you so long? Where's Carl?"

"Behind me somewhere. Where's my baby?"

"Lucy! You? You did this?" Fear paralyzed Tori. *Lucy is behind this?*

"You idiot!" Lucy screeched at Parker. "What's she doing here? That was *not* the deal!"

Parker didn't say anything for a heartbeat but his fists clenched at his sides and he looked at Lucy with dead eyes. "She followed us."

She turned to Tori, eyes glazed with rage. "You just can't

let go, can you?" She seethed. "You have to ruin everything."

Tori remained silent, fearing any comment would further enrage her tormentor.

"You've been trying to tear us apart from the beginning. But it won't work. We belong together." Lucy knelt down beside Cody. "Cody, baby? Wake up, Mommy's here."

Mommy? What the hell?

Cody stirred and looked at Lucy. "Where's Uncle Wade?"

She smoothed backed his hair. "Don't worry, darling, Daddy will be here soon."

He looked at Tori, confusion clouding his face. "Aunt Tori, what's she talking about?"

Before Tori could reply, Lucy pulled him up. "Put your coat on, baby, we have to hurry. Daddy will be waiting on us."

Cody started to whimper and Tori reached for him.

Lucy pulled out a pistol, stopping her in her tracks. "That's far enough."

"You're scaring him, Lucy." Tori tried to keep the panic from her voice. *Where are you, Wade?*

"Don't cry, baby, everything will be alright. Mommy's going to take care of you."

"Mommy's in Heaven."

Lucy pulled him close to her side, the gun wavering in her hand. "I'm your Mommy now."

Lucy looked at Parker with narrowed eyes. "Take care of her when we're gone."

"That wasn't part of the deal."

"It is now."

Lucy pulled on Cody's hand, walking to the door.

"No! I don't wanna go with you!" He broke away and ran to Tori. "Don't let her take me!"

Tori pushed him behind her. "Lucy, what's gotten into you? You're scaring him."

"It's all your fault! You're the reason he's afraid of me!" Lucy slapped her hard across the face, continually waving her gun around. "You turned him against me! Just like you did Wade!"

She blinked back tears and tried to think of a way to diffuse the situation, but one look at Lucy's wild eyes told her it would be a waste of time. Still, for Cody's sake, she had to try. "Lucy, please, let's talk about this."

"You've ruined everything." The crazy woman shook her head, stared at Tori with unseeing eyes. "It's all gone. I did it for nothing."

"It's not too late, Lucy. Stop this now before it goes any further and I know we can fix it."

"Fix it!" She screeched, "You can't fix dead!"

"Dead? What are you talking about?"

Oh God, surely she didn't mean to kill Cody?

Parker grabbed Lucy's arm and tugged. "Shut up, bitch, before I do it for you."

The red-head jerked away from him and paced the small cabin like a caged tiger. "This isn't how it was supposed to go. He's supposed to be mine; Wade will come after him. We are supposed to be together. We are a family."

She stopped and reached for Cody again. "Come on baby, please come to Mommy, we have to go find Daddy."

The terrified child grabbed Tori's waist and cried, "I don't wanna to go with you."

Lucy ducked her head, then just as quickly, turned on Parker. "You worthless piece of crap! You had one job to do! *One!* And you screwed it up!"

Parker pulled the gun from his waistband and pointed it at her. "Don't jack with me, bitch, or I'll take you out just like I did your sister."

Chapter Thirty-One

WADE WATCHED THE SCENE UNFOLDING THROUGH the window. He had to act now. Lucy with a gun was something he didn't want to deal with unarmed, but if he went in with *his* gun, the man Lucy had called Parker would likely shoot first and ask questions later.

He propped his rifle by the door and stomped his boots to announce his arrival before he opened the door.

"Wade!" Lucy threw herself in his arms. "Oh darling! I knew you'd come for us!"

He eased away from her, hand clamped around her gun hand, eyes on Parker whose gun now pointed at Tori.

Two bat shit crazy people with a gun and me with nothing.

"Cody has been so frightened, but I told him Daddy would be here soon and everything would be alright. As soon as we leave this place, everything will be okay."

Wade ignored her comments and looked at Tori. "Are y'all alright? Has he hurt you?"

Tori shook her head. "We're fine, he didn't hurt us."

Cody still clung to Tori. "Hang in there, sport. Everything's going to okay."

He nodded and sniffled.

Wade kept his hold on Lucy and eased himself between

Parker and his family. "This has gone far enough. Leave now and I won't follow." *But Doug will you sorry sonofabitch and you're lucky it will be him who stops you.*

Parker's laugh held no mirth. "You think I'm stupid? Where's your friend?"

"At the ranch waiting for the search party. You had my family. I couldn't wait."

The idiot seemed to ponder that statement a moment. "She goes with me." He nodded toward Tori. "A little insurance policy."

"I'm giving you one chance to get out of here alive, asshole. *One.*"

"I got the gun and you're giving me orders?" Parker laughed. "I don't think so."

"You're four feet away from me." Wade inched closer. "I guarantee I can make you eat that gun before you get off a shot." He eased forward. "Last chance. Leave now. Live. Be stupid. Die. The choice is yours."

Lucy picked that moment to go ape shit and grabbed his arm, trying to move him away from Parker. "No, Wade, please. He killed Karen, he'll kill you, too. We have to leave now."

Parker shuffled toward the door. "And who paid me to, you crazy bitch?"

Wade never took his eyes off Parker but this news shook him to core. "You paid him to kill Karen and my brother?"

"Can't you see? We're supposed to be together! She was in the way. Always in the way. She wouldn't let me near our son."

"He's not our son."

"Don't say that, Wade! You know he was meant to be our

son." She tried to jerk her gun hand free, eyes wide, lips twisted in a vicious snarl. "It's her isn't it? She's the reason you don't love me anymore!" She tried to jerk away from him. "After all I've done for you, you toss me aside for her!" She turned toward Tori. "I hate you! It's all your fault!" She aimed and fired.

Tori threw Cody to the floor and placed her body on top of him, tossing something in the fireplace as she went down.

Parker jerked open the front door and staggered outside.

Wade dove at Lucy as two explosions erupted from the fireplace. Lucy's next shot went wild, the third ricocheted off the rock mantle. He grappled for the gun and knocked it from her hand.

Lucy screamed and kicked but he wrestled her down and got her hands behind her back.

More shots rang out from the front of the cabin and then there was only the sound of Lucy's histrionics.

"Tori! Tori! Can you hear me? Are you all right?"

When she didn't answer, Wade twisted around and spotted the blood flowing onto the cabin floor beneath her.

Chapter Thirty-Two

"How is she?"

Wade jumped at Doug's soft spoken question. The last forty eight hours had drained him completely.

"Sleeping."

"Have you gotten any sleep at all?"

"Every time I close my eyes, I see her blood on the floor. I came so close to losing them both…"

"But you didn't. You need to focus on that." His friend sat in the chair beside him. "Sheriff Wallace has Carl in custody. Lucy is headed for the psych ward. Charges are pending."

"I forgot all about Carl. What did you do with him?"

"When I saw Lucy's Jeep coming up the drive, I knew he wouldn't be far behind. Didn't think he needed to be at the party so knocked him out and tied him up in the shed. Been singing like a canary ever since."

"Did Lucy really hire Parker to kill Karen?"

"Looks like it." He shook his head. "She is one messed up lady." He stretched out his long legs. "I heard the first shot and some guy came running out grabbing his shoulder."

"That was Parker. What happened to him?"

"Poetic justice. Lucy's first shot caught him in the

shoulder. He went down then took a shot me. My aim's better."

Wade nodded

The door opened and Sheila and Cody entered. She held a huge vase of flowers and Cody carried brightly colored "get well soon" balloons tied to a teddy bear.

"He wouldn't stay outside. Had to see her."

Cody went to the side of the bed and patted Tori's hand. "Is she gonna die, Uncle Wade?"

"C'mere, sport." He sat the bear on the floor and took the child in his lap. "She's gonna be fine. She's sleeping right now, but I promise you, she's will be fine."

Cody leaned on his shoulder. "It's my fault. She got hurt cause of me."

"No. It is not your fault and Aunt Tori would be very upset with both of us if we thought that. She would do anything to protect you. What happened is *not* your fault."

After a moment, the worried child looked up at his uncle. "What about Aunt Lucy?"

Wade exchanged looks with his sister before he could muster an answer. "She's very sick and needs special help, sport, and she will be going somewhere to get it."

"Can I stay here tonight?"

Tori would want to see him as soon as she woke up. "Sure thing, sport. We'll stay right here till she wakes up."

♡

A constant beep, beep, beep pierced through the fog of Tori's headache. She focused on the sound, trying to induce her drowsy brain to wake up and formulate an explanation.

Hospital...I'm in a hospital? How did I get here? What happened?

She opened her eyes and Wade's head slowly came into focus. He sat in a chair beside her bed, his head on the mattress, fast asleep. Cody lay beside her, one arm resting on her stomach.

The nurse checking her vital signs noticed she was awake. "How're you feeling?"

She grimaced. "Like I was shot."

The girl smiled. "You were lucky. Nothing vital hit but you lost a bit of blood." She nodded toward Wade and Cody. "Your husband and son refused to leave. I didn't have the heart to make them. Shall I wake them?"

"No. Let them sleep." She lifted her hand and raked her fingers through Wade's hair. He would need a haircut soon, too.

At her touch, he lifted his head. Tears filled his eyes as he pulled her hand to his lips. "Oh God, Tori...I thought I lost you. I thought I lost you."

"I'm fine. Cody?"

"He's fine. Couldn't bear to be away from you tonight. Like me."

"Lucy?"

"She's going to get the help she needs. You were right about her. I should've listened."

"Not your fault."

He lowered his head and kissed the back of her hand. "I love you, Tori. With every fiber of my being, I love you. I will spend the rest of my life proving that to you."

"I'll hold you to that."

She drifted off to sleep to the sound of her husband's

gentle snore and the baby sweet smell of the child beside her. *Second chances are the best kind.*

THE END

I hope you enjoyed reading about Tori and Wade. I love hearing from readers so feel free to drop me an email at danawayne423@gmail.com or visit my website, www. danawayne.com.

If you like Western Historical romances, take a peek at Emma Rae and Tyler's story coming winter 2017.

If you are so inclined, a review on your site of choice would be very much appreciated.

READ ON FOR AN EXCERPT FROM
Mail Order Groom and *Whispers on the Wind*

Mail Order GROOM

CHAPTER
One

East Texas, Spring, 1878

You've got thirty days to find a husband or I'll *find one for you.*

Her father's recent ultimatum bounced around Emma's head like a hail stone, causing her concentration to falter.

"Miss Marshall? Are you all right?"

John Ralston, the cattleman she came to Ft. Worth to see, watched with anxious eyes.

"My apologies, Mr. Ralston. I guess I am still tired from the trip."

He nodded. "I understand. It's a long trip from Bakersville." He motioned for the waitress to refill their coffee. "I wasn't aware of your father's illness until I received your telegram. I have to say, finding a woman such as yourself interested in my Herefords is unusual."

"My father told me about them after your meeting last year. I can't wait to see how they fare. How long has your herd been here? Has our finicky weather had any adverse effects on them?"

The next hour flew by, and when it ended, Emma was the proud owner of a Hereford bull and two heifers.

After Ralston left, she lingered over her coffee and savored the success of having completed not only the purchase of new breeding stock, but negotiating the sale of the herd they would bring in next month. The new purchase would be picked up then and driven back to the ranch.

He trusts me to negotiate the sale of our cattle but not to run the ranch. The smile of accomplishment faded. No matter how hard she tried, Rafe Marshall believed only a man could run Twin Oaks Ranch.

Their last conversation, still a vivid memory, played out in her mind.

"I'm dyin', girl. Doc sez I ain't got much longer. I gotta know Twin Oaks will be in good hands."

"By *good*, you mean *male*." It took tremendous effort to keep the hurt gnawing her insides from showing in her voice. "*That's* what you really mean."

He sighed and squinted. "We been over this time and again. Ranchin' ain't woman's work. You're almost twenty-six. You should've been married years ago with a passel o' young'uns for me to spoil, not runnin' round in britches and boots tryin' to do a man's job."

"I've no wish to get married, Papa, I've told you so repeatedly." *Because being married is like being property. No voice, no face, no freedom.*

He ignored her comment. "Tom Blakely over to the Lazy

B would be good."

She stared in disbelief. "You can't be serious. He's ancient. At least forty!"

"Or maybe Hank Walker."

His mention of the local attorney made her skin crawl. Hank made no secret of his interest and was prone to show up unannounced requesting she accompany him for a ride or the occasional dance.

She never accepted. He never gave up.

"I wouldn't marry Hank Walker if he were the last man on earth."

Rafe blew out a noisy breath. "I mean what I say." Pale blue eyes bored into hers. "Find a husband in thirty days or I'll find one for you."

"And if I don't?"

He paused. "Then Twin Oaks goes to my brother in Ft. Worth when I die."

That thought brought her back to the present with a jolt. Would he really give away her home, force her marry someone she didn't love? How could a father do something like this do his only child?

The coffee she enjoyed a moment ago turned sour in her stomach. Heart filled with despair, she adjusted the bow on her bonnet, and rose from the table. The desk clerk here at The El Paso Hotel mentioned earlier a new mercantile recently opened down the block. She decided it would be a great place to find gifts for her two best friends, Sarah and Mable.

Preoccupied with her father's dictate, she collided with a cowboy walking by as she exited the hotel.

Without conscious thought, she grabbed for his arms to keep from tumbling down the steps to the muddy street below. Her fingers clutched strong muscles that tightened beneath them, sending unexpected tingles up her arms.

Large hands grabbed her waist, their warmth adding to the unfamiliar sensations coursing through her.

"Whoa, there, ma'am."

His soft drawl caused gooseflesh on her arms and her gaze jerked up to his face. Eyes, grey as a storm cloud, caused her breath to hitch.

He hesitated, then set her away from him and tipped his hat. "Excuse me, ma'am. I wasn't watching where I was going." With a quick nod, he walked away.

She stood immobile for several heartbeats, then looked down at her gloved hands, surprised at the warm tingles lingering there.

The memory of those hypnotic eyes followed her the rest of the day and into the night, disrupting her sleep and making her irritable for the long journey home.

By the time she arrived two days later, she was accustomed to their frequent invasion of her thoughts.

Since her father expected an immediate report, she didn't bother to freshen up before entering his room. She removed her bonnet and gloves as she took her usual chair beside his bed. "How are you feeling today?"

"How did it go? Any problems?"

She took a breath before replying. "No, there were no problems. Mr. Ralston agreed to the terms we discussed before I left."

"I expect so since I had Leo telegraph ahead."

Her heart sank. "I should have known. I'm a woman and therefore can't do anything without a man to help me."

He clamped his jaw and remained silent.

She stood and paced around the room. "I can do anything any man on this ranch can do, even better than some, and I've handled everything just fine these last few months you've been sick."

"The only reason the men do what you tell them is because I'm still here." He struggled to sit up, then sank back on the pillows when his strength faded. "They won't listen to you when I'm dead, and everything I spent my life building will be gone."

She turned and faced him, emerald eyes stinging with unshed tears. "I don't understand how you can think so little of me."

"Don't start that nonsense again, girl, I – "

"My name is Emma Rose. Not Girl!" She hated it when he referred to her as *girl* as though she didn't even rate being called by her name. She lowered her voice. "I'm sorry your son died with my mother. I'm sorry I'm not a man." She paused a moment to gather her composure. "I finally realize no matter what I do, it will never be enough. You want me to find a husband…fine…I'll find a husband."

She stormed out of his room, slamming the door shut behind her, ignoring his demand they discuss the new foreman due to arrive soon.

Rafe glowered at the closed door, annoyed with himself for once again making a mess of things, but he lacked the time for tact and diplomacy.

He was dying.

He accepted that. What distressed him more than

the disease eating away his body one bite at a time was the thought of his only child being left alone when he died. His beautiful, smart, and head-strong Emma Rose who had the misfortune to inherit the predominant traits of both her parents. Tall and beautiful like her mother, with tobacco colored hair and emerald eyes that flashed with life or cut you to the bone, and headstrong and independent like her father.

I should've done a better job with her, made sure she knew how to be a woman. Now, it's too late.

Devastated by the death of his wife when Emma was ten, he'd closed himself off for years. By the time he realized his mistake, the void between them appeared insurmountable.

When was the last time I told her I loved her? How proud I am of her? I just want her to be happy. His brow furrowed as he tried to remember the last time he saw her smile. It shamed him to admit he couldn't.

She loved the ranch and it belonged to her. He had no intention of leaving it to his worthless brother; he merely used the threat as incentive to get her to at least look for a husband.

He wanted her to take his concerns seriously. Despite what she thought, he suffered no reservations about her ability to run the place. The men respected her and she worked hard to earn and keep their respect.

What killed his soul was the thought she would grow old alone.

Like him.

He blew out a breath and drummed his fingers on his chest. *I should've told her about the posters and the ad in the Ft. Worth paper.*

WHISPERS ON THE WIND

CHAPTER ONE

YOU LET HIM KILL HER.

The angry female voice in the pre-dawn hour jolted Cooper Delaney from a restless sleep.

Adrenalin pumping, he rolled to the right and automatically grabbed his pistol from the nightstand, fully expecting to see a stranger beside the bed.

Nothing but moonlit shadows. He swiveled his head to the left.

The room was empty.

He blinked and drew in a deep breath, trying to dispel remnants of the dream making sleep all but impossible for over a month. Always the same dream; a shadowy figure begging Coop to find her. That was it…*find me, please.* Two weeks ago, the voice changed and insisted Coop had to stop him.

Stop who? From what?

Tonight, the dream exploded into a full-blown nightmare.

He put the gun back on the table and lay down, right arm over his eyes. "Shit," he whispered as the vision replayed through his mind. *Powerful hands gripped her throat, the eerie silence punctuated by ragged gasps as she struggled for air.*

Blood trickled from her nose and the corner of her mouth. Dark hair wedged into a jagged cut across her forehead. Terror-filled eyes stared at the figure bent over her.

All the while, the voice reproached…you didn't stop him.

At forty-three, Coop considered himself a straight-forward, no nonsense lawman, well known and respected as the Sheriff of Baker County, Texas. He looked at the facts, the evidence, and made logical, rational decisions. And yet, the dream was so real, he smelled the metallic odor of blood, felt the dampness of the earth around her.

"Dammit." He lowered his arm and punched the bed. *I'm losing my fricking mind.*

It was bad enough when the voice invaded his sleep, but two days ago, he heard it at the kitchen table where he sat eating breakfast. Wide awake. This time, she warned he—whoever *he* was—would kill again.

He tossed the sheet aside and sat on the edge of the bed. Heart pounding, his breath hissed as he gulped in air. Elbows on his knees, he cradled his head in his hands. "Just a dream," he murmured, "a bad dream."

He stumbled to the window and shoved it open with an angry thrust, gasping when the rush of cool night air caused gooseflesh to prickle his sweat-coated body. "A dream," he whispered, willing himself to believe. "Nobody died." He pulled down the sash and pressed his forehead against the glass pane. "Nobody died."

When his racing heart finally slowed, he pushed away and headed for the bathroom, stopping at the foot of the bed as he tried to remember if Miss Eva had guests tonight. A curse escaped parched lips as he grabbed his jeans from a chair. *Why in the world did she want to go into the B&B*

business anyway?

Even as the thought flitted through his mind, he knew the answer. She decided he needed a wife and used the lovely Antebellum home to lure prospects. Hence, the majority of her guests were single women looking for a good time, or to change their marital status. He lost track of the propositions, both subtle and otherwise, thrown his way in the last six months. *When had women become so forward?*

He opened the door and padded on bare feet to the bathroom he shared with his son, Jason, when he was home from college. Guests used the one across the hall.

Since sleep was out of the question at this point, he threw on a shirt and headed downstairs for coffee.

Light showing under the kitchen door stopped him cold. "Crap. Company."

❖

Today is the first step of starting over.

Samantha Fowler gazed out the kitchen window, transfixed by the beauty of daybreak, convinced the magnificent sunrise was a good omen. The sky, once dark and gloomy, now showcased varying degrees of orange, blue and purple. Giant oaks, pecans and pine trees, previously hidden by darkness, sprang to life, as did the beautifully landscaped yard of the bed and breakfast she would call home for the next two weeks.

Her best friend, Barbara Walker, who grew up in Bakersville, suggested Pecan Grove B&B for her much-needed sabbatical to contemplate what to do with her life. A quick perusal of their website convinced her to give it a try. Located two hours from Dallas in rural Baker County, it was a beautiful antebellum-style home re-constructed after a fire in 1920.

Everything from the graceful columns on the front, to the upper-level porch running across the back, conveyed old-world-south. The interior was painstakingly decorated and furnished like its predecessor built in 1880. Modern upgrades included air conditioning and wi-fi, but the majority of the house retained the serene elegance and charm of the time.

"Oh, Jack, you should see this." A soft sigh of wonder arose as she took in the panoramic view. "No way could I capture this with a camera."

Her companion, a huge crossbreed dog of indeterminate lineage laying at her feet, merely grunted.

She sipped her coffee, still rooted by the window. "Don't be such a grouch. We've been up a lot earlier than this."

The mutt didn't bother to grunt this time.

"Ms. Benton said breakfast will be ready by the time we get back."

A soft groan followed by the swish of his tail on the worn linoleum floor acknowledged he heard what she said.

"No exercise, no food. Time to rock and roll, old man."

Suddenly, Jack growled low in his throat and stood in front of her, attention fixed on the kitchen door as it slowly opened.

A man, barefoot, shirt half-buttoned, sporting a severe case of bed head, strolled into the kitchen.

Every cell in Sam's body began a happy dance.

As a doctor, she was trained to quickly assess every situation and did so now. He towered over her, at least six-three or four, dark, curly hair in need of a trim touched the collar of a half-buttoned chambray shirt, while streaks of gray edged around the temples. Ruggedly handsome, his dark beard stubble projected an explicit manly aura.

Storm-cloud eyes, sharp and focused, assessed her as well.

Feminine radar pinged. Hard.

He liked what he saw.

Her fingers tightened around the cup. She attempted to speak but nothing came out. She settled for what she hoped was a smile of welcome but feared it may look more like a grimace.

Her protector didn't appear happy at the intrusion and bared his teeth in a menacing snarl.

She fumbled for the dog's collar. "Down, Jack."

Man and woman stared at each other in silence as seconds ticked by.

She reminded herself to breathe.

He cleared his throat as he ambled over to the pot on the counter. "I didn't expect company." He glanced her way, then focused on pouring his coffee. "Guests usually aren't up this early."

His voice, deep and sensual, coupled with that just-out-of-bed look sent ripples of awareness through her.

Oh my God. Looks like sin and sounds like Sam Elliott. "Oh, yes, well, we arrived late last night."

He looked around the kitchen. "We?"

His mouth moved so she knew he must have spoken, but it took a moment for her brain to stop fixating on the mat of chest hair peeking out the top of his shirt. She blinked and gestured toward the dog. "Me. And Jack. My dog. We arrived last night."

"Don't think I've ever seen a dog like him. What is he?"

An irresistibly devastating grin accompanied the question, and her stomach lurched.

She gulped in air. "Vet said maybe a cross between Mastiff and Rottweiler but even he was stumped."

The man cleared his throat—again—and looked everywhere but at her.

Warning bells sounded.

Holy crap. He feels it, too.

"Unusual coloring," the man offered at last. "Like someone splattered black and brown paint all over him."

She patted Jack's head. "Yeah. He's so ugly he's cute." *Really? That's the best you can do?*

Jack, apparently satisfied the visitor was not a danger to his mistress, lay back down with a heavy sigh.

Silence filled the room.

She set her cup on the counter. "Um, I'm Samantha Fowler. Are you a guest here, too?"

When his laser-sharp gaze fixed on her mouth, a swarm of butterflies invaded her stomach.

A muscle flexed in his jaw. "Cooper—Coop—Delaney. Guess you can say I'm a permanent guest."

Awareness bounced off the walls like a rubber ball, charging the room with explosive energy.

She let out an audible lungful of air and moved away from the counter. "Well, I think it's light enough to explore."

Jack snorted.

The edges of Coop's lips turned up. "He doesn't seem interested."

"Yeah, but he needs the exercise."

"Got a route in mind?"

Every word he spoke rolled over her in a tidal wave of

heat. A quick shake of her head sent her ponytail sliding to the side. "Just riding around, checking out the area. Got in too late last night to see much of anything."

"Well," he pushed away from the counter, "enjoy your ride." He headed for the door, stopping to speak to the dog. "Nice to meet you, Jack."

A soft rumble and a couple of weak tail thumps indicated acceptance.

Cooper grinned and walked out.

Sam closed her eyes and took a deep breath. "No. No. No," she commanded, "Hormones fooled me once. I won't let it happen again."

She nudged Jack with her toe and headed out the back door, her unhappy companion lagging behind.

What the devil is wrong with me? Sam sped down the road, tires kicking up rocks and dust. She looked straight ahead, but her mind's eye recalled the chance meeting in sharp detail. Her body still hummed with the force of his effect on it. Lust at first sight? Is that a real thing?

"Oh my God, Jack. What must he be thinking?"

Her silent companion watched intently, head cocked to one side as though listening while she ranted.

"I ogled like a fricking school girl." She shook her head, cheeks burning as she relived the encounter. "But at least, thank you God, I stopped short of drooling, though I'm sure I would have if he hadn't left when he did."

Jack's head cocked the other way, as though silently urging her to continue.

"Okay, okay, I looked. I admit it. I couldn't help it." She licked her lips. "Oh my. That chest," she murmured. "So much hair." Her fingers arched as she imagined running them through the thick mass of dark curls. "And didn't he sound a little like Sam Elliott to you? Kinda gravelly and raspy, and when he smiled—" She slapped her palm against her temple. "What the blue blazes is wrong with me? Did Paul not teach me anything?" She shook her head, sending her lopsided ponytail lower. "But his eyes, they were so, so, intense. Such an unusual color, too. Not grey, not blue; more, I don't know, like the ashes of a cold campfire or the color of storm clouds rolling in. The minute I looked at them," she paused as a light shiver rolled over her. "I swear it jolted me down to my toes." She wagged a finger at her companion. "And I'm not some sex-starved divorcee who can't control herself, either, though I'm sure he thought so. I stared. Fine. Not a crime. God took a lot of extra pains with him, and it would be extremely rude of me not to notice." She focused on the road. "My *goodness* did I notice. If ever a man was built for seven kinds of sin…"

Sam gave little thought to conversing with Jack as though he understood. In fact, sincerely believed he did. She found him beside a dumpster near the hospital two years ago more dead than alive from two bullet wounds. After he healed, they were constant companions. Paul, her now ex-husband, complained constantly about him being in the house, going everywhere with her, but she ignored his rants. Their marriage was already rocky by then, and she needed the mutt as much as he needed her.

Which no doubt explained why Paul and Jack never liked each other. Or maybe Jack was a better judge of character than her.

She sped down the road, wheel gripped in her left hand, her right waving around as she poured out her thoughts. "What did he expect anyway waltzing in there half-dressed?" She inhaled deeply and rested both hands on the wheel. "I shouldn't be surprised, though. Males in general are self-centered jerks who should be lined up and shot at sunrise." She reached over and patted Jack's head. "Well, except you, of course."

A soft whine and a thump of his tail drew her gaze.

"Again? You just went."

Another whine.

"Okay, okay." She searched ahead for an appropriate exit. Seeing what appeared to be a lane off to the right, she slowed and signaled a turn. It was little more than a well-traveled dirt lane leading to a briskly moving stream surrounded by willows, pines and an assortment of East Texas foliage. The nearest bank held a collage of mementos from past visitors, classifying the area as a primo make-out spot. Her mind's eye marked the location of beer cans, towels and discarded condoms even as she pulled under a towering pine. She rummaged in the glove box for tissues and finding them, opened the door and stepped out.

"Come on you big whiney-butt."

Jack jumped out and headed for the pine tree.

Sam headed in the opposite direction and gave a sharp, "Stay," when he turned to follow. Rounding the lone holly bush, thumbs tugging on the waistband of her pants, she saw the body.

Acknowledgements

There are so many people to whom I am indebted for their help and support in the completion of this book. To my critique partner, my editors, beta readers, fellow writers and members of my writers groups, I can never thank you enough for your encouragement, support, advice and critiques. You continue to share your vast wealth of knowledge and expertise and I am truly grateful for it.

About the Author

Awarding winning author Dana Wayne is a sixth generation Texan and resides in the Piney Woods with her husband, (and biggest fan), a Calico cat named Katie, three children and four grandchildren. She routinely speaks at book clubs, writers groups and other organizations, and is a frequent guest on numerous writing blogs.

Her debut novel, *Secrets of The Heart*, was awarded First Place—Contemporary Romance, 2017 by Texas Association of Authors, was a finalist for the 2017 Scéal Award for Contemporary Romance, Reviewers Top Pick and included on the Top 10 Books to Read This Winter from Books & Benches online magazine.

Her second novel, *Mail Order Groom,* released in April, 2017, received 4.5 Stars and the Crowned Heart from InD'tale

Magazine, 5 Stars from Readers Favorite and Books & Benches, and was included in the list of *100 Best Indie Books to Read Before You Die*. Her third book, *Whispers on The Wind*, is a romantic suspense released in March, 2018.

Affiliations include Romance Writers of America, Texas Association of Authors, Writers League of Texas, East Texas Writers Guild, Northeast Texas Writers Organization, and East Texas Writers Association.

She can be reached through her website www.danawaye.com or via email at danawayne423@gmail.com.